EVERFLAME

A NOVEL BY
DYLAN LEE PETERS

TABLE OF CONTENTS

EARTH

FIRE

WIND

WATER

EARTH

1

Chapter 1: Of Wolves and Children

"Father, why am I called Evercloud?"

"You are a mystery, my son, like a cloud that continues forever. No one can see through to what lies on the other side."

King Eveneye sat next to his son and looked at him pensively. He did not know how old his son was, but he was beginning to grow as large as some of the humans the king had seen outside of his kingdom. Eveneye was King of Bears, and as he gazed down at the human boy he called son, his mind wandered back to that fateful night, before he were king. He wondered, as he always did, if he had made the right decision.

•••

The night was humid and fireflies danced between the pines as Eveneye fished with Whiteclaw, both of them standing in a stream. The Kingdom of Bears slept peacefully in their caves, a couple of miles away from the stream. It was not common for bears to fish at night in the land of Ephanlarea, at least, not for most bears. Eveneye and Whiteclaw were among the exceptions. Both bears were full-grown and large; they were not brothers by birth, but still very close to each other. The two were often mistaken as siblings, given that they were such good friends and that they looked so much like each other. They were of the same build and had the same black fur. The only difference to someone that did not know them well, was that the fur on Whiteclaw's front, right paw was colored white, hence his name. Both of the bears held jobs in the Kingdom as prominent members of the King's advisors. The two friends had the same likes and dislikes, even the same hobbies. They counted fishing as their favorite. In fact, they were the best fishers in the Kingdom.

It was very difficult to fish at night, yet the lack of competition produced the most bountiful catches. The difficulty in night fishing was that you could not see what was happening in the water. Due to this, hearing, touch and instinct were the primary tools of making a catch.

Eveneye stood in the stream, feeling the water pass through his fur, eyes closed, and listening to the rush of the water. Whiteclaw stood in the very same fashion, six feet to the right of Eveneye. Together they were a fish-catching team, creating a gate in the stream that the fish must pass through.

Their reflexes were unparalleled. The blink of an eye might miss a catch. They were flawless in their execution, standing like meditating statues, attune to everything around them. A wolf howled in the distance. A squirrel ran through some brush. The water rushed. Whiteclaw's arm darted to the left and came up with the first catch of the night. He threw it to the shore. Neither bear made a sound. The water rushed. There was a movement on the surface of the water. Eveneye darted to his left and came up with his first catch. He threw it ashore, returned to position, and the fishing continued. They went along this way until they had caught twenty fish apiece.

"I'm hungry," stated Whiteclaw.

"Yes. Let's be done," returned Eveneye.

They waded out of the water and began to gather their catch into sacks they had brought with them. Some of the fish never made it into the sacks, as the bears snatched a few of the larger fish and devoured them. Whiteclaw smacked his lips with pleasure and grunted in satisfaction. The moon was pale in the sky and dark clouds were beginning to move across it. A rustling was heard throughout the forest as the wind suddenly picked up.

"Rain comes," said Eveneye.

"Yes," said Whiteclaw.

They fastened the sacks around their necks and began to make their way back home. Again, a wolf howled in the distance, closer though. Twigs and branches snapped under the bears' paws and the wind whipped through their fur. It became harder and harder to see where they were going as the moonlight became obscured by rainclouds. Fortunately, Eveneye and Whiteclaw could have walked the path home with their eyes closed.

The two bears had encountered far worse than rain and darkness in these woods. When they were younger, they had been caught in the woods during a blizzard and were forced to take shelter as it passed. They had made their shelter from fallen trees, and huddled underneath them for fifteen hours before the storm had finally passed. When they had emerged again, they recognized nothing of the forest and it had taken them almost two days to find their way home. There had also been a time when human hunters had ambushed the two bears on their trail home. Eveneye and Whiteclaw were fully-grown bears and they had dispatched the humans rather quickly, but not before suffering wounds from the humans' spears. They could spend a night telling tales of their forays into the forest and often did.

The woods were dense and had a thick layer of underbrush, not found in all forests. The canopy was high and wide; it was a very old forest. It was said, in the lore of the bear, that the elder bears did not choose this forest to build their kingdom, but that the forest chose them to be its protectors. This was passed down as birthright to all bears. Respect the forest; protect the forest. It was mother to them all.

Lightning flashed, thunder rumbled and it began to rain. Whiteclaw grumbled and Eveneye chuckled.

"What's the matter? We were already wet from the stream."

"That was by choice," replied Whiteclaw.

Both bears laughed heartily as lightning flashed across the night sky. Eveneye stopped laughing and perked his ears.

"Do you hear that?"

"Hear what? The rain?"

"No, it sounds like a human child, crying."

Both bears began turning their heads from side to side, trying to hear better. Contact with humans was a rarity for the bears, but it had happened enough to adult bears that they would be able to recognize the sobs of a human child. This was, in fact, the third time Eveneye had heard a child cry. The first time had been during a rite of passage that young, male bears impose upon each other. The adults disapprove of it, yet it still continues, mostly without their knowledge. During the tenth year of a male bear's life, he is expected to wake the humans in a nearby village by running through the village, roaring and causing general havoc. Eveneye had done nothing horrible during his own rampage. Yet he had still heard the cries of many children, scared at seeing a large bear charging through their village. The second time had been when he had stumbled upon a family of humans camping in the forest. Again, the crying of the child had only come from the fear of seeing him.

The cries Eveneye heard now seemed different, but he could not place how. After a moment of listening, both bears agreed that the sound was coming just west of their location.

"Should we investigate?" asked Eveneye.

"Why? We will only put ourselves in a bad situation when we encounter the adults that the child is with," said Whiteclaw incredulously.

"I don't hear other humans. It sounds as if the child is alone."

"What do you imagine yourself doing, Eveneye? Consoling the child? Coddling it until its parents return and try to attack you? They'll be a bit braver than usual if they see you around their child."

Just then, the crying became more intense and sounds of growling could be heard from the same direction. *Wolves,* thought Eveneye.

"I'm going," he said. Eveneye dropped his fish and ran off in the direction of the sobs.

"You fool!" barked Whiteclaw, dropping his fish as well, and then running after Eveneye.

Eveneye moved as fast as he could through the forest, though it was difficult in the dark and rain. He didn't know why he felt so compelled to come to the child's aid. He had never done anything like this in his life, though something inside of him told him to move on. Something inside of

11

him knew it would be wrong to ignore the cries of the child. The rain beat against Eveneye's face and mud caked his paws, his breathing grew heavy and his muscles began to ache. The cries were getting louder and louder, tearing against his consciousness. It kept him driving forward. He must save the child. Terrible visions of what he might find flashed through Eveneye's mind. The cries intensified, intermingling with the growls of the wolves and the sound of rain. Eveneye felt that he were in a nightmare he would never escape from, running toward a goal he would never reach, chilled by the rain and the screaming of a child.

Just as the bear felt he might never reach the child in time, he broke into a small clearing and found the child tied to the trunk of a tree, surrounded by a pack of five hungry wolves. The wolves were black against the darkness. All that could be seen of them were their yellow teeth, floating in the abyss of the forest. Eveneye could only just make them out. Lightning illuminated their bodies as it broke across the sky and then it was gone, leaving just the sickly, yellow teeth. Their movements seemed slow and fluid, like a snake closing in on unsuspecting prey, confident, in control. Eveneye watched the wolves closing in on the toddler, saliva hanging from their jaws. The child was screaming and seemed to be caked in what looked like blood. Eveneye did the only thing that he could. He attacked.

He was upon the pack before they knew he was there. Eveneye rose into the air, roaring with fury, and then came crashing down with his massive paws upon the first black beast, crushing its skull. The wolves were stunned and Eveneye took the opportunity to attack again. He lunged toward the closest wolf, catching its neck in his maw. The bear rose on his hind legs and shook the wolf, trapped between his jaws, biting down as hard as he could. The wolf's neck snapped and Eveneye dropped its filthy corpse to the forest floor.

The remaining wolves had again gained their composure, and now it was Eveneye's turn to be caught unaware. The wolves pounced, seemingly at once, and sunk their yellow teeth into the bear's hide. Eveneye spun and one of the wolves was shaken loose from its hold. Momentarily forgetting the other teeth sunk into his flesh, Eveneye swiped at the dislodged wolf, sending it crashing into a tree at the edge of the clearing. Searing pain returned Eveneye's attention to the two wolves, still tearing at him. He tried to shake them off, but it was no use. The wolves had gained strong holds in areas that were difficult for Eveneye to reach. One wolf was directly on top of his back, with its teeth sunk in his neck, and the other was on the right side of the bear, just below his ribs. He tried a few swipes but could not hit the wolves with enough strength to dislodge them. Then an idea struck him. Eveneye tilted his body to the right and then jumped into the air, allowing all of his weight to come down upon the wolf at his ribs. He felt the body of the wolf crush under his weight, and the hold it had on him relinquished as the life left its body.

Eveneye then tried to roll, to contend with the remaining wolf on his neck, but a massive force barreled into him, pinning him on his stomach. The wolf that he had knocked away earlier had come back at him and was now at his neck, in the same manner as the other wolf. Pain seared through the body of the bear and blood gushed through his fur. Eveneye was losing his energy and he feared that this might be his final battle. He roared and tried to shake the wolves off, one more time, but his efforts were futile. The weight of two wolves on his neck was too much, and he had lost a lot of blood. The black beasts sat upon the bear as vultures upon a corpse. Their savage teeth now stained with the blood of a would-be hero.

I've failed, thought Eveneye as the screams of the child echoed in his mind. *It's over.*

Suddenly, he heard a yelp and the fangs were gone from his neck. Eveneye rolled over and stared as his friend, Whiteclaw, stood with one of the wolves, lifeless under him and the other just a few paces from him, snarling. Eveneye thought that this wolf was the largest he had ever seen. The wolf's teeth seemed to pulse as they dripped with Eveneye's blood. For the first time, Eveneye could see the wolf's eyes and they were afire. The wolf did not know fear. Its only purpose was to kill.

Whiteclaw stood on his hind legs and roared. As he did, the wolf darted at him, jumping for his throat. With one swift move, Whiteclaw knocked the wolf out of the air, pinning it to the ground with one mighty paw. The bear clamped onto the wolf's head with his jaws and tore the beast's head clean from its body. The battle had ended.

Eveneye slowly rose and walked over to where Whiteclaw stood.

"Thank you, my brother. I owe you my life."

Whiteclaw looked at Eveneye and nodded his head. He then looked back over his shoulder at the small boy who was tied to the tree. The boy was no longer crying and it didn't seem as if he were moving at all.

Eveneye turned and walked over to the boy. He could now see that it was, indeed, blood that covered the front of the child. The bear looked over the child and could see no wound. The boy was breathing slowly. Eveneye stood, perplexed for a moment, and then bent close to the boy and licked at the blood.

"Boar's blood," he said. "It's not the child's blood."

"So?" asked Whiteclaw, now standing next to Eveneye.

"So," answered Eveneye, "that means someone tied this child to this tree and put boar's blood on it to attract the wolves."

The two bears stood next to each other, speechless at the atrocity before them. Whiteclaw was the first to speak and his voice was laced with a compassion that Eveneye had never heard from him.

"We should take the child to a human village, so that it can be cared for properly."

13

"We can't do that," uttered Eveneye.

"My friend," Whiteclaw pleaded, "I admit it. I was wrong earlier. We cannot leave this child to die in the woods, just to protect our own skins."

"I don't plan on it," said Eveneye.

"Eveneye, what are you saying?"

"I will take the child home with me. The humans do not want it. It was obviously left here to die by someone from the nearest village. I won't see this child put back into harm's way. It wouldn't be the right thing to do. I'm taking it."

"You're mad," said Whiteclaw, his eyes widening. "You don't know what you are saying. The wolves have injured you and you are not well. You can't keep this child. This is madness."

Eveneye took his claw and cut the rope binding the child to the tree. The boy sniffled, but didn't cry. Either from shock, fear, or the fact that it was just too tired, the child didn't make another sound. Eveneye took hold of the child, put him upon his back, and then headed for his home.

Whiteclaw stood, slack-jawed and dumbfounded.

"But...but..."

Whiteclaw couldn't make a sentence come out of his mouth, but it would not have mattered anyway. Eveneye had made up his mind.

High above the tree line of the forest stood Gray Mountain, home of the bears. No fires burned inside the caves of Gray Mountain, it was late into the night and everyone slept. The solitary light that came from the mountain was the Everflame. It sat upon its pyre in the highest tower of King Irontooth's castle. To the Kingdom of Bears, its size, in no way, matched its importance. The flame had burned as long as any living bear could remember and far before. It burned as a reminder of all that the bears were, and of the elder bears that came before them. For it was by their wisdom that the bears prospered. The flame was a symbol of the bears' spirit. It was the heart of each and every one of them.

Whiteclaw and Eveneye could see the Everflame's light through the trees as they approached their mountain home, just a speck of light at the top of the mountain. The rain had continued to fall during the journey home, washing the blood from Eveneye's fur as well as from the boy. Eveneye would have to dress his wounds when he arrived at his cave. As they cleared the trees and stood at the foot of the mountain, the rain abated and Whiteclaw shook off some of the moisture that soaked him. He was carrying both fish sacks, due to the events of the night. The bears' eyelids grew heavy and the boy slept on the back of Eveneye as he walked. It had been a long night and the bears were eager to see it end. Different paths led to the caves of either bear and they exchanged only a nod to each other as they parted ways. Whiteclaw watched Eveneye as he walked away. Eveneye was like a brother to him, it hadn't even been a choice to follow him as he ran toward the crying child; it hadn't even

14

been a choice to save his life. He loved Eveneye and he was afraid for him. This boy would bring scandal to the Kingdom and Eveneye's life would never be the same.

Eveneye entered his cave as his wife, Goldenheart, slept. She breathed easily and did not stir. Eveneye removed the sleeping boy from his back and wrapped him in a blanket. He stared at the boy's tiny features. *What have I done?* he thought to himself. He set the child, wrapped in the blanket, in a dry corner of the cave. The bear chose a corner set deep in the cave, hoping that if the child woke and began to cry, the sound might not reach outside. He felt ashamed that he was hiding the boy, but his earlier bravery had left him and he was now fearful of what the morning would bring. Eveneye quietly dressed his wounds and lied down next to his wife. Despite his fear, Eveneye fell asleep quickly. He would have many dreams that night, dreams of wolves and children, and dreams of being abused by the harsh voices of other bears. However, only one dream that night would endure in his memory. One solitary image, the image of a man made of lightning.

•••

As Eveneye awoke the next morning, panic rushed over him. There was a child in his home, a human boy. He quickly rose up on his feet and saw something that shook him to his core. His wife sat on the floor of the cave, throwing a stick and then watching as the small boy retrieved it and brought it back to her. They were playing fetch. Eveneye had no idea how old the boy was, two years, maybe three. He wasn't adept at guessing human age. The boy was at least young enough that he could not speak, only shriek with glee every time Goldenheart threw the stick. Eveneye was in shock, unable to move or speak, his fur standing on end.

"Even, why am I playing fetch with a human boy in our home?" asked Goldenheart so simply that it seemed to Eveneye he must still be asleep and dreaming.

"Umm...well, I... I'm...he was...umm..." Eveneye stumbled over everything he tried so say and his mind was swimming.

"He was what? Where did you find him?"

At Goldenheart's last question, the image of the wolves appeared in Eveneye's mind, as well as the image of the little boy tied to the tree. With these images fresh in his mind, the anger that he had felt toward the wolves had again risen in Eveneye. It was sobering and snapped him out of his daze.

"He was in the forest. He was in trouble. I did what I had to." Eveneye had gained his composure and began to recount the events of the prior night to his wife. Pausing after recounting the battle with the wolves to show her his injuries, then continuing with the decision to bring the boy back to the mountain. He ended his story with, "I didn't know what else to do."

15

"So you intend to keep this child?" Goldenheart asked her husband, her voice conveying her disbelief in the situation. "The King will not allow this, Even. We should sneak the child out of here tonight, and return it to the village. No one needs to know. Whiteclaw will not say anything. He will keep the secret."

"I will take the child to the King's court today and explain to him. I will show him that I did the right thing. He will see that we cannot return the child to the humans. I mean… they tried to kill him." Eveneye was calm and steady with his voice and it helped to calm his wife.

"I am afraid, Even," she said and looked down at the boy.

He was sitting on the floor with the stick in his hands, staring up at the massive bear that had helped to save his life. The boy cocked the stick back and threw it at Eveneye. The stick bounced off of Eveneye's nose and the child erupted with laughter. Goldenheart followed.

"Well," she said between laughs, "he is entertaining."

"Look, Goldie, I'm a very respected member of this kingdom. I'm a member of the council that advises King Irontooth. He will listen to me. I'll go after breakfast. You'll see. Everything will be all right."

Goldenheart looked at her husband with love in her eyes and smiled.

"I hope so, Even. I hope so."

2

Chapter 2: Defiance

It was a very busy morning in the main tunnel that led through the center of Gray Mountain and up to the King's castle. Eveneye grimaced as he made his way through. He had been hoping for the smallest amount of traffic possible. The main tunnel was where the majority of business was conducted in the Kingdom. The tunnel was about fifty yards wide with an arched ceiling that stood thirty feet high. Drawn along the ceiling were artful depictions of key events in the history of the bears. The bears were very proud of their history and any adult could name each event shown along the length of the tunnel. The walls were stark, with the exception of the torches that lit the tunnel. The walls were kept mostly clear due to the fact that merchants and traders set up booths and stands, taking up all of the wall space that was not occupied by light sources.

There were merchants and traders of all kinds. There were many stands set up where a bear might purchase things to decorate their cave. Patterned blankets and rugs of all colors hung in display, as well as tapestries to hang on cave walls. Soft mattresses filled with straw or feathers leaned against the walls of the tunnel as well.

The bears were also fine artists. Paintings of King Irontooth could be purchased, as well as recreations of some of the historical events that adorned the ceiling of the main tunnel. Strongback's lighting of the Everflame was a particular favorite.

Housewares were also a popular commodity. The metal workers were selling pots and pans, as well as grates to place over a fire for grilling. The woodworkers did a bit better for themselves, as they sold tables and cabinets for storage. Some bears had wooden doors fit to the front of their caves, though most found doors to be rude and antisocial. The woodworkers also delved into the artistic and their carvings were very popular. At the present time, it was popular to have a carving done of your family and have it hung on the wall. Eveneye had been looking into it for himself and Goldenheart, but he thought that maybe it would seem empty without the addition of a cub.

There was also a booth set up for leisure activities. Just last week, Eveneye had purchased a johnball. He and Whiteclaw were very good johnball

17

players and at least once per week, played with other bears in the Kingdom. Johnball was a simple enough sport, the goal being to move the johnball into your opponent's territory by any means necessary. They played in teams of five and the team who had crossed into their opponent's territory the most, at the end of an hour, was the victor. The johnball Eveneye had purchased was a spherical, dark-brown, leather ball with a stone on the inside for weight. The johnballs used now were less barbaric than what was used by the inventors of the game, some years back.

The story follows that a man was out hunting bear, and, rightly so in the bears' eyes, was killed by his prey. The bears who had killed the man then played a game with his head as the ball. Having previously seen that upon the man's trousers was written, property of John Hoell III, it was decided that the game would be called Johnball. To make it popular for the masses, as most bears do not enjoy playing with corpses, the ball was "redesigned."

As Eveneye passed, the activities merchant waved. Eveneye quickly turned, as if he had not seen him. He was not eager to be pulled into conversation today.

The main tunnel was also where the bears purchased their food. Breads, cheeses, fruits, vegetables, different cuts of meat and certainly fish. The fish merchants were like a little market of their own, selling all types of fish. There were stands selling salmon, mackerel, bass, trout, cod, halibut, tuna fish and sword fish, catfish, herring, pickerel, chub, carp, smelt, grouper, flounder, perch, haddock, sardines, sole, tilapia and even candied anchovies for the cubs. This section of the tunnel was always the busiest. No bear could pass through without having their mouth begin to water.

Eveneye tried to make his way through the tunnel as inconspicuously as possible. The boy was in a sack that hung around Eveneye's neck, just as the fish had been carried the night before. Eveneye was tempted to check the sack many times as he moved through the tunnel, due to the fact that the boy never fussed or even made a sound. He was remarkably well behaved and it struck Eveneye as being a little odd. He didn't dare open the sack in the tunnel, as the last thing he wanted to do was draw attention to himself. However, as he passed Hawksfoot, the old salmon merchant, his luck ran out.

"Eveneye! Hey! Let's see your catch!"

Eveneye moved quickly toward the old bear. The sooner he could get to him, the sooner the bear would stop drawing attention with his yells.

Hawksfoot was an old bear with gray fur and wide, staring eyes. He had been a celebrated fisher in his day, but had long since lost the necessary reflexes. It had not made him bitter though. Instead, Hawksfoot had turned to selling fish, which it seemed he loved just as much. He was always in a friendly mood and always eager to see Eveneye's catches.

"Eveneye, what have you brought me this morning? Night fishing again? I'll bet you've got a big catch to sell me today, don't you?" Hawksfoot ogled the fish sack with expectant eyes. He always made great profit from Eveneye's catches.

"No. Nothing today, Hawk. Just passing through today. Sorry." Eveneye tried to be casual but his words came hurried and awkward.

"You all right?" asked Hawksfoot, narrowing his eyes a bit.

"Oh, me? Fine," Eveneye chuckled. "Just up late, night fishing. You know."

"So you do have fish! Let me see 'em." Hawksfoot stepped forward and reached for the sack.

"No!" shouted Eveneye. "I mean…I can't. They're not for sale. I'm on my way to see the King."

"I should have known," said Hawksfoot, smiling. "I always said you was the smartest bear I know. You've got yourself a prize catch there and you're off to offer it up to the King. You're a keen one, Eveneye, real sharp."

"Well, you've figured me out," laughed Eveneye, visibly relieved.

"Go ahead and run on, so those fish stay fresh. Go on."

Eveneye nodded at the old bear and made his way onward. He had been so nervous talking to Hawksfoot that he was surprised that his legs still worked. As he continued through the main tunnel, the boy inside of the sack continued to behave remarkably well. Only once did the boy stir at all, and that was as Eveneye had passed by the sweet treats merchant. The smell of baked goods obviously reaching the boy through the sack.

"Be still, little one," Eveneye whispered. "I promise I'll get you something when we return."

It was a little-known fact outside of the bear kingdom, but bears loved baked goods. Pies, cookies, cakes, they loved everything. Eveneye's personal favorites were brownies. Eveneye loved them almost as much as fish. In fact, brownies were one of the things that had made him fall in love with Goldenheart. She made the best brownies he had ever tasted. They made him feel like he was floating on air. He had nicknamed them Goldenheart's Magical Brownies and usually asked for them thusly.

Eveneye had finally moved past the crowd of the market and was now very close to the King's court. He was beginning to think that he was in the clear, when he heard a strong "ahem" from behind. Eveneye stopped and Whiteclaw circled around in front of him.

"Don't do this," Whiteclaw whispered. "I'll help you come up with a better solution. Do not show that child to the King."

"It will be fine. I will make him understand."

"And what if he does not?"

"He will," assured Eveneye.

"What if you are wrong? He will order you to return that child, and

19

what then? Hmm? Will you sacrifice everything you have worked for, your reputation, your wife's reputation, everything… for that boy?"

"Please, Whiteclaw, you must trust me." Eveneye stared Whiteclaw directly in the eyes, unwavering.

Whiteclaw lowered his gaze and sighed, exasperated.

"If this is something you must do," Whiteclaw raised his eyes to meet those of his friend, "then it will not be alone."

"You are a good friend," said Eveneye, smiling. "You will not regret this."

The bears both turned and marched on, toward the castle. As the castle came into view, Eveneye could hear Whiteclaw swallow the lump in his throat.

"Trust me, Whiteclaw. I have a plan."

"Care to share that plan?"

"Sorry, I can't. You'll just have to trust me."

Whiteclaw shook his head and smirked.

The tunnel opened to the sky, just in front of the entrance to the castle. The castle rose from the mountain's peak like a giant flower, opening to the sun. The walls of the castle layered inward, like great, stone petals, disjointed, yet seamless. They came tighter and tighter until they met the lone tower that rose from the middle of the castle, like the flower's stigma. Atop the tower, burned the Everflame in all its glory. The King's castle had been carved directly from the peak of the mountain by the tireless work of the elder bears. It was the single greatest achievement in the history of the bears and each of them regarded the castle and its flame as sacred.

Eveneye and Whiteclaw approached the guard at the door to the castle, and told him that they had business in the King's court. The guard recognized them as two of the King's advisors and asked no questions as he admitted them into the castle. The door of the castle opened inward, from the middle, to reveal the beauty of the King's halls. All of the stone on the inside of the castle had been polished so smooth it seemed as though it might be liquid. The castle had many windows, so that during the day, the halls would be lit with natural light. A life-sized sculpture of each of the previous kings lined the walls down the main hall toward the King's court. Thirty-three in total, beginning with the first king of the bears, King Longbranch, and ending with King Bluestar, Irontooth's predecessor. A sculpture was only commissioned after a king's rule had ended.

Eveneye and Whiteclaw made their way to the courtroom and stood in the waiting line, just outside. There were only two parties before them who had cases to present to the King. A guard stood at the entrance to the court and told each party when it was their turn to enter. Almost half an hour passed when the party directly before Eveneye and Whiteclaw were admitted, and the two bears moved up in line. The guard returned and stared blankly at the two bears.

"You can go right in. You know you two don't have to wait in the case line."

"No," said Eveneye, "we do. We have a case to be judged by the King today."

"Come on now," said the guard. "You're pulling a goof on me, you are. You can't expect me to believe the two of you are at odds with each other."

"No. We just have something to be presented to the King," explained Whiteclaw.

"Ooooh." The guard nodded his head, rolled back and forth on the balls of his feet and then pointed at the bulging sack. "What's in the bag?"

"None of your business," shot Whiteclaw.

"Fine. Have it your way." The guard turned around and began muttering to himself.

A few minutes passed and then the sound of a gong was heard, signaling a decision by the King in the present case. The guard opened the door to the court and extended his arms, signaling that Eveneye and Whiteclaw could enter. The bears walked to the center of the room and stood upon a large star that had been etched into the polished stone. They turned to face the King, whose throne sat upon a series of ten steps. A group of five guards stood on either side of the King. The room was large and this was mostly to accommodate a sizable audience. Bleachers lined both sidewalls and the back wall. The ceiling was open to the sky so that the Everflame could be seen overhead. There were only about two hundred bears in attendance today. The room could easily fit one thousand. It rarely reached such capacity, and today's audience was rather standard. Still, it seemed a lot for Eveneye, who was seeing the courtroom from this vantage point for the first time. It took he and Whiteclaw a moment to muster their courage before they addressed the King.

"Your Majesty," said the bears and bowed before King Irontooth.

"What are the two of you doing?" asked Irontooth. "I am in no mood for pranks today."

Murmurings from the crowd washed over the two bears like a wave.

"Silence!" called the King. He then nodded at Eveneye and Whiteclaw so that they might speak.

"Your Majesty," began Eveneye, "this is no joke. I am here today to tell you of the events that befell Whiteclaw and myself last night. Whiteclaw is here as my witness of the events. I would ask that you hear my story and then, I will present you with a plan I have that will bring further prosperity to our future. Will you hear me, O King?"

"Of course I will hear you, Eveneye. You are one of my most trusted advisors. I would be a fool to ignore that which you feel you must say. But first," and the King pointed directly at Eveneye, "I need to know what is moving in that bag."

Every bear inside the courtroom moved their attention to the sack that hung around Eveneye's neck, as it was now obvious that something was trying to push its way out.

"As you wish." Eveneye took the sack from his neck and gently placed it on the floor. He then lifted back the top, and out crawled a smiling, little boy. The crowd erupted in surprise.

"Silence! I demand silence!" The crowd hushed and the King looked down over Eveneye and the child at his feet. "You had better explain yourself, and you had better do it quickly."

"Yes, Sire." Eveneye began with the events of the previous night, just as he had given them to his wife, earlier. Ooohs and Aaahs came from the crowd as he told of the battle with the wolves, but the crowd did not seem as impressed with Eveneye's decision to bring the child to the mountain. Eveneye could see that if he stopped talking, he may never get a chance to speak of his plan. So as his account of the night finished, he proceeded directly to his plan. "So, Sire, this is what I propose. This child is obviously unwanted by the humans and therefore, there is no danger of them attempting to reclaim him. I propose we keep him on the mountain and raise him as a member of our society." The murmurs of the crowd were getting louder but Eveneye ignored them and continued. "Once the boy becomes an adult, he could become an ambassador of peace between us and the humans. When the humans see that we have taken care of one of their own, they will not fear us any longer. We can begin a new era of peace and cooperation between our two societies. Together, bears and humans could reach goals we never dreamed possible. I beg of you, O King, trust in my judgment. An era of peace between bears and humans would be a great ease to our need for security. We would be able to open trade to lengths we never thought possible. Without humans fearing us, we may also be able to spread the Kingdom of Bears further than ever before. I'm sure there would be many benefits I have not even thought of. The possibilities are endless. I understand that what I ask is radical in nature, but I know, in your wisdom, you will see the truth of my words."

The King did not need to call for silence again. The crowd was too shocked to make noise. Everyone waited breathlessly for the King to speak.

"What say you, Whiteclaw?" asked the King. "Do you stand in agreement with Eveneye?"

Whiteclaw paused before he spoke, but when he did, his words rang clear.

"I do, good King. Eveneye has always had keen judgment. It has never led me astray."

Warmth rose up inside of Eveneye at his friend's kind words. He looked up at the King with a bit of confidence after they had been spoken. The King, however, began to frown and the warmth Eveneye had felt was quickly cooled.

"Eveneye," said the King. "We all know why you were given such a name. Your good ethics and morals have always given authority to your

22

decisions, even when you were a cub. You have always advised me with the best interest of the Kingdom at heart. You have done your name proud. However, I fear that today, you have brought a mark against it." Warmth and feeling alike had now left Eveneye's body. He was in a nightmare he could not escape, and he remained motionless as the King continued. "Bringing this child here was a mistake. It is not the responsibility of bears to rear a child that has been discarded by man. Did you consider what evil might reside in this child that the humans would seek to rid themselves of. Look at the child, even now; it has no fear of us. It sits placidly, staring at us. It seems unnatural to me. As for your plan for future prosperity, I say, what is wrong with the prosperity our kingdom sees on this day? We are doing just fine without the aid of humans. Bah. Humans. Humans who have made war with each other and have hunted us for game. Why would we ally with such despicable creatures? This boy that sits in front of us would probably kill you dead once he came of age. No, Eveneye, I would put no stock in humans."

"But, Sire," Eveneye pleaded, "it is my belief that a human that was reared through the wisdom of our elders would be very unlike the humans we know now. It would be better. Er…more like us. It would–"

"Enough, Eveneye. Do not try to convince me further. I have made my final decision. You and Whiteclaw will return this child to the nearest village immediately and we will speak of this no more."

Suddenly, a fire shot through Eveneye that he had never felt. He forgot where he was and whom he was speaking to. He knew only one thing, he was right and no one would take this child away from him.

"The child stays with me," uttered Eveneye through gritted teeth.

Cries of astonishment came forth from the crowd like the winds of a storm. Eveneye could hear Whiteclaw curse behind him.

"SILENCE!!" roared the King. The crowd hushed and Whiteclaw walked over to the child and gathered him up. He did not know what made him do it. Later, he would reason that it was done out of fear for the child, but from the eyes of the King, it looked like defiance.

King Irontooth looked down upon Eveneye and Whiteclaw from his throne with menace in his eyes and his lips curled.

"You two listen to me, and you listen well! If the two of you do not obey my orders immediately, I will have you removed from your positions and branded as traitors to the King! You will be banished from the Kingdom, never to lay eyes upon the Everflame again! No bear will help you, let alone look at you! Do you understand me?"

The fire intensified inside of Eveneye. He could not allow the child to be sent back to the humans, back to its death. How could this King he had followed be so heartless, so unfeeling. He began to see Irontooth in a new light and it sickened him. This king did not deserve his service. This king deserved his wrath and he unleashed it upon him.

"Oh, I understand, good King. I understand well. You would forfeit the life of this helpless boy, rather than use your brain to allow rational thought. You would mire your people in tradition and complacence, rather than see them grow through foresight and innovation. You would allow fear and ignorance to prevent the hope of a better day. You are a coward!" Eveneye then stood on his hind legs and roared more loudly than he ever had. Whiteclaw and the child trembled behind him and Whiteclaw uttered:

"Don't do this, Even. Please. Stop."

Eveneye didn't hear him as he stood there, in the center of the court. Every bear in attendance knew what was about to happen, though not one of them could believe their ears as Eveneye began to speak the words of fate.

"Oh King, you have fallen in mine eyes and I no longer stand at your side! To you, I CHALLENGE!!"

Eveneye's words echoed through the chamber like thunder. No one moved. No one spoke. Irontooth's eyes had gone bloodshot with rage. His claws had dug deep into his throne, and his jaw shook as he spoke, "So be it."

3

Chapter 3: Blood and Fire

"What's done is done, Whiteclaw. You can't be mad at me forever."

Eveneye and Whiteclaw sat in a prison cell below the courtroom with their backs turned to each other. The King's guard had arrested both of them directly after Eveneye had challenged the King. They did not know where the boy had been taken, but they knew he would not be harmed until after the ritual had been completed.

"You should have told me what you meant to do if the King refused you. I had the right to know."

"You would have tried to stop me, Whiteclaw."

"You're damn right, I would have tried to stop you!" Whiteclaw turned around to face Eveneye, furious. "Challenge the King? You are a fool, Eveneye! I should have reported that child myself! You have ruined me, you have ruined your wife, and you have sentenced yourself to death!"

Eveneye did not turn to face Whiteclaw, but he spoke calmly and clearly.

"I will complete my challenges. I will not fail."

Whiteclaw huffed and spun himself back away from Eveneye, preferring the view of the wall.

Eveneye had spoken the words of fate and challenged the King, and law said that Eveneye was now subject to challenges of his own. The reward for completing all three challenges was possession of the Kingdom, but the penalty for failure was death. Long ago, the elder bears had written this law into existence in the case of a king who was a tyrant. It was in place so that the bears of the Kingdom could choose a champion among them to challenge and dethrone a tyrant. Yet the challenges were created to be very difficult in order to deter those who would seek the throne for unjust reasons. In the history of the bears, only one new king had been crowned by this method and that was the warrior king, Blackmaw. Blackmaw was a champion of the people and they begged him to challenge the tyrant, Bloodpaw. It had happened a long time ago and was honored as one of the events shown on the ceiling of the main tunnel. No bear that lived today had been alive to witness it.

The ritual consisted of three challenges. The first challenge was of the mind, the second challenge would be physical and the third, if one should make it that far, was a duel against the king. The duel would be fought to the death.

The bears sat in their cell for what seemed like ages. There was very little light where their cell was located and they could hear nothing of what was going on in the castle around them. Eveneye worried about Goldenheart. Undoubtedly, the King had sent for her by now. She must be terrified. Eveneye cursed himself for not having protected her better.

Suddenly, the one torch that dimly lit the chamber went out. The bears could hear shuffling and clinking and then the cell door opened.

"Move and you die."

Both Eveneye and Whiteclaw could sense other bears around them and then felt the cold tips of spears. The King's guard held Eveneye and Whiteclaw at spear point, and as they did, they fit them with shackles and blindfolds.

"Consider this your funeral march," uttered one of the guards. The rest of the King's guard laughed as they ushered Eveneye and Whiteclaw out of the cell.

Eveneye and Whiteclaw were not aware of where the King's guard was taking them. Eveneye thought he had a pretty good guess though. Tales of Blackmaw's challenges were told to all bears from a very young age, and there was only one place in the entire kingdom that could host such a thing: the Mountain Arena. The King would want the entire Kingdom to witness, what he would expect to be, the death of someone seeking the throne.

Eveneye and Whiteclaw could see nothing, but continued to walk the downward-sloping path leading to their fate. Eveneye reasoned that they must be in a tunnel leading away from the castle. He could hear nothing except for the pounding of their feet. After roughly twenty minutes, the lead guard called for a halt, and Eveneye could hear a door open. The tip of a spear prodded him through the door. His shackles were removed and he heard the door close behind him. They had left Eveneye alone. The bear reached up and removed his blindfold to find himself in a large room, bisected by steel bars. *Just another cell*, he thought. But as he turned, looking around the cell, he found himself staring out at King Irontooth.

"Why have you done this to yourself, Eveneye?"

"You gave me no choice. No good bear would have sent that child back into hands that wished to harm it. I did it to save the boy's life."

"You lie. No bear can care that much for a human. I am no idiot. You have organized this whole charade as a reason to take the crown for yourself. You and your friend, Whiteclaw, seek power and that is all. Your motives are base, Eveneye, I shall enjoy watching your death."

"What do you know of my motives? I have lived my life watching the Kingdom of Bears hide from the world. That isolation has poisoned our minds and it has clouded your judgment. Our antisocial behavior has made

26

us enemies that are more powerful than we give credit. I walked into that courtroom today in your service, with the hope of saving a life, a life of no less value than yours or of mine. That child has done no injustice in this world, yet you condemn him. Why? Fear? Apathy? Neither is an acceptable reason. As I said, you have given me no choice."

"You insult your own kind, Eveneye. I think you forget what it is that you are."

"What I am has no bearing on what is right."

"It has everything to do with what is right. There is no escaping that. Your confused logic has damned you, Eveneye. Damned you and your wife and your friend."

"What have you done with them?" Eveneye gripped the bars of his cell in sudden panic.

"I've done nothing, and I will do nothing with them. Of course, Whiteclaw will be removed from his position, but other than that, I will do nothing. Your decisions will be punishment enough for them. After your death, who will be there for your wife? Hmm? What bear would marry her and take on that shame? The same for Whiteclaw, I imagine. Who knows? Maybe they will find comfort in each other's arms when you are gone." King Irontooth chuckled and turned to leave. "Oh, and as for the boy. His body shall burn upon the pyre of the Everflame, for your disobedience."

King Irontooth left the room, and left Eveneye seething with anger. *I shall not fail*, thought Eveneye. *Nothing shall stop me. Nothing.*

•••

After a short time in the cell, a guard came and escorted Eveneye to the gate of the Mountain Arena. He motioned Eveneye through the gate and closed it behind him. As Eveneye walked out onto the floor of the arena, he felt as though he had walked onto the surface of a place he had never been. He looked up, all around him, and saw that the arena was filled with the citizens of the Kingdom. What made the situation so surreal was that every single bear in the audience was silent. It was so silent, he could hear his own heartbeat. Thousands of bears, in one awkward silence. The truth of the situation was that there wasn't a single bear that dare make a sound. Who would dare to cheer a bear that would defy a King, and who would dare to jeer a bear whose defiance may gain him the crown? This was history. Today would be sacred. The bears knew how to give the moment the reverence it deserved.

The silence angered the King. He wanted the crowd to jeer Eveneye. But he did not let his anger show as he stood to address the crowd.

"My Kingdom, one of you has chosen to challenge the authority of my rule. One of you has spoken the words of fate. That bear is Eveneye, who stands before you now."

Eveneye looked up to the King's box that sat fifty feet above the floor.

27

Hatred welled inside of him and his claws scraped at the rock floor of the arena. As his furious gaze shot up at the King, he noticed two bears sitting just behind Irontooth. He looked a bit more intently at them and saw the sullen features of his wife, Goldenheart, and his best friend, Whiteclaw. Just behind them, he saw guards with spears, holding them where they were, forcing them to watch the ritual. Eveneye's blood boiled in his veins and he ground his teeth.

Irontooth turned his gaze from the crowd to Eveneye.

"Does the challenger have anything to say before the ritual begins?"

Eveneye stood up on his hind legs and shouted up at Irontooth.

"Tell my wife that I have given her my heart, and before the day is done, I shall also give her the Kingdom."

Irontooth curled his lips as he looked down upon Eveneye. His eyes were full of rage but he didn't dare to allow Eveneye's words to bait him into response. He must show his Kingdom which bear holds the steady hand.

"Raise the gate," he shouted and horns were sounded all around the arena.

A gate opened at the edge of the arena and fourteen large bears dragged a massive, wooden structure out onto the arena floor. The structure was shaped like a pyramid, with the exception of a platform at the top, and stairs at one side, leading up to the platform. It stood at least thirty feet into the air and Eveneye could not see around it. The bears dragged the structure over to a large, square board on the arena floor. They then removed the board from where it was, and replaced it with the pyramid. Eveneye looked at the structure and wondered what might lie beneath it. Once in place, the fourteen bears stood around the pyramid and waited.

The King rose from his chair and again spoke to Eveneye.

"At the top of this structure are four holes, each will drop you down through the structure to whatever lies below. Each hole will lead you to a different fate. There is also a scroll at the top of the structure with a riddle. The riddle will give you a clue as to which hole to drop through to complete the challenge. You will have a limited time to make your decision. A poor decision will result in death. Let the ritual begin now."

Eveneye looked at the pyramid and wondered why Irontooth had not told him how long he had to accomplish the task. He guessed that the riddle would explain his timeframe, so he moved over to the pyramid. He looked at the bears surrounding the pyramid as he approached. They did not return his gaze; they simply stood without moving, like statues, staring at the structure. Eveneye climbed the stairs and as he reached the top, he looked out over the crowd and noticed that some of the bears began to gasp. Some brought their paws to their mouths and seemed shocked. He also noticed, that of the bears whose eyes he could see, they were looking toward the base of the pyramid. Eveneye looked down and saw that the fourteen bears were lighting the pyramid on fire. He now understood his time limit. If he did not make his choice in time, he would be standing upon his own funeral pyre. He quickly moved over to the scroll and opened it. The riddle read thusly:

Choices four lie before
He who would seek the crown
To the right, a line of sight
May direct your decision down
Your other side, should you decide
To hear the Kingdom call
Place your fate in what you say
And allow yourself to fall

Eveneye looked to his right and saw two holes in the top of the pyramid, and to his left, another two holes. The holes were large enough for him to fit down, but not by much. He looked down into each of the holes and saw blackness. He could hear the fire crackle on the sides of the pyramid. *Calm yourself*, Eveneye said to himself. *You can do this.* Eveneye went back and read the scroll another time.

To the right, a line of sight may direct your decision down. Eveneye decided to start with the holes to the right of the scroll. He looked down into each hole and could only see blackness. He stood between the two holes and looked around the crowd. Eveneye let the words repeat in his head. *Line of sight. Direct your decision down.* Eveneye was sure that he should be looking for some visual evidence of what to do; he just didn't know how to interpret what he was seeing. Eveneye noticed that along the wall of the arena, hung the banners of the professional johnball teams that played in the kingdom. *Maybe the clue is in the banners,* he thought. His line of sight moved from different team banners as he moved around the holes. There was no clue as to where his line of sight should start from. Then an idea popped into Eveneye's head. He should stand where the scroll was and look out at the banners. He walked to the spot and looked out over the first hole. The team banner of the Flames lined up perfectly. *That has to be a bad sign,* he thought. Then he looked out over the other hole and saw the banner of the Fighting Fish. This was a more positive sign, but more confusing. *I must have been wrong.*

Eveneye decided to try the holes on the other side. He was beginning to feel the temperature go up and he could see and smell smoke. He read the second part of the scroll again. *Should you decide to hear the Kingdom call, place your fate in what you say and allow yourself to fall.* Once again, Eveneye allowed the words to play around in his mind. The other side seemed to be dealing with sight and this side seemed to be dealing with hearing. He decided to see if he could hear anything down the holes. He bent low, hung his head over one of the holes and listened. He could hear nothing, nor could he see anything. He tried the other and came up with the same result. He recited the scroll in his mind again, and 'place your fate in what you say' stood out. *Maybe I need to say something into the right hole. Maybe when I call out, something will present itself that is of some help.* He figured it was worth a shot and shouted down the first hole.

"Hello," Eveneye shouted. He received no response. Even further than that, from the echo his voice created, he could tell that the hole was very deep. *That hole must be so deep that the fall would kill me.* He moved to the other hole. "Hello," he called out again. No response. Yet this time, there was no echo at all. The hole was shallow, maybe too shallow. He would not want to choose that hole only to find himself stuck in the middle of a burning pyramid. *If only I could see.* It was getting very hot now and the smoke obscured his view of the crowd.

The flames had reached the top of the platform. His time was running short. Eveneye cursed. Then a grand idea came to him. He ran to the scroll and picked it up. He tore a piece of the scroll off and then went to the fire and lit it. He then rushed over to the shallow hole and dropped it in. Sure enough, the hole was too shallow. The walls of the hole were already starting to smoke. The hole was a trap. Thinking the other hole was too deep, Eveneye lit another piece of the scroll and headed to the hole he had lined up with the banner of the Flames. Anticipating the outcome, Eveneye backed away from the hole as he dropped the burning piece of scroll. A jet of flame shot out of the hole. The hole had been filled with some highly flammable substance. It was another trap, although, this seemed to confirm his theory about the banners.

The fire was closing in on him now and he didn't have much time. It seemed the hole that lined up with the Fighting Fish banner was the right choice. Fish were food, they were life, it must be the right choice. He began to lower himself into the hole and then heard a large splash come from the bottom. There was water down there, but he didn't know what was in the water. He decided to drop the rest of the scroll to the bottom of the hole. He heard it splash as it hit the water and then the water became a thrashing frenzy. There was something down there and whatever it was, it was not friendly. All that was left was the deep hole.

Eveneye spun and looked at it from across the platform. Flames were everywhere now and the smoke was burning his eyes. Just then, a giant, cracking sound ripped the air and the pyramid jolted. The flames were consuming it. *I'm out of time*, thought Eveneye. He quickly resigned himself to his fate and dashed for the deep hole. As he ran to it, the pyramid continued to break underneath him. Without a second thought, he launched himself into the hole and disappeared into the blackness.

The crowd could see nothing. The pyramid had become a great bonfire. Everyone expected the worst. Irontooth smiled from his high seat and turned his gaze at Goldenheart. Her face was wet with tears, though she made no sound. Whiteclaw sat emotionless.

"Let this be a lesson to the both of you," sneered Irontooth.

Irontooth turned back toward the crowd and inhaled the smell of smoke that had filled the air. He smiled and sighed in satisfaction, relishing the moment. He wanted to watch the pyramid until it became a pile of ash and he wanted every bear in the kingdom to watch it too.

As Eveneye fell, he closed his eyes, bracing for an impact that would never come. He had flung himself down the hole, headfirst, in a free fall. However, his body quickly came flush with the wall of the hole and it began to change his direction. Eveneye realized that the hole did not go straight down and was, in fact, an angled slide. The slide eventually came level and Eveneye skidded to a stop. He was in complete blackness but he could feel the walls on either side of him. He knew from which direction he had come and decided to continue in the opposite one. It was not long before Eveneye ran into a staircase, and as he began to climb it, pride welled up inside of him as it became clearer that he had chosen correctly. He came to the last step and hit his head on the ceiling. He pushed at it with his paw and it gave way. It was a trap door in the floor of the arena, and Eveneye pushed himself up and out of it.

Members of the crowd began to point as they noticed his presence, some sixty yards from the burning pyramid. As more of the crowd noticed, they began to cheer, no longer able to conceal their natural inclination to support the underdog. Whiteclaw and Goldenheart began to cheer as well. The guards raised their spears to the bears' throats and they were quickly silenced.

Irontooth shook with rage, unable to speak. Eveneye ran across the arena floor until he was under Irontooth's box and shouted at him.

"Irontooth," he called. "Tell my brother, Whiteclaw, that he shall help me rule this kingdom so that my heart never becomes as poisoned as yours."

Irontooth shot out of his seat and bellowed into the smoky air.

"Begin the second challenge now!"

This time, Irontooth gave no instructions to Eveneye and there was no doubt that this was done purposefully. The fourteen bears returned through the gate, yet one came back out carrying a johnball and motioned for Eveneye to follow him. The arena floor already had markings for johnball and Eveneye was led to the far end of the johnball field. The bear gave the ball to Eveneye and said, "Your goal is the opposite end of the field. When you hear the horns sound, you may begin. You must score only once."

Eveneye nodded and the bear turned and left the arena. Eveneye looked around and saw nothing in the arena other than the burning pile of wood that was once the pyramid. He kept his senses sharp. He knew that any moment his obstacles would be presented to him and they would most certainly be deadly. He took the johnball and waited, ready to run.

The horns sounded and a gate opened on the opposite side of the area. Gasps came from the crowd as ten giant wolves came, barreling out of the gate. The wolves were at least as big as the ones he and Whiteclaw had battled the previous night. Eveneye's wounds ached and his eyes narrowed. Despite his injuries, he had better battle more effectively than last night or it would cost him his life.

He immediately dropped the johnball and began running toward the fire. The ball would be no use to him unless he could kill all ten wolves. He had an idea and he quickly reached the perimeter of the blaze and turned toward the charging wolves. He stood on his hind legs and roared at the approaching pack. It did not slow them and Eveneye realized he would have to be fast. As the first two wolves reached him, they leapt into the air, going straight for his throat. Eveneye anticipated their jump and fell to the ground, as the wolves overshot him and landed in the flames. The next two wolves were immediately behind them, and Eveneye used their momentum against them, slashing at the first with his claws while sidestepping the other. His blow met the wolf under the chin, stunning it. The second wolf that he had sidestepped tried to stop itself, but could not until it had just passed Eveneye. He lined the wolf up and kicked it, sending it into the blaze. The stench of burning flesh and hair now permeated Eveneye's consciousness and sent adrenaline coursing through his veins. The wolf Eveneye had slashed came back at him and he was ready, swiping at it and knocking it into the fire as well.

Four down, six to go. Eveneye again stood on four legs and roared at the pack. They had grown wary of the fire and were no longer flinging themselves at him. It was now Eveneye's turn to go on the offensive. He flung himself upon the pack with reckless abandon. He took his claw and uppercut the first wolf under the jaw, lifting it into the air. With his other arm, he slapped a wolf to the ground. Stepping on its head with his hindquarters, he crushed its skull. Another wolf dove at him and he swung the wolf, impaled on his claw, down at it. The wolves came crashing together and rolled to the side, stunned and wounded. Eveneye used the small diversion and quickly darted at another wolf, catching its hind leg in his teeth. He crunched down and broke the wolf's leg. When he released it, the wolf fell to its side. Eveneye then clamped his jaw to its neck and ended the wolf's life. There were now four wolves left. The two Eveneye had knocked to the side were back on their feet, although one had been severely wounded under the jaw.

The wolves were now afraid of Eveneye and circled him, looking for a weakness. Eveneye had an idea of how to bait them in, though it would take all of his strength. He rose up on his hind legs and roared toward the ceiling of the arena. The wolves took the bait and launched themselves at him as he looked toward the sky. Immediately, he felt the searing pain of fangs in his flesh. All four wolves were upon him, hanging from his body. The weight was immense and it took all his strength to remain upright. Slowly, he gained his balance and took a step toward the fire, then he took another step and another. The crowd stared in awe as Eveneye, carrying four immense wolves, took one final step toward the fire and then fell backward upon it. The two wolves on his back were crushed between Eveneye and the burning wood. They relinquished their hold, and as soon as they did, Eveneye rolled. He then pushed himself up and off of the wolves that were on his stomach, crushing them against the fire as well. Eveneye was off of the blaze but the fur on his legs was on fire. He rolled on the arena floor and smothered it. The wolves were dead, but Eveneye had suffered severe burns on his legs.

He limped over to the johnball and picked it up in his mouth. The crowd began to cheer. They routed Eveneye onward as he limped, with the ball in his mouth, all the way to his goal. Once Eveneye had crossed the opponent's territory line, he dropped the johnball and called out to Irontooth.

"Irontooth! Tell my Kingdom to cheer louder! For my victory is their own!"

Irontooth stood from his chair and turned his back on the arena.

"It is time that I end this," he uttered through clenched teeth. Irontooth began to leave his box, but stopped short and stared at Goldenheart and Whiteclaw. Then he turned to one of his guards.

"When I have taken the life of that traitor, kill those two."

"Yes, Sire," answered the guard.

The crowd continued to cheer Eveneye and as he stood on the floor of the arena, he felt his strength waning. *I shall not fail*, thought Eveneye. *Just one last challenge.*

The horns sounded and the gate opened again. This time, Irontooth himself walked into the arena. The crowd quieted instantly, as if suddenly aware that their cheers for Eveneye had also been cheers against their King. Irontooth was bigger than Eveneye and as he walked toward the wounded bear, it was evident that rage was also on his side.

Eveneye closed his eyes and pictured his wife. He loved her more than anything in the world. He would not let her life continue without him, having to bare his disgrace. He would not leave her with that burden. The bear thought of his wife being shunned from the Kingdom and a fire rose in his belly. He gritted his teeth, furrowed his brow and opened his eyes. Irontooth stood directly in front of him and unleashed his wrath.

Irontooth swung and caught Eveneye on the side of the head with his paw, knocking him to the ground. He followed with another blow to Eveneye's ribs and then stepped on one of his burned legs. The pain was unbearable and the bear cried out. He rolled away from Irontooth, narrowly missing another blow to the head. Irontooth, however, would not let him escape. He pounced on Eveneye, pinning him on his back. Blow after blow came to Eveneye's head. His wounds had weakened him. Eveneye's vision began to blur as blood dripped into his eyes. Irontooth had control. Eveneye was going to die. He could hear Goldenheart cry out from far above as he drifted away.

Eveneye's mind drifted far above the scene of his wife, walking through the roads of the kingdom. Bears, along the sides of the road, were assaulting her with slurs and pelting her with rotting food. Whiteclaw wasn't far behind her, being taunted by children and stabbed at with spears. They were being banished from the mountain, sent far from the light of the Everflame, far from their home. Storm clouds formed in the sky and lightning flashed in the distance. At the top of Gray Mountain, the Everflame burned and upon its pyre, laid the body of a small boy.

"No," grunted Eveneye. He opened his eyes to see Irontooth on top of him, afire with vengeance.

"What did you say, you maggot?"

"I said, no."

Eveneye swung both of his arms up at Irontooth, sinking both sets of claws into the King's throat. He brought his hind legs up under Irontooth and pushed him off, rolling him over. Eveneye kept his claws in Irontooth's throat, rolling with him and ending up on top of him. Then, Eveneye bent his head down to Irontooth's ear.

"Tell whatever it is that waits on the other side of death that my life has only just begun."

And with those words, Eveneye tore Irontooth's throat out, defeating him and claiming the Kingdom. He stood and unleashed a primal roar as his Kingdom chanted his name.

4

Chapter 4: Rumors

Eveneye had never forgotten those words.

Why have you done this to yourself, Eveneye?

Those words haunted him, Irontooth's image haunted him, and the sculpture of Irontooth, standing right outside of his courtroom, haunted him. It had been fifteen years since he had killed Irontooth, but those words stayed as fresh as if they had just been spoken.

Why had he done it? Back then, he had been so sure of his convictions; so sure that his motives were just. But from time to time, he doubted himself and his decisions. He had taken another bear's life. It had not been in self-defense. Yes, it had been legal, but was it necessary, was it just? He had disagreed with Irontooth and had been backed into a corner. It was Irontooth or the boy. But was it?

Even the bears of the Kingdom had these questions. No one brought them to Eveneye, now that he was King, but Eveneye was no fool and he had heard the rumors. No one was displeased with how Eveneye ruled over the Kingdom, but some questioned his motives. Many more questioned his plan for the boy. An ambassador of peace, was it madness? Was he forcing a horrible fate onto the boy? Was he forcing a horrible fate onto his kingdom?

The bears had accepted the boy, or at least the majority had, and as King, Eveneye was able to provide him with everything a child could need. But the boy was grown now, and his fate was almost upon him. A fate Eveneye had sentenced him to when he had killed Irontooth. Eveneye felt that the boy was still too young, but the questions had already begun. When? His advisors had asked him on different occasions. When would Eveneye's plan for peace begin? When would the boy be ready? The truth was that Eveneye didn't know, and he was afraid that the Kingdom might force his decision before he had made up his own mind.

Eveneye thought back to those first few years after the ritual. They had been some of the happiest in his life. He and Goldenheart, playing with the boy and enjoying the leisure of being royalty. It had all seemed like such a dream. Lately, however, it seemed like sand falling through an hourglass. He could even pinpoint the exact event that had shattered his perfect little dream world, because it had broken his heart.

Papa, why am I different?

Even now, when he remembered it, his chest would tighten. What had he done? What horrible fate had he damned this boy to? That boy's entire world was the bears. Yet, if he stayed in the Kingdom, he would grow to be an incomplete man, never knowing the love of a woman or the miracle of seeing his own children. He would never completely fit. Yet, if he left the Kingdom for the world of man, he would be a man with no past and no one to help him. Would he even fit in man's society, having been raised by bears? His only hope rested on Eveneye's plan for peace. Eveneye had put this boy's only hope in a society that was both bear and man, and it scared him to pieces.

Eveneye sat next to Evercloud in the castle tower, looking out over the kingdom with the Everflame burning directly behind them. Both father and son would come up to the top of the tower to meditate or speak to each other, if they should please. It was something they had been doing together for a while now. Evening was upon them and the sky was shades of pink and violet, its hues becoming cooler as time passed. Eveneye had had enough of his own thoughts and decided he'd like to hear of his son's day. He looked over at the young man, his long, matted hair hanging around his bare shoulders. Evercloud wore leather pants and shoes but the bears hadn't seen the use for anything else during warm weather.

"Evercloud, what is it that happened today that made you ask about your name earlier?"

"Oh, nothing much. Riverpaw and I were having a discussion about names earlier, and I realized that I didn't know how I had received mine. I think that I had always assumed that it was because my skin is pale compared to a bear's fur, like the clouds are paler than the sky. But after Wintersun said it was because I had clouds for brains, Riverpaw and I began thinking on it."

"Why would Wintersun say that of you?"

"Only because I had told him that his true name was Fishface."

"And why would you do that?"

"Because he had said that Riverpaw played johnball like a female. Which was only Wintersun being sore, as Riverpaw and I had just won a match against he and Redcoat."

Eveneye chuckled heartily.

"I'm glad to see you getting on so well with your friends."

Evercloud smiled and climbed to his feet.

"Father, I've been meaning to ask if you and Uncle Whiteclaw might teach Riverpaw and I to night fish sometime? We are both very eager to learn."

"So it would seem," said Whiteclaw as he entered the room. "Riverpaw just asked me an hour ago. I told him yes, on the condition that the two of you continue to achieve high marks in your studies."

"Of course, Uncle. Thank you."

"All right, now run and tell your mother that the King is needed for an emergency meeting and it might take a while."

"Yes, Uncle." Evercloud said his goodbyes and then left the room.

"Emergency meeting?" asked Eveneye.

"Yes, I have the rest of the advisors assembled. We shouldn't waste time."

Eveneye rose to his feet and followed Whiteclaw down the tower steps. He knew what this meeting would be about. Eveneye had been expecting this for some time. His advisors were going to demand action on the plan for peace, or at least a timetable. Eveneye didn't want to think about it. So, as he and Whiteclaw made their way to the advising room, he figured that he would lighten the mood with talk of their sons. Whiteclaw had married soon after the ritual, and he and his wife, Autumnbreeze, had given birth to Riverpaw not long after.

"Did you hear? Our boys won a johnball match today."

"No, but I can't say I'm surprised."

"Yes, I should send a gift to Wintersun's and Redcoat's fathers for teaching their sons to be good sportsmen and taking it easy on a lesser opponent. My boy is lucky to have such kind friends."

Whiteclaw looked at his friend in confusion.

"Eveneye, when was the last time you watched your son play johnball?"

"Well," he hesitated, "I suppose that it has been a while. Why?"

"Well, first off, your boy is as large and capable a man as I have ever seen. Should he walk into a human village right now, they just might mistake him for a bear. Secondly, I assure you, no one is taking it easy on him. He is a very good player."

Eveneye beamed.

"Well, I'll have to make some time to see him play."

The bears had reached their destination and entered the room. All the advisors were seated around the table and Eveneye and Whiteclaw took their places. Eveneye didn't wait for someone else to begin.

"All right, I already know what this is about, and I have to say that I would ask you to have a little more faith in my ability to know when the time is right. I–"

"Er, Your Highness," interjected Oaktongue, a small, brown bear with a nasally voice, "I don't think that this meeting is about what you think it's about."

"Yes," added Forestmoon, "this meeting has been called to address a rumor that has been coming from outside of the Kingdom."

Eveneye looked around at his five advisors quizzically. This was definitely not what he was expecting and he was not prepared.

"Sire," said Whiteclaw, always addressing Eveneye more formally in front of others, "we have reason to believe that one of the Ancients has returned to our world."

"You can't be serious," returned Eveneye. "What evidence do we have of this?"

"Not a lot," answered Oaktongue. "Just a rumor, really. But the rumor has spread. Our scouts have heard the same rumor in the North of Ephanlarea as well as in the South, and it would seem that the rumor originates in the West."

Gray Mountain was located in the middle of the land of Ephanlarea. Eveneye knew it was uncommon to hear the same news over such a vast area, unless there was some validity to it.

"Well," and Eveneye shrugged, "continue."

"The rumor is this," continued Oaktongue, "a footprint has been found around the area of the White Mountains. The footprint of a giant griffin, to be exact."

"Tenturo," uttered Eveneye.

"Yes, Sire," said Oaktongue, "it would seem so."

A vast span of time had passed since the Ancients had been a part of the world. It had been so long that some bears believed the Ancients to be fiction, created by the elder bears. This rumor seemed fantastical. Eveneye spoke:

"I do appreciate being informed of this rumor and I would like to be updated with any new information that may arise, but I hardly see why I have been called to an emergency meeting that has me missing dinner with my family. I cannot justify taking action on a rumor, even if it is concerning the Ancients. Please, tell me you weren't expecting me to take a rumor at face value."

Now it was Whiteclaw's turn to speak.

"No, my King, not exactly. We did not expect you to believe this rumor. Yet this rumor, true or false, causes an issue that we need to address. Namely, the effect it will have on Evercloud's life."

"Oh, I see." Eveneye stood up and paced around the room for a moment. The other bears didn't dare interrupt him as they knew this was a delicate matter, but Eveneye didn't take very long to come to his decision. "Send for the boy."

"Excuse me, Sire?" said Forestmoon.

"You heard me. Have a guard retrieve the boy. It's time that he be told…everything."

5

Chapter 5: The Ancients

Evercloud entered the advisors room for the first time in his life, and it felt sacred. His father and five other bears sat at a round table of mahogany. There were no windows and the room was rather small. Four torches lit the room dimly, just one in each corner. As Evercloud looked around the room, each bear looked up at him with seemingly different expressions.

He first looked upon Oaktongue, smallest of the bears at the table, who seemed to be indifferent. Forestmoon, however, seemed nervous and jittery. His frame, which was thin by bear standards, almost seemed to vibrate with unease. This did not help Evercloud's own nerves. Sitting next to Forestmoon was Firerock, a large, gray bear. The bear was scowling at Evercloud. He hoped that Firerock's name served as an indication that the bear always had an unpleasant disposition, and that it wasn't due to Evercloud's presence. The next advisor, Redriver, seemed rather happy, by Evercloud's measure. That helped calm Evercloud's nerves a bit. However, all nerves were cast aside and replaced with confusion as he looked upon his uncle and then his father. Whiteclaw beamed at him with obvious pride. This would have been a great comfort, were it not for the fact that his father's face seemed so tortured and morose. Evercloud tried to remain balanced as he greeted each of the bears individually, although he was sure that he must have seemed apprehensive.

"Please, my son, be seated." Eveneye pointed at an empty chair across the table, right between Oaktongue and Forestmoon. Evercloud smiled and took his seat. "We have called you here today to teach you a bit of the history of the world. This is something that no man knows. It is a piece to a puzzle that has been lost to man for a very long time. In fact, this group has been in debates, for the majority of your life, as to whether you should be told at all. This information, it is believed, could be very dangerous in the hands of men." These words seemed to explain each bear's reaction toward Evercloud. "Recent events, however, have caused me to remove the issue from debate. I believe that it is now necessary to tell you these secrets. Better that you hear it from us, than from rumors that will undoubtedly spread through the Kingdom. If you are ready, I will have your uncle tell you of the Ancients. He is a better storyteller than I."

Evercloud's mouth was dry as he spoke.

"I am honored to have this knowledge bestowed upon me and I am ready."

"Then we shall begin," said Whiteclaw. "Once, there was nothing. Or at least that is the word that we use to describe what there was. You see, Evercloud, at one time, our world was made up of things that we have no words for and no images for, things our minds cannot conceive of. So we say that once, long ago, there was nothing, and we imagine it as infinite blackness.

"All we have as a clue to our origin are the teachings of the elder bears. Though even they do not know of true origins. The first things they have told us of were the Ancients. The Ancients were strange creatures. Not at all like the creatures of today's world, but at the same time, very much like many of the creatures we know. There were four of them and they controlled the elements of our world.

"There was the mermaid, Chera, who controlled the water. There was Bahknar the dragon, who controlled the element of fire. Tenturo the griffin, who had the head and wings of an eagle, but the body of a lion. He controlled the air. Finally, there was Densa. Densa was a gigantic beast, who most closely resembled a gorilla, and he controlled the element of earth.

"Each of these Ancients created many creatures to populate the earth. It is believed that it was Densa who created the Kingdom of Bears. Man, however, was another story. The Ancients wished to create a creature that embodied a bit of them all. So they gathered together and drew upon all of their strength. Densa created the form and Chera added to it water. Bahknar used fire to give it warmth and then Tenturo breathed into it air. This was the way in which they created man. Man was to be the connection between all creatures. Man was to be the balance. The Ancients also gave unto man some of the powers of the elements. They gave man slight control of wind, water, earth and fire, so that man could help the world flourish. The Ancients had created a utopia and man was their bastion of peace. The earth saw ages of prosperity for itself and all creatures.

"But then the Great Tyrant came and destroyed the utopia of the Ancients. It is said that the Great Tyrant possessed a power that the Ancients did not. It is said that he could summon the lightning from the sky. The Ancients were powerless against him. The Great Tyrant hunted the Ancients, hell-bent on destroying them. Given little choice, the Ancients fled from the earth, never to return.

"The Great Tyrant took control of the creatures of the earth, driving them apart. Mankind became his slave and he forbade them from controlling the elements, under the penalty of death. The Great Tyrant had cast an ominous cloud over the earth and ruled it for many ages. After a time, mankind forgot its powers. It was not long before the entire world had forgotten what it once was. It was now a world afraid, amid the storm of the Great Tyrant.

"The elders say that over time, the Great Tyrant's rule became more and more distant, until it seemed as though he had disappeared. To this very day, we do not know if the Great Tyrant still controls the earth or if he has gone and left the world that he destroyed."

Whiteclaw stopped here to see if Evercloud had understood everything and to see if he had any questions.

"So," started Evercloud, "I mean no disrespect, but are these just stories or are they true?"

"We take no offense, Evercloud. In fact," and Whiteclaw glanced over at his King, "there are many bears who have their doubts. Though the majority of the Kingdom does believe this account to be true."

"Does this mean that I can control the elements?"

"The truth is that we don't know. Outside of the elder's teachings, there is no record of any human with these abilities."

Eveneye, at this point, interjected.

"I understand this is confusing for you, Evercloud. I have labored under the weight of whether to tell you this or not for many years. I only want what is the best decision for you and for this kingdom. I only want to keep you from danger."

"What danger?" asked Evercloud. "I don't see the danger in hearing these stories."

"Well," said Whiteclaw, "I was about to get to that. You see, rumor has been circling the land outside of this kingdom of a giant footprint in the West, the footprint of a griffin. Many inside the kingdom, as well as outside, believe this may be the marking of the Ancient, Tenturo."

"And Tenturo is dangerous?" asked Evercloud.

"Well, no," said Whiteclaw, slightly confused. "I mean, he shouldn't be."

Oaktongue took Whiteclaw's hesitation as an opportunity to step in.

"The danger is, Evercloud, that you may wish to explore the truth in this rumor. There is thought that you may wish to search for the Ancient, in hope of regaining the power that was given to man... There is also the fact... that some...believe you should."

At this, Eveneye shot Oaktongue darts from his eyes and the small bear cowered.

"It is my decision whether the boy goes or not. If it is to be debated, I would ask you to save your feelings for another time."

"Perhaps this is a matter we should address directly, my King," added Redriver.

"Fine," said Eveneye. "Evercloud, return to your mother and let her know I will be a bit longer."

"Father, I have something to say." Evercloud stood up as he said this and it surprised the bears. It was not strange for them to be in the presence of

41

Evercloud, but Evercloud had only just become a man. It was odd for them to hear words of authority coming from him. No one knew quite how to handle it.

"Speak, my son. What is it that bothers you?"

Evercloud took a moment to choose his words wisely. He knew that he had little chance of being allowed to stay in the room, and he had better not say the wrong thing.

"I want to thank all of you for allowing me to hear of the Ancients. I feel very honored to have been accepted by the Kingdom. I understand that I am the King's son, but I also understand that I am a man and that it may be difficult for you to place faith in me. I owe the citizens of the Kingdom, as well as the King, my life. With that said, I am a man, and will not have my fate decided without my own input. You have had faith in me, accepting me into your Kingdom, and you must now continue to have faith that I will make my decisions with the Everflame in my heart. I wish to be present for this debate."

Evercloud, once again, took his seat and he kept his gaze upon his father's eyes, waiting for a response. There was no immediate reaction, but Evercloud thought that, as he looked upon his father, he could see the smallest of grins break across his mouth. Then Eveneye stood, as his son had, and addressed him.

"As I look upon you this evening, my son. I am proud and I know that the decisions that I made, years ago, were the right decisions. You may sit with this esteemed group of bears and your input will be considered. But first, let us go to the dining hall and eat something. This promises to be a long night."

Eveneye, Whiteclaw and Evercloud sat at their own table in the dining hall. Many citizens of the Kingdom were taking their meals in the dining hall this night, creating enough noise as to allow for private conversation.

"Do you think I overstepped my bounds?" asked Evercloud.

"I don't think so," said Whiteclaw. I think you were assertive, yet respectful. I'm sure that the others understand your feelings."

"It reminded me of when you were younger," began Eveneye with a smile.

"Oh, here comes another Evercloud story," said Whiteclaw.

"What?" quipped Eveneye. "Do I tell many of these?"

"No, of course not," Whiteclaw said with sarcasm, and then winked at Evercloud.

"How about you eat your meal and be quiet, so that I can talk to my son, you old grouch."

Whiteclaw chuckled and Eveneye began again.

"It reminded me of your first day in school, Evercloud. I was so afraid that you might hate it and that the cubs might give you a hard time. When I came to collect you later that day, I asked your teacher how it went. I'll never forget how proud I was to hear what she told me that day. She told me that you had stood up to some cubs that were bullying a weaker cub. Oh, what was that little cub's name?... It doesn't matter. Anyway, she said that the bullies had left and then you stayed and helped the weaker cub with his work that day. She told me that you were a natural leader and that I had done a very good job with you."

"I think I sort of remember that," said Evercloud. "But why did today remind you of that?"

"You aren't afraid to take a stand for what you feel is right. You did it then and you did it today. It's a good thing."

Evercloud nodded and continued to eat his meal, thinking on his father's words.

"I think we'd better finish up," said Whiteclaw. "Firerock's starting to shoot us daggers from across the hall."

"Is he always like that?" asked Evercloud.

"Unfortunately, yes," said Whiteclaw. "Can't really blame him, though. I'd be angry all the time if I looked like he does."

Evercloud smiled and Eveneye rolled his eyes.

"We'd better go," said Eveneye.

As they all returned to the advisors room, Eveneye briefly took his son aside, just outside of the room.

"These conversations can get ugly sometimes. Do what you can to not take anything too personally. The beginning to our plan for peace is convincing those bears that do not believe in it to agree to its merit. In a way, your actions here will go a long way to convincing certain bears that humans can be beneficial allies. If you were to act inappropriately tonight, it might be difficult to counteract the repercussions. You have to remember, at our core, bears are as afraid of humans as humans are bears."

"I won't fail you, Father."

Eveneye smiled at his son and they entered the room. Evercloud worried that it might be his father who might not remain collected. Everyone took a seat and Eveneye began the debate.

"So, tonight we need to come to a decision concerning the rumor of the Ancient and what action should be taken. As we usually do, we will go around the table and state our positions. After we have all spoken, we will debate. I'll begin." Eveneye shuffled in his seat and gazed around the table. "As you all know, I do not necessarily believe in the tales told by our elders. It is my charge to make decisions that protect the interests of the Kingdom. So my position is quite simple. Without greater proof than mere rumor, I believe it would be foolish to give this possibility our attention until we are presented with further information. Furthermore, I believe it is time to explore our options concerning our plan for peace with the humans." Eveneye smiled. "It would seem our boy has become a man."

43

The bears nodded in agreement of the final statement and the floor now belonged to Whiteclaw.

"Thank you, King. As you all know, I believe wholeheartedly in the teachings of the elders. Although this is naught but a rumor, I do believe it should be investigated. However, I agree with the King that it is time to implement our plan for peace. Someone should investigate the rumor, but not Evercloud. He is needed here."

"Thank you, Whiteclaw," followed Forestmoon. "I, too, believe in the teachings of the elders and I fear this rumor of the Ancient's return. If, in fact, one or all of the Ancients have returned, we need to know as soon as possible. Those who hope to have amiable relations with them should not ignore beings so strong. I agree with Whiteclaw."

Redriver came next.

"I agree with the King. We cannot throw our resources into the ring with rumors. If our imminent future lies in this plan for peace with the humans, then we must put all our efforts toward that goal." Redriver shrugged. "What do we have to gain by tracking down an Ancient, anyway?"

"Unfortunately," began Oaktongue, "I don't agree with any of you. Who are we to use this boy as some political pawn? We are doing fine without the aid of humans and we have been." Eveneye grimaced. "What is the rush in this plan for peace? Let the boy go find the Ancient. If it were I who had lost a part of my history, I would wish to regain it."

Now it was Firerock's turn.

"I like none of these options. This plan for peace has still given me no reason to endorse it. I do not trust men, they are vile." Now Evercloud knew why his father had warned him. "Let us not forget, they tried to kill one of their own. A bear would do no such thing. Also, the boy should not be allowed to look for the Ancient. Why would we wish to see humans have more power, to hunt us further? Let us, instead, continue our lives and forget about these dreams."

Lastly, the turn came to Evercloud. Firerock's words had stung him, but he kept his promise to his father and did not let his emotions get the better of him. Instead, he focused his energy into making his position known.

"What authority do I have? How can I be an ambassador of peace? Who will listen to me? In my own kingdom, I am viewed as an outsider. You just heard testimony of the distrust for humans. What have I done to change those feelings? Nothing. And what of the world of man? What authority do I hold over them? I am no king of men, no champion of the people. They will not listen to me. I must find the Ancient and regain the powers men once held. Only then, will I command authority. I will use these powers justly, so that this kingdom will trust my actions. And with these powers, the world of man will take my words seriously. With authority, the plan for peace will work. I must go and find the Ancient."

No one had considered the fact that humans may not listen to Evercloud. The realization came as a shock to them. Oaktongue was the first to respond.

"I agree with Evercloud. With the power of the Ancients, there is no chance that the plan for peace could fail. Besides, it is what he wishes to do. We should not stand in his way."

"I will agree with Evercloud as well. He brings up a very valid point," added Redriver.

Evercloud beamed. Had he done it? Had he convinced them?

"The boy may have changed Redriver's mind, but not mine. I keep my original position." Firerock pounded his paw upon the table.

"I'll stand with Evercloud," said Forestmoon. "His words make sense."

That was four of the seven. That was a majority. Evercloud knew this was not a majority rule decision, but he could not help but be hopeful. Whiteclaw now took his opportunity to speak.

"I understand that this is a difficult decision for everyone, and I understand that there are many factors that weigh on each decision. It would seem to me that the largest factor involved in this discussion is whether Evercloud should be focused on the plan for peace or with finding the Ancient. I understand that both these issues are important to all citizens of the Kingdom, however, in these situations, it is best to look at things logically. Both issues concern Evercloud, but Evercloud is not needed to address both issues. I volunteer myself and my son, Riverpaw, to travel the land and search for signs of the Ancient. Evercloud can stay here and work with this group on the plan for peace. Should Riverpaw and I find further evidence of the Ancient, then we can reevaluate the situation."

"But, Uncle," started Evercloud. Eveneye shot him a glare as soon as the words left his mouth and Evercloud quickly remembered his promise. Eveneye began to speak before anyone else could add their thoughts on the matter.

"I have heard all of your positions and I believe that I fully understand where each of you is coming from. Each of you speaks for the Kingdom and you must remember that I do as well. The majority of the Kingdom believes in the existence of the Ancients, so I give any matter concerning the Ancients great respect. Yet, the fact still remains that we have nothing but a rumor as evidence. Evidence of the distrust between the humans and ourselves permeates everything we do. Its evidence sits in this very room. It makes no logical sense to me to sacrifice minds and bodies to a rumor, when there is an actual issue they could be focused on. We have scouts that move through Ephanlarea to bring us news. I say, have patience, and let them do their job." Eveneye now turned his gaze upon his son. "As to the issue of your authority, Evercloud. You carry the authority of the Kingdom and every bear that is a part of it. Do not take that power so lightly."

"I apologize, Father. I meant no disrespect."

"I know that you did not. There is no need for apology." Eveneye looked around the room and it seemed that no one had anything else to add. "I believe that this meeting is over, for now. Let us gather again, two days from now, to discuss the plan for peace."

Everyone nodded their heads in agreement and got up to leave the room. Eveneye stayed back and kept his son, so that he may speak to him privately. Alone, Evercloud felt he could speak to his father more freely.

"Father, you know that I love the Kingdom. I would do nothing to jeopardize it. However, your words do not reassure me the way you had hoped they would."

"How do you mean, Evercloud?"

"I may have the body of a man, but still, I have done nothing to prove my worth as a man. If I carry the authority of the Kingdom of Bears into the world of man, will they not fear it instead of embracing it?"

"I understand your concerns, my son, but you still do not allow for the possibility that this is an issue we can resolve through conversation. You are but our key into that conversation."

Evercloud looked at his father with doubtful eyes.

"I suppose."

"I think that it is late, and I think that we should reserve any further conversation for the morning."

Evercloud nodded and then followed his father out of the room.

As the castle fell into slumber, the mountain lay silently beneath it. The Everflame burned bright against the blackness of the sky. It was a clear night and if you took your eyes away from the flame, you could see the stars. They twinkled brightly in the sky and if anyone in the Kingdom had been stargazing that night, they may have noticed that one star in particular seemed to be getting slightly larger, minute-by-minute.

6

Chapter 6: Lights In The Sky

When morning came, Evercloud got up and ran to his uncle's cave to wake his cousin, Riverpaw. There were no lessons to attend on this day and he was eager to tell Riverpaw of the night before.

"Wake up, you mountain of fur." Evercloud pushed his cousin's shoulder, trying to wake him. Riverpaw rolled over slowly and scowled at Evercloud.

"This had better be a dream."

"Come on. Get up. Let's go fishing." Evercloud bent low and whispered into his cousin's ear. "I attended the emergency meeting last night."

Riverpaw shot up, wide-eyed. Evercloud put his finger to his mouth, signaling silence. Riverpaw understood and both of them quickly made for the cave's exit.

"Not so fast, you two," Whiteclaw spoke from behind.

"We're only going fishing," said Riverpaw.

Whiteclaw walked over to Evercloud and Riverpaw and gave them a knowing look.

"Evercloud, I don't expect for a minute that you would not share what happened last night with your cousin, but by the Everflame, do not let anyone else hear you."

"We'll go far into the forest, Uncle. I promise."

"This must be good," whispered Riverpaw.

The two cousins made their way off of the mountain as fast as they could. Weaving their way down the road, through bears pulling carts of merchandise, and elderly bears out for a morning stroll. One grizzled, old bear cursed them as they bolted past. Once they had made it to the forest at the base of Gray Mountain, they slowed to a walk and caught their breath. It was a beautiful day and very warm. They might run into other bears on a day like today, so neither of them spoke to each other until they had walked about a mile into the forest.

"So, out with it. We're in the clear. What happened?"

Evercloud related the meeting to Riverpaw with the best accuracy that he could. Riverpaw's eyes were wide with surprise. He couldn't believe what he was hearing.

"So, they finally told you. I didn't ever think that they would."

"How long have you known about the Ancients?"

"It's been years. They told us about the Ancients when we were young, but we all had to swear to keep it from you, under penalty of death."

Evercloud chuckled.

"Death? Come on."

"I'm serious, Evercloud. They scared us pretty good."

"Well, it doesn't matter anyway. They're not going to let me do anything about it."

"It's too bad. I wish your father had let me and Pop go and look for the Ancient. That would be a great adventure."

Evercloud and Riverpaw had almost made their way to the stream, when their stomachs began to grumble.

"We didn't eat anything before we left and I'm starving," moaned Riverpaw. "Sit on the bank of the stream and I'll catch us a meal."

"I know how to catch a fish," said Evercloud indignantly.

"I didn't say that you didn't, but by the time you find a long stick and sharpen the point with a rock, I'll have us a meal already."

"Well, when you put it that way."

Riverpaw chuckled and slowly crept into the stream. Evercloud sat down on the bank and began to toss a stone he had found into the air. He watched Riverpaw, standing in the stream, the sunlight sparkling on the surface of the water. The air was hot and dry and the day seemed to have a dreamlike haze to it. He heard a splash and Riverpaw had caught breakfast. Riverpaw tossed the fish to Evercloud and he began to eat. It wasn't long before Riverpaw joined Evercloud on the bank and ate his catch. They finished their meal and then sprawled out on their backs, staring at the clouds.

"So," started Riverpaw, "you must be pretty excited to start this whole plan for peace thing, huh? I mean, it's gonna make you pretty important."

"To tell you the truth, Riverpaw, I really wish that I didn't have to do it. I just don't really know what everyone thinks I'm going to be able to do."

"Well, aren't you at least excited to meet some other humans?" asked Riverpaw, yawning.

"No. Not really." Evercloud watched a butterfly flit through the air. He knew that he wasn't a child anymore but he just didn't know if he was ready for this responsibility. "What if I don't know how to be human?" Riverpaw didn't respond so Evercloud continued. "The Kingdom is all I can remember. What if I don't know how to be like a human anymore? Maybe I've been gone too long. I don't know, Riverpaw. What do you think? ... Riverpaw?"

Snores came from Riverpaw. He had fallen asleep. Evercloud felt the grass between his toes and fingers.

"You're right. I shouldn't worry about it."

Evercloud laughed to himself as his own eyelids began to get heavy. The sun was bright today. The day was almost perfect, as if it had been drawn from the pages of a fairy tale story. As Evercloud fell asleep, the clouds began to take shape in his mind. They seemed as if they were taking the shape of a man, a man in the clouds.

•••

Bahknar said that men are dead. Men are dead, Bahknar said. Bahknar said that hope is dead and lost forever more.

"What?... What did you say, Riverpaw?" Evercloud sat up and rubbed the sleep out of his eyes. He didn't know how long he'd been sleeping, but Riverpaw was still asleep next to him. "Wake up, Riverpaw… Riverpaw, I heard something. Get up." Evercloud shook Riverpaw and as he did, he heard it again.

Bahknar said that men are dead. Men are dead, Bahknar said. Bahknar said that hope is dead and lost forever more.

"There it was again. Did you hear it?"

"Hear what?" Riverpaw was groggy from sleep and slow to his feet. Once he had his senses about him, he saw Evercloud walking away from him into the forest. "Hey, where are you going?" he called.

"I think it's coming from over here."

"What are you talking about?" grumbled Riverpaw as he began to follow Evercloud through the forest. Riverpaw followed Evercloud for a couple of minutes and was just about to stop, when he heard it himself. Evercloud was just a few paces in front of him now, and the bear saw Evercloud stoop to the forest floor and cup something in his hands. Evercloud stood back up as Riverpaw reached him and looked over his shoulder.

"What is it?" asked Riverpaw.

"It's a mouse," answered Evercloud as he opened his hands to reveal a small, white mouse. The mouse looked at Evercloud and spoke.

"Bahknar said that you were dead." Evercloud and Riverpaw stared, wide-eyed at the mouse. "But you looks alive to me."

"Ask it a question," whispered Riverpaw.

"Do-Do you speak of Bahknar the dragon?" asked Evercloud.

"That depends," said the mouse. "Who wants to know?"

"We do. My name is Evercloud and this is my cousin, Riverpaw. Tell me, mouse, has the Ancient returned?"

"Put me down first."

Evercloud put the mouse back on the ground and it looked back up at him.

"Bahknar has never left," said the mouse and then scurried away, disappearing underneath the roots of a nearby tree.

"Wait!" called Evercloud. "Where can I find him? Mouse! Come back!"

"Evercloud," began Riverpaw. "We have to tell your father. We have to tell the King what just happened."

49

"Yes… You're right." Evercloud smiled and patted his cousin on the shoulder. "Let's go."

Riverpaw smiled back at him.

"Get on my back. I'll run all the way to the castle and you can shout to everyone we see the news we've discovered."

Evercloud leapt onto Riverpaw's back and they were off. The trees flew past them and Evercloud whooped into the air. The wind felt good on his face. Evercloud couldn't remember the last time he had felt this good. This news they had would change everything that had been talked about the night before. Evercloud was sure that finding the Ancients would now become priority over everything. What was peace between bears and humans, when there could be peace throughout the whole world?

"The Ancients live!" shouted Evercloud into the forest air, wanting to believe.

Soon, Riverpaw and Evercloud broke clear of the forest and onto the roads of Gray Mountain. The roads were filled with bears and Evercloud began shouting to everyone in sight. However, no one seemed to notice Evercloud and Riverpaw. Everyone was standing in the streets, staring blankly up at the sky. Riverpaw stopped running and skidded to a stop.

"Evercloud… Look…"

Evercloud and Riverpaw looked into the sky to see what everyone else had been staring at.

"Riverpaw, what…what is that?"

There, floating hundreds of feet in the air above the Everflame, was what looked like a giant ball of lightning. Everyone stood with their mouths agape, unable to believe what they were seeing. The giant ball of lightning was slowly moving to the north, and when you squinted your eyes, it seemed as though, sitting in the middle of the ball, there was a figure of a man.

"I've never seen that before," said Riverpaw.

"We'd better find my father. I don't have a good feeling about this."

At once, Riverpaw began running toward the castle. The mountain was silent except for Riverpaw's pads against the stone. It was as if time stood still all around them. From Riverpaw's back, Evercloud continued to look into the sky. He noticed that dusk had fallen on the mountain. *We haven't been gone that long, have we?* he thought to himself. The giant ball shone bright against the violet sky. As he continued to look up, he noticed that he couldn't find the setting sun. All of a sudden, he wasn't so sure that it was dusk that he was seeing or if it was just some sort of illusion created by the giant ball. The air was warm but a chill ran the length of Evercloud's back. He lowered himself closer to Riverpaw's back as the bear continued to run for the castle. Evercloud felt vulnerable. He felt like a line had been crossed and there was no going back. He swallowed and hung onto Riverpaw as hard as he could.

Evercloud could see the castle now, and as they approached, the doors swung inward. Riverpaw ran until he was inside the castle walls and then came to a stop, just in front of two guards who were barring their way.

"Evercloud. Riverpaw," spoke one of the guards. "Your families are at the top of the tower. Please continue on to the tower without delay."

"Thank you," said Riverpaw and he continued on.

Riverpaw continued to move as fast as he could, up the tower stairs. Evercloud could hear his own heartbeat matching the rhythm of Riverpaw's strides. They reached the room that housed the Everflame and each saw their families, visibly relieved to see them. Goldenheart rushed over to Evercloud and threw her furry arms around him.

"We were so worried. Where have you two been?"

"We fell asleep," said Evercloud, muffled through his mother's embrace. "What is that thing in the sky?"

Goldenheart released her son and turned her sullen eyes over to her husband. Eveneye looked at his wife and then to the young man he called son.

"We are... not... sure."

The King's words came cautiously from his mouth, as if he were not sure that he wished to let them go. Whiteclaw came over and put a paw on his shoulder.

"It may be wisest, Even, to assume the worst."

The King sighed and dropped his shoulders. After a moment, he looked up at his friend.

"Unfortunately, Whiteclaw, I think that you may be right."

"It's the Great Tyrant, isn't it?" said Riverpaw as he stood next to his mother. "He has returned, hasn't he?"

Everyone looked at Riverpaw with a mixture of pain and astonishment. The King was the first to speak.

"We are not positive. We don't know this for sure. But... I don't know what else it could be."

"Father," began Evercloud, "something happened to Riverpaw and I in the forest that may tie into this strange event." The room turned their attention to him like confused children looking for an answer to the most important question in the world. "Well... we fell asleep by the stream and... we were woken by a voice." He looked to Riverpaw for assurance and Riverpaw nodded him on. "The voice turned out to be coming from a mouse; a little white mouse. He kept repeating a rhyme."

Evercloud told the room of the rhyme and of the white mouse. Expecting to have his discovery swept away as coincidence and foolishness, he was hesitant with his delivery. He had lost the bravado he and Riverpaw had held in the forest. His words seemed juvenile now, especially with the concern of what was now taking place. Riverpaw had to prod him on through the story

51

in different places. He was no longer sure that what had happened to them in the forest was even of any importance. When he had finished recounting his tale, he found it difficult to meet the others' eyes. For some reason, he felt ashamed, as if he had just mocked the severity of the situation. The room was grim. The bears looked to Eveneye for wisdom and he merely stared at his son. Whiteclaw was the first to break the silence.

"Eveneye... My King... What say you?"

Eveneye gazed at his friend and as he met his eyes, he seemed to realize his place again, as well as the importance of what he was about to say.

"I say...that I was wrong." Everyone seemed puzzled by his remark, with the exception of Whiteclaw. "I believe our sole purpose, now, is to find the Ancients, or at least do all that we can to. I cannot explain away that thing in the sky. Without it, it is easy to dismiss our other information as rumor and coincidence. But if that thing in the sky is what we believe it to be, then these rumors may be our only hope for salvation. We must find the Ancients." Whiteclaw nodded in agreement and everyone else remained silent. Eveneye spoke again. "Riverpaw, I need you to retrieve my advisors. We will need to hold an emergency meeting. I also wish for you to be present at this meeting."

Riverpaw rose to his feet with alacrity, beaming with pride.

"Yes, my King. I am honored."

"Go now," said Eveneye, "and make haste."

Riverpaw left the room at once and then, Eveneye turned to Goldenheart and Autumnbreeze.

"I need the two of you to gather all the castle's servants and have them prepare a feast to be held in the arena. I wish for the entire kingdom to be there. Tonight we will celebrate and honor what may be the greatest quest in the history of the bears."

Eveneye then motioned to both Whiteclaw and Evercloud and they departed for the advisors room.

It did not take long for Riverpaw to round up the King's advisors. With a giant ball of lightning floating across the sky, they had already made their way into the castle in preparation for just a meeting. As Eveneye, Whiteclaw and Evercloud entered the room, the advisors were already seated and waiting. The three new arrivals took seats and Eveneye began speaking at once.

"I thank all of you for attending this meeting at such short notice. I respect all of you very much and your opinions have always held great weight in my mind. Though as I speak to you now, it is without the intention to spark debate. I have brought you here to give forth decree." The bears around the table glanced at each other, obviously worried but trying desperately not to show it. "With the appearance of this entity in our sky, I have decided it is in the Kingdom's best interest to prepare ourselves for the worst possibilities. I, at this time, would say that two things are true of this entity in the sky. The first truth being that we do not know what it is or what the significance of its appearance is. The second truth being that the worst possibility is that it is the return of the Great Tyrant and all of our lives are in peril. As I have already said, we are dealing in uncertainties. However, it would be foolish to wait for further proof before we act. With that said, this is what I have decided our course of action shall be. As I speak, a banquet is being prepared in the Mountain Arena to be attended by every citizen of the Kingdom. It is to be a celebration to honor both the Ancients and our champions. We, my brothers, are these champions. At this banquet, I will announce two things. The first announcement will be the creation of the Protection League. Four of you shall have prominent roles in this league. Firerock, it will now be your priority to train the bears of the mountain to defend themselves. We bears have never had a problem defending ourselves, but we may, for the first time in our history, be confronted with powers stronger than our own. Forestmoon, it will be your charge to construct a barrier around Gray Mountain. No longer is it safe for creatures to come and go from our home, unchecked. Redriver, I wish for you to create an armory. There very well may come a day when every able-bodied bear will need to be equipped for battle. Lastly, Oaktongue, I wish you to head a communications team. We need eyes and ears all over Ephanlarea so that we are fully prepared. Our small number of scouts will no longer suffice. I will oversee the league, but it is the four of you who hold its power. Do you understand?" The four bears nodded their heads. "The second announcement is that I will be sending out a search party to look for the Ancients. Whiteclaw will head the group and he will be accompanied by both Riverpaw and Evercloud." Riverpaw and Evercloud beamed at each other. This was exactly what they had wanted. Others, however, did not share their enthusiasm and found they could no longer hold their tongues. Firerock spoke:

"Sire, is there truly to be no debate on these decisions?"

"No, Firerock, and I will tell you why. There are very few facts I base these decisions on, very few, indeed. It is a gut feeling and a gut feeling is not a matter to debate. Secondly, I am king and leader. The responsibility falls on me and so should the failures, if it is to be so. But we need solidarity. We must unite. A bear that second-guesses himself in times of action cannot lead a kingdom. No bear would follow me, nor should they. It is not station alone that leads our Kingdom, but also decisiveness and passion. Our Kingdom deserves my strength, now more than ever. I, in turn, need yours."

Oaktongue rose to his feet and gazed at the King.

"You have mine, my King."

"Mine as well," said Whiteclaw.

After Whiteclaw, the other bears echoed him in turn, as did Evercloud. Last to stand was Firerock and he spoke thusly:

"My King, I have a confession. The day that I became one of your advisors was one of the happiest days of my life. I was so happy to be able to serve the Kingdom alongside you. You, who had shown more courage and strength than any other bear I had ever known. I was in awe of you. But during my time on this board, you have disappointed me. Your lack of decisiveness had changed my opinion of you. I longed to see the power you had exhibited during your ritual challenges. Tonight, you have shown me that you are still that bear and I am honored to call you my King. I give to you every ounce of strength I possess. Long live, King Eveneye."

At this, everyone in the room, with the exception of the king himself, echoed these last words.

"Long live, King Eveneye."

"Thank you," said Eveneye. "All of you. You double my heart in size. I would now ask that you all prepare yourselves for a celebration tonight. For it is tonight that we give to our Kingdom its heroes."

7

Chapter 7: For The Kingdom

"Evercloud, you've been silent ever since the end of our meeting with the advisors. Are you all right?"

Evercloud was beginning to feel the enormity of what was happening. He didn't know how to begin processing it. His head was swimming with everything that had transpired. It was a lot to take in.

"I'm fine, Father. It's just…" Evercloud paused. He had so many questions.

"Don't hesitate to talk to me, Evercloud. You will be leaving soon and I don't want anything unresolved before you go. Please, ask me anything."

Evercloud saw his father's concern and it eased the words out of his mouth.

"Well, how did you come up with this plan so quickly? I mean, it was as if you already had it laid out."

"You are very perceptive. In fact, I did have it mapped out. It was a plan I hoped that I would never have to use, but it was important to have it ready nonetheless. You see, Evercloud, often times, it is best to prepare for any situation, regardless if that situation should present itself or not. You would do well to remember that… Was that all that was bothering you?"

"I know that you have never really believed in the Ancients. So, I was wondering if you really think that they and the Great Tyrant have returned or if this is something that needs to be done just to appease the Kingdom?"

"It is true that I have not taken the stories of the Ancients as truth in the past. Even still, I do not know if I believe these stories in their entirety. However, it would be ignorant of me, at this point, to not admit that at least part of these stories are true. As I said already, there are things going on that I cannot explain. It would be foolish of me to not consider all the possibilities. I believe a better answer to your question, however, would be that I would never send you off on such a quest if I did not believe that you wouldn't find *something*. Does that make sense?"

"Yeah. I guess so." Evercloud still looked bothered by everything that swirled around in his brain. He decided to continue with the questions. "What about me? What about… my abilities?"

"What exactly do you mean, your abilities?"

"Well… I'm not a bear. How am I going to defend myself on this quest? What if we should come under attack?"

"You are more capable than you think, Evercloud." Eveneye paused. "I think your questions may be better suited for after the celebration. Some things may be revealed to you that may quench your curiosity."

Eveneye put his arm around his son and nodded as they stood outside the King's box seats at the arena. Goldenheart waited inside, as did Whiteclaw, Autumnbreeze and Riverpaw. Evercloud nodded back at his father with a grin.

"Come on," Eveneye said to the boy. "Let's join the others. I guarantee this will be a night that you never forget."

They entered the box and looked out over the arena. As Evercloud gazed out onto the arena floor, he couldn't believe his eyes. The entire floor of the arena was covered with tables and chairs and the bears of the Kingdom were already feasting on all types of food. The smell of cooked meats and hot breads filled the air. Evercloud had never seen such a spectacle.

"How did the servants put this together so quickly?" asked Evercloud in astonishment.

"Preparation," said the King. "Nothing is impossible if you have planned accordingly."

Evercloud noticed that at one end of the arena, there was a raised platform with a podium and some chairs behind it.

"We'll be going down there after we've eaten," said Eveneye.

In the King's box, a table was set up with many of the same foods that sat on the tables below. Seated at the table were Goldenheart, Whiteclaw, Autumnbreeze and Riverpaw. Eveneye and Evercloud took their seats at the table and began to join in the feast. Everyone filled their plates high with the exception of Evercloud. The enormity of the night had stripped him of his appetite. Riverpaw sat to his right and nudged him with an elbow.

"Eat something. You don't want to have to make your speech on an empty stomach."

"My sp-speech?"

"Riverpaw, you're making more of this than it is," chided Whiteclaw and then turned to Evercloud. "You won't be expected to make a speech, but when you are presented, you'll be expected to say a few words. It's not a big deal."

"Don't worry, sweetheart," added Goldenheart. "Just let it come naturally."

"Yeah, sweetheart," added Riverpaw with a mouth full of potato. Evercloud jabbed him with an elbow.

"All right, you two," said Eveneye. "Before we go down there, I want to go over the procedure. I'm going to spend a moment speaking to the crowd while the two of you and the advisors will be seated behind me. I will address the concerns of the entity in the sky with the announcement of the Protection League. As each position is announced, that bear will come to the podium and say a few words. Pay attention, so that you can see how it is done. After the announcement of the Protection League, I will announce our search for the Ancients and each of you will take a turn at the podium. When you are speaking, be sure to thank the Kingdom, and whatever you say, do not make mention of the Great Tyrant. Just because we think he has returned, doesn't mean that we should cause hysteria by announcing it as fact. Understood?" Both Riverpaw and Evercloud nodded to the King. "Good. Now let's finish our meals."

The bears continued to eat and Evercloud managed to force down a pork chop. Once they had had their fill, King Eveneye stood from the table with a smile and nodded. It was time.

Evercloud and the three male bears left the King's box, after saying their goodbyes to Goldenheart and Autumnbreeze, and made their way down to the arena gate. As they stood just outside of the arena, Oaktongue, Forestmoon, Firerock and Redriver joined them. Now that they were all present, a guard sounded the arena horn and the gate to the arena opened.

"I think I'm going to be sick," muttered Riverpaw. Evercloud chuckled. "Who's the sweetheart now?"

As they entered the arena, the crowd began to cheer. Every bear in the Kingdom rose to their feet for their King and his advisors. They reached the platform and everyone except for the King found a seat. As Eveneye came to the podium, a hush fell over the crowd. Everyone was very eager to hear what he had to say.

"Tonight, we celebrate and honor our past, our present and our future. We celebrate and honor our great Kingdom. We look to the light of the Everflame, which burns to remind us of the bears that came before us, and of the elder bears, whose teachings we guide our lives by today. It is now, more than ever, that we look to their wisdom to guide us through these mysterious times. Times in which we hear rumors of Ancient beings retuning to our land. Times in which unknown entities pass through our skies. It is not with fear that the elders would have us face these mysteries, but with a sound mind and a courageous heart. It is with my mind and heart that, tonight, I give you answers to your questions. And I answer you with the Protection League. This league, headed by my advisors, will serve to protect Gray Mountain and all its inhabitants. The League's first order of business is to create a wall around the base of the mountain, allowing us to better monitor traffic, in and out of the mountain, as well as preventing passage to those who may wish us harm. The department in charge of the wall's construction, as well as the monitoring of traffic, will be known as the Department of Fortifications, and as its head, I give to you Forestmoon."

Forestmoon rose to his feet and the crowd roared in approval. He took his place at the podium and silenced the crowd, so that he might speak.

"I wish to thank my King, and also, thank my Kingdom. For it is only through your power that we are able to achieve such wondrous heights."

The crowd, once again, erupted with cheers and Forestmoon gave the podium back to the King. Eveneye raised his arms and the noise of the crowd fell.

"The next step in the process of the Protection League will be in the creation of an armory, so that any bear who wishes to defend their Kingdom may do so with the finest weaponry available. The department in charge of this feat will be known as the Department of Armaments, and as its head, I give to you Redriver."

It was now Redriver's turn and the Kingdom gave him a matching response.

"All praise be to the Kingdom. I thank the King for this wonderful opportunity and I pledge to serve my Kingdom with honor."

Again the crowd cheered, but the King was not finished.

"What good are weapons in the hands of the incapable? I would not see my Kingdom defend itself without the proper knowledge and training. Any bear that wishes to become so, will be trained to be a ferocious warrior. For this, I give you the Department of Disciplines, and I give to you Firerock."

Firerock received the largest cheer so far. He was the most popular advisor in the Kingdom, due to the passion with which he spoke. He was widely regarded as the Kingdom's voice.

"Thank you, my King. You do me great honor. It is with great pride that I serve you, my Kingdom. You are the blood that flows through my heart. Together, we shall become as strong as the mountain. Together, we shall burn like the Everflame!"

The crowd erupted and it seemed the mountain might explode. Oaktongue leaned over to Whiteclaw.

"How am I supposed to follow that?"

Whiteclaw shrugged and smiled. Riverpaw and Evercloud turned to each other with nervous looks. Neither of them looked ready to take the podium. As the crowd lulled, Eveneye spoke.

"Finally, concerning the Protection League, no amount of defense is enough without knowledge of what we are up against. It is now important to have eyes and ears all around our land of Ephanlarea. For this purpose, I give you the Department of Information and Oaktongue."

Firerock had stirred the crowd into a frenzy and Oaktongue was happy for it as he took the podium.

"Thank you. Thank you, everyone. I promise to serve you justly and inform you with ferocity!"

The crowd, already primed, exploded. However, Oaktongue's ridiculous statement was not lost on Evercloud and Riverpaw.

"Did he say 'inform you with ferocity'?" giggled Riverpaw.

"Don't joke," returned Evercloud, trying to stifle his own laughs, "or he may try to enlighten you severely."

This was too much for Riverpaw and he threw his head back in a giant guffaw. Throwing his back against the chair, it tipped over and he fell off the back of the platform. The crowd went silent but Riverpaw jumped up quickly, embarrassed. Seeing that he was all right, the crowd went back to cheering, now laughing as much as anything else. Eveneye, once again, made to quiet the crowd, but it took a little longer to quell them this time. All of the laughing had taken the nerves right out of Evercloud and Riverpaw. They were comfortable now, with the knowledge that they could say almost anything when their turn came. Again, the King began to speak.

"I said this would be a celebration, didn't I?" The crowd gave one more cheer before quieting. "The Protection League will begin recruiting tomorrow. If any of you would like to volunteer, you know where you will be able to find the appropriate department head. Now, with the Protection League out of the way, we move to the next item on our agenda. Addressing the rumors that have been circling the Kingdom. We've all heard the rumors of the possible return of the Ancients. I'm sure that you are all wondering about their validity and what it might mean for you. Well, I'm sorry to inform you, my friends, that we have no answers for you at this time." The crowd moaned. "But fear not, my Kingdom. As your King, I find this to be as unacceptable as you do, and I refuse to allow your questions to go unanswered forever. That is why I have put together a search party. I swear to you. If the Ancients have returned, we will find them!"

The crowd cheered, and shouts of 'long live, Eveneye' were heard.

"I give to you your searchers. Whiteclaw, Riverpaw and Evercloud."

The frenzy of the crowd continued as the three walked to the podium. There was no waiting for perfect silence anymore. Whiteclaw began speaking over small bursts of jubilation.

"Thank you, my King, and thank you, my Kingdom. We shall not return to you without an answer."

The crowd roared and it was Riverpaw's turn.

"Thank you, King Eveneye, and thank you, King- er- thank you, my Kingdom."

Riverpaw shuffled aside as the crowd continued to roar, but the roaring didn't last long. As Evercloud took the podium, the arena went dead quiet. Evercloud's heart jumped into his throat and he looked at his father.

"Speak from your heart."

Evercloud took a deep breath.

"It has been some time now that I have lived among you. So long, that I know nothing outside of this Kingdom. You have taken me in, protected me and accepted me. For this, I thank you from the bottom of my heart. My only wish is to be able to repay each and every one of you. I am proud to serve you, in any way that I can. This Kingdom is the most important thing in the world to me. For in my heart, I am a bear." At this, the crowd began to cheer and a smile broke across Evercloud's face. They were cheering him. They had accepted him. "And I will find the Ancients for you!" shouted Evercloud. The crowd cheered even louder, becoming more and more excited. "And I will regain the ancient powers that were once given to man!" The arena went silent. Evercloud had gone too far. He knew the bears feared this and what it might bring for their future. He said the only thing that he could to win them back. He raised a fist into the air and yelled, "For the Kingdom!"

It seemed as though the roof of the arena might come crumbling down. This was the loudest it had gotten all night and some in the crowd began chanting, *E-ver-cloud, E-ver-cloud.* The King, seeing his opportunity, edged Evercloud away from the podium before he could say anything else and Evercloud took his seat next to Riverpaw.

"I didn't know you could do that," Riverpaw said, slack-jawed.

"Neither did I." Evercloud looked around, and his eyes met the gaze of Firerock, the large bear nodded in approval and Evercloud nodded back in gratitude. *My father was right,* thought Evercloud. *I will never forget this night.* The King stood at the podium with his arms in the air, trying to calm the crowd.

"Please. Please. Just one more thing." The crowd quieted. "Tomorrow brings the beginning of the Protection League and with that comes a great deal of work. Tomorrow also brings the departure of our searchers. So please, let's make this night the greatest celebration any of us have ever seen. Let us honor those who will serve us. I give you music and I give you drink." A band entered through the arena gate and through other gates, kegs of ale were rolled in. Eveneye raised a paw into the air and shouted, "For the Kingdom!"

"For the Kingdom!" returned the crowd.

The merriment began and Eveneye turned to smile at his son. Evercloud smiled back, and Goldenheart and Autumnbreeze arrived to join their families on the arena floor.

The band played into the night and the bears danced and danced. Evercloud received more compliments on his words than he had thought possible. Most importantly, though, he hadn't seen his parents this happy in quite some time. Riverpaw must have danced, at least once, with every female of his age. Evercloud thought that Riverpaw might have had a little too much ale. The young man was feeling much better now. He wasn't as worried now that he had the support of the entire Kingdom behind him.

As the night wound down, the bears prepared to retire to their caves. It had been a very long day for Evercloud and he welcomed the thought of a soft mattress. His father found him sitting amongst a group of older bears, each telling him that he was the most well-mannered human they had ever seen.

"Can I speak to you for a moment, Evercloud?" Evercloud thanked the bears for their company and joined his father. "How are you feeling?" Eveneye asked the boy as he put a paw on his shoulder.

"I feel good. Tired, but good."

"No more concerns?"

"No. Not really."

"Not concerned with how you might defend yourself, as you were before?"

"Well. I'll have two bears on my side, won't I?"

"Yes, you will," said Eveneye, nodding his head. "Still, I think I may have something to ease your mind even more. Follow me."

Evercloud looked at his father curiously, but heeded his words and followed him as he walked out of the arena.

"What about Mother?"

"She's going to meet us at home," said Eveneye. Evercloud followed his father along an upward-sloping path, away from the arena and back to the castle. They didn't say much to each other on the walk, mostly because Evercloud was tired and because Eveneye didn't want to give away his secret. Eveneye led his son into the castle and then down the hallway that led to the courtroom.

"We're going to the courtroom?" asked Evercloud.

"We are," replied Eveneye.

Once they were in the room, Evercloud noticed a chest at the room's center.

"There's something I want to give you." Eveneye walked over to the chest and unlocked it. He took something out of it and made to hand it to Evercloud. "I had our finest metal-smiths make it for you. It should make defending yourself much easier." Evercloud's eyes widened as his father handed him the weapon. "Now, you too, have a claw."

The weapon Eveneye had given to his son looked like the claw was made of pure gold, yet it was hard as steel and light as a feather. It was a long piece of metal that extended from his elbow to his hand, and coming out of the end at the hand, were three eight-inch blades that extended like a claw.

"Go ahead and put it on."

Evercloud saw that there were leather straps to secure it to his arm. He strapped it on and gazed at it in wonder.

"I had the metal extended down to your elbow so that you could use that part as a shield, but it ties to your arm so that your hand is still free. Do you like it?"

"It's incredible," said Evercloud, still in amazement. "I've never seen anything like it."

"I know that men usually fight with swords, but–"

"I'm not a usual man, Father. I don't know what usual men do. I know what bears do, and that is as it should be."

Eveneye smiled at his son.

"I just wanted to give you something to show you what you mean to me, Evercloud. You'll never know how important you are to me. I owe you so much."

61

"It is I who owe you, Father. You saved my life and you made a kingdom of bears accept me. You owe me nothing."

"No, Evercloud, you don't understand. You are my only son. The only son I will ever have. The only one that I *can* ever have." Evercloud looked at his father, uncomprehending. "I and your mother are unable to have offspring, Evercloud. We tried for many years, unsuccessfully, and then you came into our lives and we didn't need to worry anymore. You filled the void in our hearts that would have never gone away, had you not come along. You were a miracle for your mother and I. You saved us from sadness." Evercloud still looked at his father as though he did not completely understand. "I tell you this now, Evercloud, so that you can see my motives for saving you were selfish. It was not for the greater good. It was what I wanted. It was a decision for me. I see you worry yourself everyday with what others want of you and how others will perceive you. Wanting to do good for this kingdom is noble, but it is not all there is to life. Don't forget about you. Don't ever lose yourself, my son." Eveneye embraced his son. "I love you, Evercloud."

"Thank you, Father. I love you too."

•••

When Evercloud woke up the next morning, it was as if he had woken up as a different person. He felt surer of himself, less awkward. He wondered when he would leave. Evercloud crawled out of bed and made his way toward the kitchen where he found his mother and father eating breakfast. There was a plate, already made for him and he sat down, said good morning, and began eating.

"How did you sleep?" asked Goldenheart.

"Well," said Evercloud with a stuffed mouth.

"You're not nervous about leaving?"

"No," Evercloud swallowed, "why would I be?"

Goldenheart didn't respond. Eveneye spoke for her.

"Your mother cares for you, Evercloud. She worries."

"I'll be all right. Uncle Whiteclaw will be there and Riverpaw too. Nothing bad will happen."

A call came from the entrance to the Eveneye and Goldenheart's cave, and in walked Whiteclaw, Riverpaw and Autumnbreeze. Autumnbreeze had a pack with her, full of all of her things.

"Is Aunt Autumn staying here?" asked Evercloud.

"Yes," answered Eveneye. "She'll be staying here until the three of you return."

"Almost ready to go, Evercloud?" asked Whiteclaw.

"Yeah. Let me just grab my claw." Evercloud ran back to his bed. He had left his claw lying next to his mattress. He grabbed it, fastened it to his belt, and returned to the others. "All right. I'm ready now."

"What is that?" asked Riverpaw, gawking at the weapon that hung from Evercloud's belt.

"That's my claw."

Riverpaw looked at his own claw, then back at Evercloud's and shrugged. Evercloud turned to his mother and gave her a hug.

"Don't worry about me, mom. I'll be fine and I'll be back soon."

"Just be careful, Evercloud, and remember that I love you," said Goldenheart, giving her son a kiss.

"I love you too." Then, Evercloud turned to his father and gave him a hug. "Don't you worry, okay? I'm gonna make you two proud."

"I know you will, son."

Autumnbreeze gave her goodbyes to her husband and son and then all six of them walked out of the cave to the main road, heading down the mountain.

"Where are we headed first, dad?" asked Riverpaw.

"Well, there are rumors of Tenturo to the west. So we're going to start west. Evercloud, you'd better ride on Riverpaw's back, otherwise I don't think that you could keep up."

Evercloud jumped onto his cousin's back.

"You ready for this?" asked Riverpaw.

Evercloud smiled. "I've been waiting my whole life for something like this."

"Then we're off," said Whiteclaw, and he and his son went barreling down the mountain.

Eveneye, Goldenheart and Autumnbreeze watched them go, all the way down the mountain, until they disappeared into the forest.

"Oh Even, he'll come back to us, won't he?"

"Of course he will, Goldie. Of course he will."

FIRE

8

Chapter 8: Regret

The world is cracking apart. It can't exist this way much longer. I feel guilty. I feel like this is my fault. I never should have let this happen. I should have fought. I could have found a way, I know that I could have. But now… It's too late.

This world has run its course, or at least it doesn't have much longer. Humans are a failure. My failure. I have failed them… Am I wrong? I wish that I were. I wish we had seen this coming. How could we have been so blind to forget about it? Forget that it might care? That it might wish to be involved? That it was more powerful than the rest of us combined? We were so naive, so self-assured and so wrong. We were so wrong to ignore it… and so wrong to discard him.

If I could start it all over, I would have kept him. How could we have thrown him away like so much trash? He was ours, our creation, we owed him so much more and now…

Everything will die.

I will die.

For myself, it will be just, as it is my fault. But as for the rest? This is not justice. This is as wrong as I was. Alas, what hope is there?

Men are dead.

They just don't know it yet.

9

Chapter 9: Need

Edgar hated when his mother had him run errands. He would purposefully try to make himself scarce when he could see that supplies were low. It wasn't that Edgar Shein was a lazy child. It was simply that Edgar Shein was an unpopular child, and the bullies would always find him when he went into the village alone. Especially Pritchard Barton. Pritchard Barton had already bloodied Edgar's nose on three occasions, as well as stolen money from him and even embarrassed him by taking his clothing, forcing him to run home nude. Edgar's mother, Rachael, felt horrible about how her son was tormented, but with Edgar's father gone so often on long trips, she had little choice but to send Edgar on errands.

Edgar's black locks hung past his eyes as he walked into the village of Hammlin. Gazing down at his feet as he walked, the small, pale boy looked miserable. He knew he had to help his mother. He didn't blame her at all. It was his father he blamed. Edgar's father, Joe, worked for the Holy. He was a missionary and he had been gone for more of Edgar's life than he had been present for. The boy resented him for it. He felt Joe should be at home, taking care of him and his mother, not off in other lands. Edgar didn't even feel right calling him father.

As Edgar started passing houses in the village, he changed his posture. He couldn't afford to hang his head now. He had to be on the lookout at all times. As his eyes surveyed his surroundings, he wished that his father were there. But as Pritchard Barton's yellow teeth came sneering around the corner of the blacksmith's shop, Edgar's sentiment changed and he cursed his father's name.

"You know, I would have thought, by now, you'd just stop showing your ugly face around here, Shein."

Edgar reacted the same way that he always did when he saw Pritchard Barton. He kept his head straight, walked as fast as he could and prayed to the Holy that this would be the time that Barton let him go. Unfortunately, as they always did, Edgar's prayers went unanswered.

"I'm talkin' to you, you little insect," shouted Barton as he picked up a stone along the side of the road and hurled it at Edgar, hitting him on the shoulder.

Pain shot through Edgar's shoulder and arm but he didn't stop walking. *Please make him stop. Please make him stop*, thought Edgar. However, Pritchard Barton wasn't alone today. His crony, Joe Stockton, was with him and Pritchard loved to show off.

"I think the little girl's gone deaf," laughed Stockton.

"He ain't deaf...yet," sneered Barton as he picked up another stone.

"Put that stone down, you little bastard!" Murray the Blacksmith came rumbling out of his shop and grabbed Pritchard Barton by his ear. "If I catch either of you little hooligans terrorizing people again, you'll get the back of my hand. Got it?"

Murray released Prichard's ear and the boy almost tripped over himself in retreat. Scuffling in the street and kicking up dust, the two bullies ran away as fast as they could. Edgar couldn't help but grin due to the shocked and embarrassed look on Pritchard's pimpled face, the bully's fat cheeks turning scarlet. The smith walked over to where Edgar stood and put his big hand on the boy's shoulder.

"You all right, boy?"

"I'm fine, Sir. Thank you, Sir."

Edgar looked up into the big man's bearded face. Murray was an intimidating man and although he had just helped Edgar, the boy wasn't exactly comfortable in his presence.

"You running errands for your mum again?"

"Yes, Sir."

"Well," and Murray extended his hand down the road, "let's get em done then, shall we?" Edgar couldn't believe his luck. The blacksmith had stopped Pritchard Barton and now he was escorting him through the village, just like his own personal guard. "What do you need to get today, Edgar?"

"Mum asked for salt, sugar, and bread," answered the boy.

"Where's your dad gone off to this time, eh?"

"Don't know, Sir... He never says."

Murray grumbled to himself. It was obvious to Edgar that the blacksmith felt the same way that he did about his father's absence. Edgar had begun to feel much better, but with the topic of his father back in his mind, he was falling back into a depression.

"How's your mum doing up at the farm?" asked Murray.

"She's all right, Sir. Busy, but doing fine."

"Now that's enough of that *sir* stuff. I appreciate the manners and it goes to show your mum's doing a good job with you, but you can call me Murray. Sound good?"

"Yes, s- I mean, Murray."

Murray smiled down at the boy as they entered the bakery and Edgar smiled back. Once Edgar had purchased what he needed, and he and Murray had returned to where the blacksmith's shop was located, Murray stopped and looked down at Edgar.

"I got something inside the shop I wanna show you before you go back to your mum."

Edgar nodded his head and the two of them left the cobblestone road and walked into the shop. Sunlight came through the windows of the blacksmith's shop, revealing a good amount of dust in the air. The shop was rather dingy and it seemed obvious to Edgar that Murray didn't clean things very often.

"I live just through that door, there at the back of the shop. It's small, but it's just me, so I figured there's no sense in having a whole house. What I wanted to show you is back there. Follow me."

Edgar followed Murray through the door into his living quarters. Murray wasn't being modest when he said it was small. There was a bed, a table and a chair, what looked like a closet with a curtain hanging in front of it, and a door that Edgar assumed led outside to an outhouse. There was leftover food still on the table and the bed had not been made. Edgar was not used to such untidiness, and as children sometimes do, he let his curiosity get the best of him.

"Why don't you have a wife, Murray?"

Murray looked down at the boy sullenly and pursed his lips. Edgar suddenly realized that he should have kept his mouth shut.

"Well," Murray said with a sigh, "I was married for a time. Her name was Andrea. She was the most beautiful woman in the village." Murray then turned away from Edgar. "But she took ill and passed on a couple of years ago." Edgar was ashamed of himself and began to say he was sorry, but Murray cut him off. "Enough about the past. Let me show you what's in the closet."

Suddenly, Edgar realized that he was in a strange man's house and became uneasy. Murray had been nice to him and had helped him, but he didn't know him that well and wondered if it wasn't a mistake to follow him into his shop. Murray reached the closet and turned to Edgar with a smile, and when he saw the cautious look on Edgar's face, he chuckled.

"Come on, boy. I ain't gonna hurt ye." Murray began to draw the curtain to the side and said, "Now be quiet. I think they're sleeping."

As Murray moved the curtain aside, Edgar's eyes lit up. Lying at the floor of the closet was a female wolfhound with five pups, all huddled together.

"The big one's name is Tiffa." As Murray spoke, one of the puppies lifted his head from his mother's leg and walked over to Edgar, wagging his tail.

"Can I pick him up?" asked Edgar.

"Course you can. Go ahead."

Edgar bent down and picked up the puppy. It was like a big ball of brown fuzz. Edgar held the dog in his arms and it licked his face.

"What's his name?" asked Edgar.

"Well, he doesn't have one yet," said Murray. "Thought you might want to give him one, since he's yours now."

Edgar looked up at Murray, slack-jawed, the puppy still licking his face. "Really?"

"Yep. He's yours. I can't take care of all these dogs. Plus, he likes you."

Edgar's face lit up and he slumped down to the floor, letting the little, brown puppy bounce all around him.

"There's something else I want you to have, Edgar." Murray reached under the mattress of his bed and pulled out a small dagger with a black handle and a red stone on the hilt. "Now, that Pritchard Barton is a sight bigger than you, his head's not right and he don't fight fair. Anytime your mum sends you on errands, you can come see me first and we'll go together, but I might not always be here. So, I think that you should keep this with you."

Murray handed the dagger to Edgar and the red stone shined bright as Edgar held it in his hands.

"I don–"

"Hear me out, Edgar. I'm not saying you should attack Pritchard Barton, but if he puts you in a dangerous situation, that dagger might be your only way out... Not everybody knows right from wrong, Edgar. Far worse, sometimes people think that they do, when they really don't. It's okay to protect yourself."

"Thank you... I-I don't know what to say." Edgar stared down at the puppy in his lap and then at the dagger in his hands. "Mother and Father are real strict with the Holy. I don't think they'll let me keep the dagger... They probably won't let me keep the dog either."

Murray pursed his lips and nodded his head. Edgar's reaction wasn't quite what he had expected. Murray didn't say anything for a minute and Edgar began to feel ashamed. Edgar was just about to say that he should probably leave, when Murray spoke again.

"Well, I'm just going to have to convince your mum then. Let's go."

Edgar stood up with the puppy in his arms. "You're going to come home with me and talk to my mum?"

"Yep," Murray nodded. "Let's go." A smile broke across Edgar's face. He couldn't believe the luck he had run into today. "Oh, and Edgar."

"Yes, Murray."

"You still need to name that dog."

Edgar and Murray walked silently for the first mile of the trip to the Shein's farm. The day was beginning to break into dusk and the sky was a mixture of blue and pink. Edgar had hid the dagger on the inside of his shirt. He didn't want his mother to see it until Murray had talked to her. Edgar held the puppy in his arms and placed a hand in front of the dog as they walked through trees, so as to protect its head from low branches. There was a dirt road that led to the farm but it was only the fastest route while on horseback. A straight path through the forest was the best route on foot. Edgar worried what his mother would say to Murray. He was already attached to the dog, and even more than that, he didn't want to lose the blacksmith's friendship. With Murray on his side, he'd never have to worry about Pritchard Barton again. The puppy looked up at Edgar with his little, blue eyes, panting and wagging his tail, when Edgar, as children usually do, came to an obvious name choice.

"Blue," stated Edgar.

"What's blue?"

"I've decided to name the dog, Blue."

"He looks like a Blue. Good name." Murray smiled but didn't say much else on the matter. Edgar didn't feel much like talking anyway. He was too busy thinking of all the things he was going to teach to Blue.

As Edgar and Murray emerged from the forest, a large field of tall grass spread out before them. On the far side of the field, up on a small hill, was Edgar's home. The pair waded their way through the tall grass until they reached the gate to Shein farm. A small, wooden fence that only came up to Murray's waist, opened with a creak. Edgar could see candlelight coming from the windows of the small, white house that rested on top of the hill. The sky was beginning to show shades of violet as Edgar and Murray reached the porch. Edgar handed Blue over to Murray and instructed him to wait on the porch while he fetched his mother. Murray held the dog up to his face and looked into the dog's eyes.

"You're just too cute to say no to, aren't you? Yes you are. Yes you are."

Murray cooed at the dog and ruffled the fur on its head, not noticing that Rachael had come out onto the porch.

"What can I help you with, Murray?"

"Rachael," said Murray, startled and embarrassed. "I- uh- good to see you."

"Good to see you too, Murray. Edgar said there was something you wanted to talk to me about."

"Well, actually, it was Edgar that I wanted to talk to you about."

Murray now noticed how tired Rachael's eyes were. She was a small woman with mousy, blond hair. Too small, Murray felt, to be living out here, all alone, with her husband far away. His heart went out to her as it had for the boy, when he had spotted him out his shop window.

"He hasn't been making trouble, has he?"

"Oh no, not at all. Actually, it seems as though some bullies in town have been making trouble for him and I was hoping to have a talk with you about it."

"I know the older children pick on him, Murray, I do. But I'm just too busy to escort the boy around. With Joe gone, I just don't have enough time."

"I know that, Rachael, and well, that's where I wanted to help. You

70

see, I want Edgar to have this dog for protection." Murray held up Blue. "He's just a pup now, but he'll grow and be real loyal. Wolfhounds always are. Plus, every family should have a good dog they can count on."

"I appreciate your concern, Murray, really, I do. But I don't have the extra food for a dog, let alone the time to spend taking care of it."

"Well, I can help with that too, Rachael. You see, I haven't had too much to keep me busy since Andrea passed away and I was hoping that I could help out with some things. I'm not asking for anything for it. It's payment enough just to have something to do. And I hope I'm not out of line saying so, but I just can't bear to watch you with your hands so full when I've got extra time on my hands. What with Joe being gone so often."

Rachael stared at Murray with a sharp look in her eyes and Murray was afraid that he had gone too far. Murray found himself too uncomfortable to meet Rachael's eyes and briefly let his gaze move past her shoulder. Edgar was standing in the doorway, listening.

"So, can I keep Blue?"

Murray glanced back toward Rachael and was surprised to see her looking slightly downward with a grin on her face. She shook her head and turned to Edgar.

"Edgar, go back inside and put another plate on the table." Then Rachael turned back to Murray and smiled. "I do expect that you'll be staying for dinner. You can't expect me to let you go hungry on my watch."

Murray couldn't help but to smile back at her.

"Can't say no to that."

Rachael stepped aside to usher Murray in through the door and as he made his way past her, she touched him gently on the hand. He stopped and looked down at her.

"Thank you, Murray."

Murray looked into her blue eyes and something moved inside of him. All of a sudden, he felt very shy.

"My pleasure, Rachael."

Edgar, Rachael and Murray talked and laughed as they ate dinner and nobody's smile shone bigger or brighter than Edgar's. *How did I get so lucky?* he thought to himself and snuck Blue a scrap of meat from the table. It was obvious that Edgar had taken to Murray and although Rachael was wary that the boy might find in Murray a substitute for his absent father, she just couldn't do anything to prevent his happiness.

As they finished dinner, Rachael gathered the empty plates and brought them into the kitchen. Once Edgar and Murray were alone, the boy began his questions.

"Did you ask about the dagger, Murray? I didn't hear you say anything about the dagger."

Murray looked at Edgar and winked. "Your mother doesn't need to be bothered with every little thing, Edgar."

Edgar smiled and lifted Blue onto his lap.

Later that night, after Murray had left for the village, Edgar lay wide-awake in bed, going over the day's events in his head. He was so happy. He couldn't remember any other time in his young life that he had been this happy. He pet Blue and the puppy returned the affection by licking his arm. Edgar looked out his bedroom window and found the biggest star in the sky. Then he made a wish that Murray were his father.

10

Chapter 10: A Storm

Over the next few weeks, Edgar's happiness continued to grow. Murray had fulfilled his promise and was spending a lot of time helping out on the farm. There was nothing he wasn't a great help with. He worked in the vegetable garden at a speed that neither Edgar nor Rachael could dream of matching, even on their best days. He was able to keep the barn in much better order, mostly due to his ability to lift heavy objects, that previously, only Joe had the strength to tackle. He was handy with repairs and had fixed two drafty windows as well as some loose boards on the porch. He even spent time teaching Edgar how to hunt in the forest. All this, and he was still able to keep his smithing business in operation.

Also, Blue seemed to be growing at an exponential rate and the dog's affection for Edgar hadn't waned. He and Edgar were inseparable. All of Edgar's free time was spent playing fetch with the dog and teaching him tricks. Blue had quickly mastered the art of rolling over and shaking hands and was now tackling speech on command. Murray was greatly impressed with Edgar's ability to train Blue.

"It won't be long before Blue will be able to accompany us on hunting trips," Murray had told Edgar. "Then he'll be a dog able to earn his keep."

Edgar was thrilled with the prospect of hunting with Blue. At night, Edgar would tell Blue stories he had made in his head of how their hunting adventures would unfold. He would weave wild stories of giant deer with ten sets of antlers that could breathe fire and fly. The dog would sit calmly and listen to everything. He was the best friend Edgar could have ever hoped for.

Edgar wasn't the only Shein that had found a greater happiness since Murray's arrival. Rachael was finding that her life had become easier, and she now had time to enjoy the little things again. She was able to spend more time teaching Edgar reading and writing. Their clothes were now properly mended in a timely manner, instead of days in tatters. Her dinners, as she now had more preparatory time, were all the more sumptuous and the house was something she was once again becoming proud of. In fact, there were times in the evening when she sat on the porch in the rocking chair and knit, as relaxed as could be, while Murray, Edgar and Blue roughhoused in the field. She marveled at the seemingly endless reserve of energy that Murray possessed. The man was truly a blessing from the Holy.

There were many times when Edgar would go into town, early in the morning, to help Murray in the shop. Murray would teach the boy his trade as he would complete his work. After only two weeks of helping at the shop, Edgar had presented his mother with a crudely made, but nonetheless functional, fork.

"I made it for you, mum," he beamed.

Everything seemed to be going perfectly for Rachael and Edgar. Though, at night, Rachael would toss and turn in bed, unable to fall asleep. She couldn't help but worry over what Joe would think of this situation when he returned from his mission. Would he understand that she had desperately needed the help, or would he be angry with her that she was unable to fulfill her duties as his wife? Would he be upset that another man was spending such a large amount of time with his son? Would he be jealous? Would he have faith that this arrangement was innocent, or would he think that he had been cuckolded in his absence? Rachael worried about all these things, although, her worries would often manifest themselves into frustration and then hostility toward Joe. How dare he be upset, she would think. It was he who was gone so often, causing her and Edgar to have so much on their plates. What sort of father was he to Edgar? What sort of husband was he for her? She thought back to when she had first met Joe. She had been so young; so impressionable. She had thought he was such an important man. After all, he worked for the Holy.

Through her youth, men who worked for the Holy had always been able to provide greatly for their families. They were always the most respected families in the village. Rachael didn't feel respected by her community, she felt pitied. The men in her youth were not missionaries, they were preachers, and they never had to leave the village. They could provide for their families and still be there for them. Joe was only able to do the first of those two things, and lately, he was having a hard time with that.

In the beginning of their relationship, Joe would come back from his missions with ample compensation, more than enough for the family. That was not the case anymore and Rachael was finding it harder and harder to make ends meet. There were many times she had implored him to take a stationary position. She was even willing to uproot her life to another village, if that were necessary. Joe always rejected the requests, for one reason or another. He liked where they were living. He was only suited for missionary work. Whatever excuse he could find. She had tried everything to make it work, so why should she feel guilty?

However, whenever she arrived at this question, she knew why she felt such guilt. She didn't want to go back to the way things had been before Murray. She didn't think that she could go back. It had been so much work…

74

and it had been so lonely. She couldn't deny it. Murray was taking away her loneliness. She would lay in bed and think of the way that Murray would smile at her, the way he was always trying to please her and look out for her. Just like he was…

She cursed herself for her thoughts. She was married to Joe. She had taken a sacred vow. Yet, she could not deny her feelings for Murray and those feelings were growing stronger and stronger every day. She would watch him in the garden sometimes or watch him when he was in the field, playing with Edgar, and find herself imagining that this was her family and that Joe wasn't part of the equation. Imagining that Murray was her real husband and imagining that Edgar was her real son.

She could remember that night so vividly. Joe had returned from one of his missions with a tiny child. An orphan, he had said. He had saved the child after savages had murdered its parents. The boy was no infant, yet too young to understand anything. She had sworn to Joe that she would raise the boy as if it were her own and love it just the same. And she had…she did. Edgar was Rachael's whole life, she couldn't imagine living without him. She would never do anything to jeopardize his happiness, and regardless if she was using this to justify her own feelings or not, she would not send Murray away. She knew that he was making her boy's life better. She knew Murray cared and that was enough justification for her.

Perhaps this is part of the reason Rachael's feelings grew for Murray. Perhaps it was also part of the reason why she did not push her feelings for Murray away. She tried to hide them, of course. But as feelings do, no matter how deeply hidden, if given time, they find their way out.

One particular summer night, as the sun was beginning to dip below the horizon, when Edgar had gone up to his room with Blue to retire for the night, Murray stood at the doorway, preparing to leave for his shop. Murray and Rachael's goodbyes had been increasing in their awkwardness with each passing night. Lingering moments. Uncomfortable pauses. It was as if both of them were waiting for some inevitability to happen that simply never did.

"Well, thank you for dinner, Rachael. As always, it was delicious." Murray bowed his big head as he said this, trying to hide any red that might be apparent on his face and forgetting that the gesture was futile, given that he towered over the diminutive woman.

"You know, you don't have to say that every night," Rachael said with the same guarded smile that she had been forcing herself to use around Murray.

"I know…I guess I… I don't know what else to say," Murray chuckled bashfully.

Then Rachael's better judgment faltered. Her words were almost a reaction.

"You could stay here tonight, I mean, in the guest room. The wind has picked up and it looks like it's going to rain. You could go back early in the morning. No sense in getting wet from the rain. I mean–"

"No…I really shouldn't…the rain should hold off."

Just as Murray's words escaped his mouth, rain began to pour from the sky. Rachael and Murray looked at each other and laughed.

"Come on, I'll show you to the guest room." Rachael grabbed Murray's hand and made to lead him away, but Murray wouldn't budge. Rachael turned back to Murray. "What's wrong?"

"Rachael, I can't stay the night here."

"It's pouring down out there. Don't be silly."

"Rachael, there's something I'm ashamed to admit to you, but I think that it's about time that I come out with it. You're a married woman and…I would like to think of myself as a respectable man. You see… I have…feelings for you, Rachael, and I know it's not right. I don't know why I'm telling you this. I'm sorry."

Rachael's body moved without a thought as she threw her arms around Murray. They looked into each other's eyes and kissed.

Murray never did go home that night.

•••

Thunder rolled across the land and shook everything underneath the sky. The rain continued throughout the night in torrential sheets, thrown across the land by violent gusts of wind. The weather pounded Shein farm, drowning out all other sound and leaving the air inside the house damp. The storm was all that existed to Rachael and Murray, apart from each other as they lay in bed. Wrapping the two lovers in their own cocoon of noise, separating their consciousness from the outside world, nothing existed but their new love for each other.

They were oblivious to the skittering of a small mouse across the floor, as it darted from a leaky wall into the dry safety of another. They couldn't hear the snores that came from both Edgar and Blue as they slept through the storm in the room upstairs. They couldn't even hear the rocking chair as the wind knocked it back and forth, rapping against the wooden porch. They heard none of it.

So as the gate to Shein farm swung open and closed, they never heard its creaky warning. They were oblivious to the impending doom of each footstep of large boots as they walked up the porch. Deaf, even, to the front door as it opened and then closed, like the sealing of a casket. However, in the dark of the bedroom, where Rachael and Murray held each other in the throes of passion, a sound, cunning and sharp, suddenly cut its way into the minds of the two lovers. Gasping with shock and spinning to greet their shining intruder, Rachael and Murray found themselves at the mercy of a man scorned. Joe had returned, with a rapier at Murray's throat and wild vengeance in his eyes.

76

"Seems I've been gone far too long."

Murray was speechless, he couldn't move. He knew that his death was standing in front of him. Rachael jumped out of the bed, scrabbling for her clothes and pleading with Joe.

"No, Joe! Please!"

Sweat poured from both Murray and Joe's brows. One man hot with panic, the other with rage. Rachael continued to plead. Joe didn't say a word. He was motionless, poised to strike at any moment. Only his face revealing the gravity of what he was about to do, contorting as he battled with himself. Murray finally gathered the air to speak, rasping, begging for his life.

"Don't kill me, Joe. Please. Don't kill me. I'm sorry. Joe. Please. Forgive me."

Hearing Murray's voice had ended the battle in Joe's head. His face became resolute and he straightened his shoulders.

"You're forgiven," Joe said and plunged the tip of his rapier deep into Murray's throat.

"Nooooo!!!" came a yell at the bedroom door. Rachael and Joe spun to find Edgar, eyes wide at the horrific scene. Tears began to stream down his red face and he gasped for air.

"Edgar?" Joe's hardened face grew soft as he realized what the boy had seen. "Come here, Edgar. I'm sorry you saw that. Edgar? Please." Slowly, Joe began to walk toward the boy but the damage had already been done. Joe had become a monster to Edgar and he ran, screaming, from the house, Blue right on his heels. "Edgar!" Joe shouted after him. "Come back, boy! I'm sorry! I had to!"

The rain pelted Edgar's face, mixing with his own tears, but he didn't stop running. Nothing could stop him from running. Joe had killed Murray. Edgar had loved Murray, more than he had ever loved Joe. Joe didn't care about him, didn't care about his mother. He only cared about the Holy and his stupid missions. Edgar could barely see where he was going and tripped on a tree root. Blue was right on top of him, making sure that he hadn't been hurt. Edgar reached up for the dog, still crying as the rain came down.

"You're all I got now, Blue." The dog licked Edgar's face and the boy held him, sobbing in the rain. Edgar sat there for sometime before he regained himself. Soon after, the rain stopped and a cool wind followed it, chilling Edgar to the bone. He shivered. "We need shelter," said Edgar. Blue wagged his tail in agreement.

The boy stood up and began making his way through the forest again, this time heading toward the village. It wasn't long before Edgar and Blue had reached the outskirts of Hammlin. They stayed quiet as they slipped into the village, careful not to make any sound, trying to stick to the shadows. They reached Murray's shop and stealthily made their way inside. Once inside,

Edgar lit the hearth and he and Blue settled down with each other, beside the fire, and promptly fell asleep.

●●●

"What have you done!" cried Rachael.

Joe turned on her with venom. "What have I done?! What have *I* done?! How dare you say that to me, you whore?!"

Rachael fell to her knees as the tears fell from her cheeks. "I'm s-sorry," she wailed and covered her face with her hands. "Where is my son? We have to find Edgar."

It's moments like these that define the true nature of a person. The world seemingly spinning out of control, your mind darting from one issue to another. Instinctual priority takes over. Situations such as these will reveal a man's soul.

Joe stared at his wife as the night flew through his mind. *She's raving*, he thought. *She's betrayed me.* His adopted son had run away into the night, after he had killed a man that he had found sleeping with his wife. Rachael was reaching for him now. Pleading with him. Crying. She needed to find the boy. *The boy isn't our blood. The woman has betrayed me. The body is bleeding. The body.* The man that Joe had killed was bleeding in his bed. He had to get rid of the body. Joe pushed his wife away from him.

"We can find the boy later. We need to get rid of the body."

Joe's eyes blazed maniacally. Rachael backed further away, disgusted. She no longer loved this man and she wasn't sure how long it had been since she had. She spit at Joe's feet and ran for the door. Joe didn't pursue her. He had business to take care of.

11

Chapter 11: Darkness and Rage

Edgar woke with a start, as if out of a bad dream. He looked around, expecting to see the comfort of his bedroom, only to find himself dirty and cold on the floor of Murray's shop. The events of the previous night came rushing back into his mind, a cruel reminder that the nightmare was real. The sun still hadn't crept up over the horizon yet. Edgar rubbed his eyes and looked down at Blue, who was still asleep. The hearth was still lit and Edgar edged closer to it, rubbing his arms to get his blood flowing. The sky was becoming lighter and Edgar's senses were beginning to sharpen as he stretched his body. Suddenly, Edgar realized that Tiffa, Blue's mother, should be somewhere. Murray had sold the other puppies, as they were too much for him to take care of, but he had kept Tiffa. Edgar walked around the shop and back into Murray's living space, but the wolfhound was nowhere to be found.

As Edgar began to wonder if he should look outside for Tiffa, he heard the front door to the shop slam shut. He spun around, only to find an evil, yellow grin staring him in the face.

"Well, well, look who's back without his blacksmith for protection." Pritchard Barton stood in the dim light with his arms folded, snickering. "And if you're looking for that old wolfhound, well…she ain't around to help you neither."

"What did you do with Tiffa?" growled Edgar.

"Sold her to a traveling merchant. Didn't think that idiot blacksmith would mind. Seemed like he had his concerns elsewhere." Pritchard looked down at Blue, who had just woken up. "Maybe I'll sell your dog too."

Blood boiled in Edgar's head and he clenched his jaw.

"You're not gonna touch my dog…or I'll…I'll–"

"You'll what, Shein? Just what do you think a puny, little scab like you is gonna do, huh?"

Edgar's hand went down to his belt and found the dagger Murray had given him. He pulled it from his belt and pointed it directly at Barton's head.

"Don't touch my dog."

Barton laughed, unfazed by Edgar's attempt at bravery. He looked down at the dagger Edgar held in his hand and then looked around the room. Pritchard's eyes went to the hearth and he saw a log, only half taken by the fire. He slowly edged his way around Edgar, closer and closer to the fire. Edgar watched him with tunnel vision, waiting for Pritchard to strike. As Pritchard reached the fire, he slowly bent down and retrieved the log, brandishing it like a torch. Edgar hadn't expected that and stepped a few paces back from Barton. The bully, realizing that he, once again, had the upper hand, began to taunt Edgar.

"C'mon, Shein, let's fight for the dog. That dog probably doesn't want a worm like you for a master anyway. You weakling. I bet he doesn't even like you. Why don't you just go run back to your mommy before the sun is up? Go run to her bed and cry that you had a bad dream."

Edgar's mind flashed back to the rapier as it pierced Murray's throat, the blood pouring down his chest, his mother crying and his father's eyes like fire.

"NOOO!!" Edgar screamed. He couldn't hold himself back and he lunged at Barton with the dagger clutched so tightly, his knuckles had gone white. Edgar was blind with rage and his movements were wild. Pritchard Barton easily sidestepped Edgar's thrust and countered by plunging the smoldering log into Edgar's face. Edgar screamed and fell to the ground, dropping the dagger.

The pain was intense. He brought his hands up to his face but couldn't touch it. His face seared in agony. Edgar moaned, rolling on the ground, writhing in pain. He tried to open his eyes. He couldn't see anything. The world was black. All that existed was pain. Edgar tried to scream but nothing escaped his mouth. Slowly, sound trickled in to his consciousness. Yelling, and what sounded like growling. It was so faint that Edgar wasn't sure if he was really hearing things or if the pain was beginning to drive him mad. He strained against the wall of pain and suddenly, his hearing came back in a rush.

"Get off me, you mutt!" yelled Barton.

As soon as Pritchard Barton had hit Edgar with the log, Blue had attacked him, latching onto his arm. Blue knocked the bully to the ground, thrashing his jaws, trying to tear Pritchard to shreds. Edgar could hear everything perfectly now, though he could still see only blackness. The dog was growling and Edgar could sense that he was out for blood. Edgar tried to scrabble to his knees, fighting against the pain. Then he heard scraping metal across the stone floor and he knew that Pritchard Barton had found the dagger he had dropped. Edgar was paralyzed in fear.

"BLUE!!!" he yelled. But it was too late.

Pritchard Barton lifted the dagger and repeatedly stabbed at the dog that had him pinned to the ground. Blue yelped and fell away from him. Edgar fell to his hands and knees, crawling through the blackness to the place where he had heard the yelp. Closer and closer Edgar crawled, groping the air to find the dog.

Then he found him, a warm, fuzzy heap upon the rock-hard floor. Edgar ran his hand over the dog and felt the warm, wet flow of blood. "Blue," he sobbed, "no."

There was no sound from the dog, no movement. Blue had died.

"That bastard dog deserved it! It bit me, Shein! Your ugly dog bit me and I'm bleeding! Serves it right it's dead!"

Edgar no longer felt the pain. The sound of Pritchard Barton became more and more faint until he heard nothing but a low hum and the pounding of his own heart. The beat of his heart grew louder in his head until it shook his body with every new beat. His legs and arms began to tingle with heat, and it was spreading. It had reached his stomach and made him nauseated. His body shook and the heat continued to rise in intensity. He was cold with sweat but burned inside like a fever. Then the heat reached his head, filling the blackness of his world. Edgar slowly rose to his feet and turned to where he knew Pritchard Barton was standing. Every muscle in his body was screaming for blood, as if each and every one had its own insatiable hunger. The drumming of his heart grew louder and louder in his head until it was deafening. He clenched his jaw and ground his teeth until he was sure that they would shatter in his mouth. Then, the blackness of Edgar's world exploded into a white rage.

Edgar screeched like a wild animal and leapt at Pritchard Barton, knocking him over and pinning him to the floor. Barton screamed but Edgar heard nothing. He balled his fists together and began pounding Barton's face as hard as he could, feeling the warm gush of blood flow over his hands. But he did not stop. He scraped and dug at Barton's eyes, ripping, tearing. He lunged his head at Barton's throat and sunk his teeth in as far as he could. Biting down, he ripped Pritchard's flesh away from him. The drumming in Edgar's head never ceased and he continued to pound Barton with his fists. Edgar could feel the bones of Barton's face cut into his hands, but the rage would not let him go. Edgar would never stop. There was nothing left in his world other than rage. He must annihilate Pritchard Barton.

The villagers heard the screams and were struck with horror. The screams of a boy would bring any good person running. These were not the screams of a boy in trouble and they were not the screams of Pritchard Barton. These were the screams of a feral beast, a demon, a fiend. The frightened villagers proceeded with caution as they came closer to the blacksmith's shop. The screams continued, deep, guttural, and desperate. It took three grown men to pry Edgar off of what was left of Pritchard Barton. Edgar never stopped thrashing, his screams becoming more carnal with the rush of each new breath. The men carried Edgar, writhing in their arms, to the doctor, and only a few minutes after he had given Edgar a sedative did the boy calm down. Finally he gave up his fight, the white rage faded back to blackness, and Edgar faded into a deep sleep.

12

Chapter 12: Revelation

Joe sat on his porch in a rocking chair as he watched the wind whip across the field. The sun had been beaming down for a few hours and had evaporated all of the wetness left from the previous night. Joe packed his pipe full of tobacco and began to puff at it nervously. Rachael hadn't come home. The boy hadn't come home. The body was buried under the porch and anything that blood had gotten on had been burned. *I've made a mess of this,* thought Joe. *I never should have spared that boy. I should've been stronger in my faith.* The day was hot but the breeze made it nice. He wished that he could enjoy it. His mind wouldn't stop.

Should he go looking for them? Should he wait? As Joe sat, pondering his regrets, a horse and rider came into view through a group of trees. Joe raised an eyebrow and made to stand, but thought better of it. If he seemed too eager to greet the rider, he may give away that something was amiss. So Joe continued rocking and smoking as the rider came nearer and nearer to the farm. It wasn't odd that someone should come out to the farm, so Joe couldn't be sure that this visit concerned his wife and son…or the blacksmith. However, the rider was traveling with some haste. Joe's heart was in his throat, but he was disciplined enough not to let it show. He sat and smoked and waited.

As the horse reached the gate to Shein Farm, the rider quickly dismounted. Without even tethering his horse, the rider opened the gate and began walking quickly up to the porch where Joe sat.

"Rachael! Rachael!"

"Rachael ain't here, Bob."

The man coming quickly up to the porch was Bob Grennel, the town baker. When he heard Joe's response, he dropped his shoulders and uttered a sigh of relief.

"Oh, Joe. Thank the Holy you're here, Joe. It's Edgar. He's with Doc Aron. You'd better come, right away, and Rachael too, Joe. She should come too. Right away. Did I hear you say Rachael's not here?"

Bob was speaking a million miles an hour. Obviously, something bad had happened to the boy. Now Joe's worry couldn't be avoided, and he jumped out of the rocking chair.

"Tell me what happened, Bob." Joe's eyes narrowed on Bob Grennel and Bob took a second to catch his breath.

"Calm down, Joe. Edgar is with the Doc, like I said. He is hurt bad, but he is alive."

"Tell me what happened, Bob." Joe's eyes became more intense and Bob took a step back.

"Well, we don't know exactly. But…well, maybe you should sit down to hear this, Joe."

"I'm fine where I am," Joe shot at Grennel.

"Okay, Joe. Okay, just calm down. Like I said, we don't know exactly how it went down, but it seems your boy and Pritchard Barton were in a fight and…I…I don't exactly know how to say this, Joe." Grennel wiped a bit of perspiration from his brow. "Joe. Edgar killed Pritchard Barton."

"What?" Joe was stunned.

"Yeah, we found the two boys in the blacksmith's shop. Edgar was on top of Pritchard, pounding his fists into him. It took three of us to pry him off. Nobody really knows what happened."

"All right, Bob," Joe nodded. "Let's go."

"Wha-what about Rachael?"

"She ain't here, Bob! Now let's go!"

Joe ran to the barn and got his horse, sparing no time at all. Bob got back to his horse, eyes sunken from the day's events, and fell once, before successfully mounting his horse. Both men rode as quickly as they could to Hammlin. *He doesn't know,* thought Joe. *He doesn't know anything.*

•••

Joe walked into Doc Aron's office and saw who he guessed was Edgar, lying on a cot. It was certainly a child, but there were bandages all around it's head with the exception of a hole for the nose and a hole for the mouth. Joe didn't see any other major injuries, but the child had cuts and scrapes all along it's arms and legs and a few on the hands that had been stitched up. Joe tried to walk over to the bed, but he couldn't. His body was frozen.

"I'm sorry that you have to see Edgar like this, Joe," said Doc Aron as he walked into the room.

Joe started and Doc Aron pointed at a seat over by a desk. The Doc sat down behind the desk and Joe slowly sat down in the seat on the other side. Doc took out a pipe, not unlike the one Joe had been smoking just an hour ago, and lit it. Smoke filled the air as Doc began to speak, giving Joe the feeling that he was in a dream.

"I'll start with the big stuff," said Doc Aron. "Edgar's alive and from what I can tell, barring any major infections, he should continue to live a long life. That's the good news." Doc took another long pull from his pipe. "The bad news, Joe, is that it seems as though Edgar was burned in the face, quite

83

badly. So badly, that his eyes were burned as well. He'll probably have scars on his face and, more than likely, he'll never see again."

Here Doc stopped and looked at Joe as if they were acting parts from a play that Doc had known for years, playing his part effortlessly and looking up at the other player as if to say, *your line.*

"How did it happen?" asked Joe.

"Well, we can only assume that there was a fight between your boy and the Barton boy. We also found a dead dog in the shop. Apparently stabbed with a dagger that we found close by. Also, we found a half-charred log outside of the hearth that we assume was the cause of your boy's burns."

Thinking swiftly, Joe interjected with a well-placed question. "Where was the blacksmith through all this? He must know something."

"We were hoping you might be able to answer that question, Joe." Joe's heart jumped into his throat. "I don't know if you were aware of the situation or not, but over the past month or so, the blacksmith has been doing extra work for your wife. We had hoped that you or she might know his whereabouts."

After Joe realized that he wasn't being accused of anything, he thought frantically for a plausible lie. He quickly realized that his wife would never give him away, as she was just as guilty of adultery as he was of murder. She had as much to lose as he did. The boy was the only witness left. At this point, Joe came up with a story and decided to roll the dice on the boy, hoping that the trauma Edgar had gone through had somehow stripped his memory of the blacksmith's demise.

"Truth is Doc, and I'm a little embarrassed to say this, I don't even know where my wife is. You see, I came back last night to an empty house. I was preparing myself to come into town, hoping to find her and Edgar, just before Bob Grennel showed up. Now, with my wife and the blacksmith gone and Edgar being found in his shop, well, I just don't know what I'm supposed to think."

The Doc shook his head. "I'm sorry, Joe. I know this must be real disturbing for you. All of it."

A knock came at the door and a rather heavy man poked his head through the doorway.

"Hope I'm not interruptin'," said Sheriff Daniels.

"Uh, no. Come on in, Sheriff," said Doc Aron.

"I know you're dealing with a lot right now, Joe," the Sheriff said with a slightly bowed head. "But we need to talk."

"Yes, Sheriff," nodded Joe.

"I'll give you gentlemen some space." Doc Aron got up from his desk, and proceeded to leave the room.

"As you can imagine, Joe, Mrs. Barton is in an uproar. She wants full charges brought against Edgar and the blacksmith. There's nothing you need to worry about though. We know the Barton boy was a bully to all the younger kids, and given what happened to the dog and to Edgar, it's pretty clear that your boy was actin' in defense. However, I do want to ask you some questions about the blacksmith. We have an obligation to find out what level of responsibility he has in all this."

"Doc Aron just told me about the blacksmith, Sheriff. This was the first I had heard of him doing any work for Rachael. I'm afraid I don't know the nature of his involvement with my family."

"Would you happen to know his whereabouts?"

"No, Sir. I'm sorry. I returned just last night to an empty house and I still haven't seen Rachael."

The Sheriff looked surprised at this revelation and scratched his beard for a second.

"Joe, had you ever noticed, maybe some time in the past, the smith looking at Rachael in a funny way or maybe makin' a pass at her?"

This was, so far, going exactly where Joe had hoped it might. "No... I mean... I don't think... You don't think they might have–"

"No. No. I'm not saying anything, Joe. I just think, at this point, it's best for us to have all of the information that we can." Sheriff Daniels shifted uncomfortably in his seat. He was, all of a sudden, finding it hard to meet Joe in the eyes. "Well, I'll let you know if we find anything else out, Joe. In the mean time, take care of that boy. If it's not too much trouble, I'd like to stop by in a week or so and talk to both Edgar and Rachael. You know, after the boy's healed up and ready to speak."

"Of course, Sheriff. I'm sure Rachael will be back at the house by now. Probably just went off looking for Edgar and got a little lost in the woods. She's a smart woman. I'm sure she'll find her way back or I'll find her on my way back."

"I'm sure you're right, Joe, and like I said, any information we gather, I'll be sure to let you know."

"Thank you, Sheriff, Holy be."

"Holy be, Joe."

Joe stayed the night at the Village Inn. Doc Aron had said that he'd like Edgar to stay with him overnight before going home. Joe told Doc he wanted to stay close, in case Edgar's condition changed.

In the morning, Doc told Joe that Edgar was fine to go home and gave Joe a salve for Edgar's burns. Doc Aron made Joe swear to come back quickly if anything were amiss with the boy and Joe obliged. Edgar was awake now, for the first time since Joe had come to town, but his head was still wrapped in bandages. Joe walked over to him to let Edgar know that he was there.

"It's me," Joe said. "It's your Papa."

Edgar said nothing.

"He might not talk for a while, Joe," piped Doc Aron. "Sometimes when children go through traumatic experiences, they stop talking for a few days. I wouldn't let it bother you, just keep an eye on it."

Joe thanked the Doc, brought Edgar outside and sat him up on the horse. He then mounted the horse himself and they headed for home.

•••

Weeks went by and Rachael never returned to Shein Farm. Joe began to think that it was for the best. How would the two of them ever be able to get past the events of that night? He still loved her though, and hoped that she was all right. For weeks, Rachael was all that he could think about. Crying himself to sleep at night, yet unable to motivate himself to search for her. He knew that this was his punishment. He knew that he deserved everything that he got.

Edgar still wasn't speaking. Sheriff Daniels had been by a few times, but he couldn't get Edgar to even acknowledge his presence. At the end of the last visit, Sheriff Daniels declared the case closed and told Joe that he wouldn't bother him any more. He said that Mrs. Barton would just have to deal with the fact that Edgar was blind and mute and that the blacksmith was never going to come back. The Sheriff didn't say anything about Rachael. It was nothing any of the townspeople wanted to talk to Joe about. They all believed that Rachael had run off with the blacksmith and they felt great pity for Joe.

Doc Aron had been by as well. He had done multiple checkups on Edgar.

"I'm sorry, Joe. Blindness is all that afflicts the boy. He just doesn't *want* to talk."

Joe wasn't sure that Doc was right about Edgar's speech, but about a year later, Doc's diagnosis was proven correct. One night, Joe woke to find Edgar standing at the end of his bed, screaming. The boy had scared Joe so badly that he was sure he was going to have a heart attack.

"Edgar!" Joe yelled over him. "What's wrong? Are you all right?"

The boy stopped yelling but didn't say a word. He just stood at the end of Joe's bed, staring at him in the darkness. The vision chilled Joe to the bone. The scars across Edgar's face had healed a dark red and brought an eerie emphasis to the milky-white orbs that were Edgar's eyes. Joe had tried to make Edgar wear a cloth around his eyes, given the fact that they were useless. However, Joe had wanted Edgar to wear the cloth simply to avoid the boy's gaze. Much to Joe's dismay, Edgar would not keep it on, taking it off as soon as Joe put it on him. Joe shivered as he looked at Edgar standing there, looking like a corpse in the moonlight. Joe jumped out of bed and escorted Edgar back to his room.

Unfortunately, this did not spark the beginning of regular speech for Edgar. He continued to be silent with the exception of random outbursts every few months. On one occasion, Joe and Edgar had been seated at the dinner table in the middle of a meal, when suddenly, Edgar began to speak.

"I ate that boy," he said and twirled his fork in his hand as the light glinted off of its edges.

"What?" said Joe, and slowly placed his own utensils back on the table.

"I tore his flesh away with my teeth and then I swallowed it."

Joe put one hand to his head as the other reached for his whiskey glass. That was all he could do to cope now. Joe couldn't leave the farm very often, due to Edgar's blindness, leaving him unable to do his work. They were barely getting by, surviving mostly on charity from villagers who had taken pity on them. Joe felt trapped, so he escaped to the bottle. Soon, his actions became as random and wild as Edgar's.

Joe would rant and rave and drink himself unconscious on most nights. Choosing to keep himself in rooms far away from the boy he called son. Sometimes, he would run outside and scream obscenities at the sky until he was hoarse in the throat. It never affected Edgar at all. He took the same place, every night after dinner, in the rocking chair out on the porch, staring out into the blackness of his world. He never changed his demeanor and never reacted to Joe's tirades, with the exception of one particular night when Joe had decided to make the boy the target of his animosity.

Edgar was sitting in the rocking chair, staring out into nothingness, unaware of how red the sunset was this night, when Joe started in on him. Sweaty and slurring, Joe plopped a chair down on the porch next to Edgar and stared drunkenly into the boy's eyes.

"What are you starin' at?" Joe paused, so drunk that he couldn't keep his eyes straight. "I *said* what are you starin' at!" Joe screamed, inches from Edgar's face, blasting him with spittle and noxious fumes. Edgar didn't even flinch. "You can see him, can't you? I bet he's talkin' to you right now, isn't he? Yeah, he is. I knew it. He won't talk to me anymore. I failed! I was not faithful…I was disobedient." Joe stumbled to his feet, picked up the chair and heaved it off the porch. "Do you know why I failed, son? Do you know why he won't talk to me anymore? Huh? It's because I didn't kill you." A manic grin came over Joe's face and he began laughing wildly. "Can you believe that? He wanted me to kill a baby! But now I know why. Now. Now I know why." Joe sauntered over to Edgar and put his reeking face, inches from the boy's. "Because he knew that you…would ruin…everything. You brought that blacksmith here and he ended up dead. You made your mother leave. You killed that poor Pritchard Barton. And look at me." Joe stood to full height and took a few steps back, spinning around. "You ruined my life!" Joe stumbled and fell onto the porch, then he began to cry. Lying on his back, he bawled like a child. "But that's what I get, for not having enough faith in him. That's what I get…you know, that was the last time he talked to me. That was it. After I brought you here, he never talked to me again. After that, I had to go find odd jobs in other villages so that your mother wouldn't think less of me."

Joe stopped his crying and sat up. "But you don't even know what I'm talking about, do you? Do. You. You don't even know what I was. Well I'm gonna tell you. I'm gonna tell you everything. Whether you want to hear it or not." Edgar hadn't moved a muscle until this point, but now he turned and looked directly at Joe, his useless white orbs burrowing into the drunk. "It was *he* who used to talk to me, Edgar," continued Joe. "The Holy himself. He would tell me to do things for him. It was easy at first. Little stuff…I think he was testing me…but then, he wanted me to kill…he would tell me who to kill and where to find them, and after I did it, I would find my pockets full of gold. I was an assassin for the Holy himself. And I never asked questions. Not once. Until you." Then Joe started crying again. "I'm not your father…and Rachael wasn't your mother. I killed your parents because the Holy told me to, and I was supposed to kill you, but I didn't. I was too weak. I didn't have enough faith in him, and now look at what's happened." Joe put his hands to his face and continued to sob. "You won't even talk to me."

Edgar stared into the blackness, toward the man before him, and moved away from the rocking chair, kneeling down so that he could be face to face with Joe. He grabbed Joe's hands and moved them away from his face. Joe stopped crying and looked at Edgar as the boy said:

"You should have killed me, Joe."

13

Chapter 13: Ghosts

Seven years passed since Edgar had lost his sight. He was now a full-grown man. In fact, he had grown quite bigger than Joe. Joe's problem with alcohol hadn't helped his dwindling stature. A once-proud man, standing at full height, Joe now limped everywhere that he walked, humpbacked and slouching. No longer able to take care of Edgar, it was Joe who needed help. In fact, Edgar had become quite able to take care of himself. It had taken a few years for Edgar to adjust to his blindness, but his other senses had become far more acute, and he was now able to move along, unassisted, even through areas he had never been to. The blindness had made his hearing more acute and he had somehow developed a kind of sixth sense, able to sense his surroundings through the movement of air or possibly through temperature change. It had become virtually impossible to come within twenty feet of Edgar without his knowledge. Not that Joe was in any shape to be sneaking up on anyone these days. Now it was Joe who spent the majority of his time sitting in the rocking chair, gazing off of the porch.

With Edgar's new abilities, he had regained a once-lost freedom. He began to spend his time wandering the forest that bordered Shein Farm. He would go on long hikes through the forest, testing his ability to retrace his path accurately. He was constantly trying to increase his distance each day, as an explorer would blaze new trails through new lands. On occasion, after walking a great distance, Edgar would seat himself under a tree and meditate. Keeping perfectly still and calm, animals would often come right up to him before realizing that he was there. Edgar had begun testing his ability to catch squirrels by staying still until they were close enough to grab. He had been successful on one or two occasions.

The anger and frustration that had once boiled inside of Edgar had begun to ebb away into a cool serenity. Through his meditation, he had come to terms with what had happened to his eyes, to Blue and to Murray. Edgar had even come to terms with Joe, not with any conversation, but within himself. He now pitied Joe more than anything. Of course, Joe had killed his parents, but the man was obviously insane, believing that the Holy himself had commanded the act. Joe wasn't causing harm to anyone any longer, with the exception of himself. Edgar felt that the man had received his punishment already. He had lost his wife, his physique and his mind. Joe was a shell of a man.

Edgar still wondered about his mother from time to time. He felt just in referring to her as thus. He had truly loved her and she had truly loved him. She had raised him as best as she could and he couldn't blame her for what had happened with Murray. He also couldn't blame her for fleeing Joe that night. Edgar's curiosity about his mother rested in the events that took place after that. Where had she gone? Why had she not returned? Was she alive? Edgar had assumed the worst. He assumed that she had died. He could not understand why else she would not have returned. She certainly would not have returned for Joe…but for him? Sometimes Edgar thought about trying to find her, but the prospect always seemed overwhelming. He had become more able and more in tune with his surroundings, but these were small steps in contrast with a quest to find his mother. And although he tried not to think about it often, there may be a good reason that she never came back.

On this particular day, Edgar walked slowly through the forest, moving just a bit further than he ever had before. In one hand, he carried a staff that he had whittled from the thick branch of a dying tree. The other hand Edgar used to protect his face from low-lying branches. The day was warm and dry and the ground cracked underneath his feet. Edgar was sweating quite a bit now, as the day crept into afternoon. Feeling he had made a good distance, Edgar searched for the shade of a large tree to rest under. Once found, he removed his flask and drank deeply. The day seemed warmer than usual and Edgar found himself growing sleepy in the shade of the tree. His thoughts began to wander and he found them resting, once again, on the issue of his mother's disappearance. Edgar found frustration begin to worm its way into his thoughts. He should be able to search for his mother; he should not allow his disability to limit him. Not only that, but how could he give up on her? What kind of man was he, to assume that she were dead? That is something Joe would do; something Joe had done. What if she were in trouble? Edgar's worries would not leave him alone.

All of these thoughts about Edgar's mother raised another issue in his mind as well. What would he do with his life? What would be his purpose? If Edgar could not even go out into the world to inquire into his mother's whereabouts, did that mean he would have to spend the rest of his life on the farm? He couldn't allow that. In fact, he hated being at the farm. It was the reason he had begun to venture into the forest in the first place.

Edgar leaned back against the tree and took a deep breath, staring out into the blackness of his world. He directed his senses outward, allowing himself to hear and feel the forest. The warmth of the sun poured over him and he could feel, from the direction of the heat, that it was only a few hours past midday. As Edgar allowed his consciousness to converge with all that was around him, he began to feel an absolution. He would not stay at the farm much longer. He would go out into the world, and though he did not know what his ultimate purpose would be, he became very sure of one thing. He would find his mother.

Edgar felt a light breeze, heard the sound of a lark in the distance and his breathing became light and easy. It was not long before he fell into slumber, beneath the branches of the large oak tree.

•••

Edgar woke and immediately noticed that the heat of the day had changed drastically. *How long have I been asleep?* he wondered. Edgar stretched his arms and legs and began to get to his feet. As he tried to shake off the sleep, he became increasingly aware that something was very odd. He felt the heat of the sun upon him, but it was a much cooler heat than he had ever experienced. It was making it very difficult for him to discern what time of day it was. Also, though the heat was cooler, it somehow seemed to be more intense, as if the sun were closer to him. Something was wrong. He thought his senses must be confused due to the recent nap, so he decided to sit back down underneath the tree until things had returned to normal.

Though, as Edgar sat under the tree, he was sensing that things were increasing in their weirdness instead of normalizing. After a moment or two, Edgar came to the conclusion that he had not woken from his sleep after all, and was, in fact, still in a dream. He decided to relax and allow himself to be carried through the dream. Edgar felt the sun of his imagination moving across the sky. It was moving at a much faster rate than the real sun ever did. He started to view his dream as a mystery. This sun was cooler, closer, quite possibly smaller, and moving more quickly than the sun of the real world. He allowed his senses to flow outward, unimpeded, toward the imaginary sun. He used his memories of light and heat to conjure an image of what this sun looked like. He held the image there in his mind's eye. His imagination painted a picture of a dusky sky with a small sun traveling over the land, a few hundred feet above the ground. His imagination began to release the thought that the heat source was a sun and instead embraced an image of a mystical orb of light, and the orb seemed to be moving in his direction.

Edgar's arm itched and he reached down to scratch at it. *That's funny*, he thought. *I've never dreamed of an itch before.* He stopped his hand from scratching his arm. Why should he scratch an imaginary itch? It was, in fact, only detracting his imagination from the much more interesting orb in the sky. He didn't want to lose it, as often happened in dreams when one's mind wanders. The orb was traveling closer still and Edgar wondered if he would wake up if it got too close, much like one might wake up abruptly, when dreaming of a long fall.

Unfortunately, the itch had returned. Edgar tried, once again, to force it out, but found that he was unable to ignore it this time. Angered by his inability to control his own dream, he reached down and scratched at the itch vigorously, pressing his nails into his flesh hard and thinking, *that will show it.*

Pain? He had cut his arm with his nails. Suddenly and shockingly, it became very clear to Edgar that he was not in a dream at all. Edgar quickly got to his feet and refocused on the sky. The orb of heat was getting closer to him and seemed to be picking up speed. Should he run? He was still a long way from being able to run through a forest. He would inevitably knock his head on a tree. There was no escape for him. The heat seemed to be flying at him now. He was sure that whatever it was, it intended to collide with him. Edgar stood his ground and braced himself for whatever might happen.

Just as Edgar was sure that this thing would collide with him, the heat flew directly over his head and seemed to land a few meters behind him. There was no sound. The forest had been undisturbed. No birds flew, no leaves rustled, no small animal ran along the ground, everything was perfectly still. Edgar turned his body toward the heat and realized that it was not coming from an orb. The heat seemed to be coming from the body of a large person. He marveled at how anyone could give off such a large aura of energy.

"Hello, Edgar."

It spoke to him. Edgar found his mouth dry and out of practice. A response didn't come easily from his lips.

If you would rather communicate like this, we can.

The being had touched his mind and Edgar found that he was able to communicate without speech.

I... Who are you? asked Edgar

You know who I am, Edgar. It has been a great many years since I have come to this world. It is for you, that I have chosen to return.

Are you the same one who revealed himself to the man, Joe Shein?

I am. However, I have never revealed myself to Joe Shein in the way that I am revealing myself to you, Edgar, but it is true that I communicated with him.

Why did you ask him to kill? Why did you ask him to kill me?

It is true that Joe Shein served me as an assassin, and I have my reasons for each task that he was given. However, it is untrue that Joe Shein was asked to kill you. That is a command that he created with his own mind. That is the reason that I ceased communication with him. He had become disloyal. His service was no longer a viable option.

Why didn't you stop him? Why did you let him kill my parents? Why did you let him kill Murray?

Edgar, I know that there are many things that are difficult for you to understand. I would ask that you have faith in me. Can you have faith in me, Edgar? Edgar nodded his head. *Good. That makes me happy, Edgar. It is your faith that has brought me to this world. I want you to serve me, Edgar. I want you to be faithful to me. I demand unfaltering faith, Edgar. Can you give that to me?*

Yes.

Do you believe that I created this world, Edgar?

Yes.

Do you believe that I created you?

Yes.

And do you believe that my nature is good or evil?

Good. Of course, good.

Than what must you assume of those who would go against my wishes?

That they are evil.

Very good, Edgar. I can see that I was not wrong in choosing you. It is important that we understand each other. Are you ready to accept your first mission, Edgar?

Yes.

Good. You must kill Joe Shein. Edgar's eyes widened and he swallowed hard. His thoughts betrayed him. *Your faith shall always be there to give you strength, Edgar. Do not worry about your condition. I wish to bestow upon you a gift. Open your mouth, Edgar.*

Edgar did as he was asked, even though he shook with fear. He could see nothing but blackness, but he could feel the Holy closing in on him. The being extended an appendage and placed an orb of heat into Edgar's mouth.

Swallow, Edgar.

Edgar did as he was told and immediately felt changes occurring all over his body. It was something foreign, something powerful. It felt like being close to a lightning storm. Edgar felt a surprising surge of strength flow through his body. He clutched the staff in his hand and felt the wood give under the pressure. He squeezed tighter and the staff snapped in half. He bent down and picked up one of the pieces and hurled it into the woods. It flew further than he dreamed possible. His strength was amazing.

Then, suddenly, the blackness of Edgar's world began to slowly fade away into a deep blue. Edgar stepped back, startled as the light inside of his head grew in intensity. It became lighter and lighter, beginning to bend and weave patterns in the air around him. It made shapes as it danced in front of him, like ghosts in the air. He looked down toward his feet and saw a plane of blue underneath him, as if he were walking on water, and then slowly, the shapes of little sticks and rocks came up out of the flatness. He looked back up and saw the most radiant light he had ever seen, in the shape of a man, standing in front of him. The light around the man danced and folded until it had created the shapes of trees. Edgar reached his hand out toward it and there in front of him, was the outline of his hand as it reached up toward the sky. Edgar smiled and moisture formed at the corner of his eye. A single droplet made its way down his cheek and fell to the ground.

I can see…I can see.

Edgar looked back up to where the Holy stood and saw a man made entirely of light, enclosed in a transparent orb. The surface of the being's body crackled and glowed.

Thank you, my Holy.

You are most welcome, Edgar. Be on your way now and fulfill your mission.

Yes, my Holy.

Edgar turned from the being and felt the heat disappear behind him. He could see. The Holy had given him the strength and vision to be his most faithful servant and he would not fail. He looked at the light that swam around him like smoke in the air, outlining everything in the world in tints and shades of blue. He saw the trees, the ground and his own legs. He turned and began to walk back to the place that he would no longer call home, to the man he would never again call father and to a world that would never again give to him its pity.

14

Chapter 14: The Messenger

Edgar walked across the field before Shein farm as his world of blue ghosts swirled around him. The grass was tall and he allowed it to brush against the palms of his hands as he walked through it. It swayed in the evening breeze. Edgar took fistfuls of the grass into his hands, squeezing and feeling the strength in his forearms. He was the chosen one. He had a purpose.

Edgar inhaled and the scent of lavender came to him from the flowers across the field. He heard the trees sway in the wind. All of his senses were heightened now. He was only just coming to the gate of Shein farm and he could smell the alcohol, undoubtedly reeking, from Joe's breath. He could see him rocking in his chair upon the porch, scowling and drunk. Edgar didn't bother to stop and open the gate as he approached it. He merely kicked it in, the wooden slats busting apart.

Joe stood from his chair and glared down at Edgar as he walked up to him from the gate.

"What are you doing!?" Joe yelled down at Edgar.

Edgar didn't respond, only proceeded walking toward Joe, the smell of alcohol increasing with each step Edgar took. The sweet scent of lavender was no longer present, just the cloying presence of the alcohol. Joe yelled at Edgar again, but he didn't hear it this time. His blood had begun to pound a rhythm in his head like war drums. He tensed his shoulders and felt the electric crackle of power surge through his muscles. He clenched his jaw and his fists, preparing for his task.

Joe had killed Edgar's parents.

Joe had killed Murray.

Joe had driven away Rachael.

Joe had defied the Holy.

Joe was evil.

As Edgar reached the porch and began to climb up the steps, he saw for the first time that he could remember, Joe's eyes. They were afraid and meek. Edgar took no pity on them. He moved forward with astonishing quickness and grabbed Joe by the head with both hands. Edgar squeezed and tried to crush Joe's head as the electric energy coursed through his body. Joe was no match for Edgar's power. Nothing could stop him and the drums beat on.

Joe was drooling and leaking from the nose, and the drums beat on.

Joe screamed and his jawbone cracked, and the drums beat on.

Joe grasped at Edgar's arms and swung wildly at him, and the drums beat on.

Joe looked into the fiery whiteness of Edgar's eyes and pleaded for release.

"Forgive me! Holy creator, forgive me!"

Edgar held Joe's head in his hands and lifted his feet off of the porch. He brought the man's face close to his and whispered to him through clenched teeth.

"I absolve you. I shall deliver you. I am your messenger."

Edgar squeezed one last time and then dropped Joe's lifeless body to the porch. He picked up the lantern that had been sitting next to the rocking chair and threw it through a window. It exploded in the house and Edgar walked off of the porch, toward the gate.

The scent of lavender filled Edgar's nose again, and as he walked across the field he let the grass brush his palms. Behind him the fire rose into the sky as Shein farm burned to the ground, erasing a life Edgar would never know again, erasing everything Edgar had once been.

Erasing Edgar.

Blue ghosts danced around Edgar as he raised his eyes to the sky.

I am the Messenger.

WIND

15

Chapter 15: A Rite of Passage

The days had begun to feel very long for Evercloud and Riverpaw. Their quest to find the Ancients hadn't been filled with as much excitement as they had hoped. As the oppressive sun beat down upon Evercloud, he thought back to those first few days when they had embarked upon this quest. Evercloud and his cousin had been at the height of excitement. Running through the forests of the Kingdom, nothing could stop them. Whiteclaw had given them a direction for travel and that was all they needed. There was many a time when Whiteclaw would tell the two cousins to reserve their energy.

"The journey we are on shall be a long one," he had said.

Evercloud and Riverpaw paid him no mind though. There were fish in every stream and wonder behind every tree. Every breaking twig they heard in the forest was the footsteps of the Great Tyrant's minions and every breeze through the treetops spoke of an impending doom only they could save the world from. Evercloud and Riverpaw had entertained themselves verily. Whiteclaw had found them to be amusing on a few occasions, but for completely different reasons that he never shared.

When the travelers had finally left the confines of the forest, they were met by the grandiose expanse of the Ephanlarean plains. This had been energizing for all three members of the Kingdom, each one feeling, for the first time, that they truly were on the precipice of a great adventure. The grass reached all the way to the horizon and the sky looked bigger and brighter than Evercloud had ever remembered seeing it. For a long moment, they stared wildly into the great beyond, each imagining great adventures in their heads.

However, conditions and spirits were now soured and the reality of the task at hand had become clear. Without the shade of the forest trees, the sun came at them in a relentless assault, mocking their progress from its perch in the sky. The terrain had little to no variation and provided little fuel for the imagination. Riverpaw had had enough of the sun.

"Are you sure we're going the right way?" he nagged.

"I told you to reserve your energy, didn't I?" snapped Whiteclaw. His demeanor had become rather salty.

The long march was getting to everyone. Food was hard to come by in the plains, as there were less sources of water in which to fish. Grumbling stomachs were becoming a normalcy. The food situation had, in fact, gotten so bad that Whiteclaw had informed the cousins that they were going to have to start hunting the buffalo that roamed the plains.

"I've never eaten buffalo before," said Evercloud in a doubtful tone.

Whiteclaw snickered. "You've never starved to death before either. Which would you like to try first?"

The severity of the situation was driven home to both Evercloud and Riverpaw with that statement. Yet it only further damaged their morale.

It did not take them long to come upon a herd of buffalo, as it seemed they roamed the plains in large numbers. Whiteclaw motioned for the other two to come closer to him and then he whispered to them, "Watch what I do, so that you can do this later."

Whiteclaw got down on his stomach and began to crawl slowly, out to where the herd was grazing. It seemed to the cousins that he was moving at a snail's pace. Riverpaw and Evercloud waited for some time as Whiteclaw exacted his plan.

"This is taking forever," Riverpaw whispered to Evercloud as they watched from a distance.

Suddenly, Whiteclaw shot into the air and began to sprint toward the herd of buffalo, his massive legs thundering across the ground. Evercloud and Riverpaw watched in anticipation as they laid their bodies flat against the grasslands. Whiteclaw was gaining quickly on the pack as they ran from his ambush. The two cousins could not believe the speed with which Whiteclaw could run. They had both greatly underestimated his ability. They had always believed that he told them to slow down and save energy because he had gotten too old and could not keep up. That was obviously not the case, and in less than fifteen seconds of pursuit, Whiteclaw had pounced on a buffalo and the hunt was over.

•••

The plains seemed to never end. A whole week had not gone by and again, they were without easy food. Whiteclaw informed them that another hunt was necessary. Soon, they reached a herd of buffalo and Whiteclaw turned to Evercloud and Riverpaw.

"Your turn."

Riverpaw and Evercloud looked at each other, hoping that the other would volunteer.

"I can't run fast enough to catch buffalo," said Evercloud, shrugging his shoulders.

Riverpaw huffed. "I guess it'll have to be me then."

Riverpaw lowered himself to the ground and began to crawl toward

99

the herd of buffalo. This time, it was Whiteclaw who watched with Evercloud from a distance. Riverpaw made his way closer and closer, taking care not to move too quickly. Whiteclaw commented that he was showing good patience for his first attempt. Once Riverpaw had gone far enough that he didn't dare to creep any closer without spooking the buffalo, he jumped to his feet and began his pursuit. Riverpaw ran as fast as he could but he was no match for the buffalo. He returned to Whiteclaw and Evercloud, dejected and out of breath.

"I'm sorry," he said, "I'm not fast enough."

Whiteclaw patted his son on the shoulder. "These animals have been running for their lives since birth. You have not. It will be a while for your legs to gain the strength they will need to hunt buffalo, but it is important that you tried. Maybe if you and Evercloud put your heads together, you'll be able to figure out how you might aide each other. We'll move on for now."

The travelers continued west and it was not long before another herd of buffalo appeared upon the horizon. They stopped at a good distance and watched as the buffalo grazed.

"Have either of you come up with anything?" asked Whiteclaw. "Think of what you can do, not of what you cannot."

"I can chase the buffalo," said Riverpaw.

"I suppose I can crawl toward them, maybe even further than the two of you, because I am smaller. Maybe I could get close and hope that they come near me." Evercloud looked at the bears but neither of them seemed keen on the idea.

After a moment of thinking, Riverpaw spoke up. "They probably wouldn't just stumble upon you, Evercloud. But…Maybe I could chase them toward you and then you could ambush them.

"Good," said Whiteclaw. "I knew that the two of you could come up with a plan. Now get to it, I'm starving."

Riverpaw and Evercloud huddled together to get their plan straight and then they headed off, crawling in opposite directions. They crawled out, away from each other, and continued moving until the buffalo were in between them. Evercloud had crawled out with his golden claw strapped to his arm and from there, he would stay as low as he could to the ground and wait as Riverpaw chased the herd in his direction. When the buffalo were close enough, Evercloud would leap up and slash at the throat of a buffalo. Evercloud had achieved his position and now all he could do was wait. As he lay in the grass, the entire world was silent. No birds, no insects, no wind, not a sound except for his own breathing. As time passed, the silence made him paranoid and he became impatient. *Where are you, Riverpaw?* Evercloud thought. Then he heard Riverpaw's roar come across the plains, followed by the rumble of the herd. Evercloud dug his toes into the dirt and lifted his body up, just enough so that he could see the herd. They were coming straight for him. Evercloud dug his toes even further into the dirt and readied himself for the attack. He moved his hands out in front and kept his elbows bent so that he would be able to get a good push off of the ground. He looked like a wildcat ready to pounce. His claw, strapped tightly to his right arm, glinted in the sun. The buffalo were almost upon him now and they had no idea that he was there. The plan was working perfectly. The fear of Riverpaw chasing them had dulled the buffalo's ability to sense Evercloud. Evercloud's heart beat faster and faster and the rumbling of the herd increased in volume and shook the ground, harder with each passing beat of his heart. *NOW*, thought Evercloud. *NOW. GO.* Evercloud didn't move. He was frozen. His heart was beating so fast and the sun was so hot. He stared at his claw in the light.

"NOW!" Riverpaw roared from behind the herd. "Evercloud! NOW!"

The heat was intense and Evercloud's limbs wouldn't move. He had no control over them at all. The herd saw him now and began to scatter away. Evercloud's vision began to tunnel as the herd moved further and further away from him. He had failed. He had frozen.

"What happened?" Riverpaw asked as he approached Evercloud, still crouching on the ground.

"I-I froze. I'm sorry."

Whiteclaw was running toward them with worry etched upon his face.

"Is he hurt?" he asked as he approached. "Was he trampled?"

Evercloud raised himself up on his knees to show that he was all right and then he lowered his head in shame. "I'm sorry, Uncle. I froze. I couldn't move my limbs."

Whiteclaw narrowed his eyes and visibly clenched his jaw. "Get up," he uttered.

"Uncle, I–"

"Get up!" Whiteclaw roared and Evercloud quickly stood on his feet. "I will coddle you no longer, boy!" Whiteclaw took a few steps toward Evercloud and glared at him. "Look at me when I speak to you!" Evercloud raised his eyes to the ferocious bear, and Riverpaw slightly backed away. Neither Riverpaw nor Evercloud had ever seen Whiteclaw this angry. It scared them both. "Do you think this is a game, boy? That this is all for fun? Your grand adventure? You wanted this and now you have it. This is real. I will not allow you to act like a child any longer. The Great Tyrant has most likely returned and we have been charged with finding the Ancients. We carry the fate of the entire Kingdom in our hands and you can't muster the courage to kill a buffalo? I will not tolerate this. You will face much tougher tasks before this quest is through and some may very well mean life or death. Will you freeze in the face of death? I will not place my life and the life of my son in the hands of a spoiled boy with dreams of heroism. Do you understand?!" Evercloud was shaking now, but it was not out of fear that he was losing control of himself, it was out of anger. "We cannot afford for you to be a boy any longer. If it's the last thing I do, I will teach you to be a–"

"A what?!" Evercloud yelled. "A bear? I'm not a bear!" Evercloud turned and stalked away from the two bears, seething with anger.

Whiteclaw called after him, "A man, Evercloud. It is time that you become a man."

Evercloud walked for a while, but his anger did not abate. It stayed with him, mostly because he had been embarrassed and also because he knew that he was wrong. He kicked at the ground and cursed at the sky. *Why did I freeze? Why? What is wrong with me?* Evercloud chastised himself for his inaction. *How can I learn to become something I know nothing of? How can I become a man when I have never known one?* Evercloud sat down and pulled grass out of the ground, throwing it into the wind. *And how does he even know what a man is like?*

Then, something became clear to Evercloud. Whiteclaw *didn't* know what a man was like. He wasn't really asking him to be a man. What he was really asking him to do was to be accountable for himself and to hold up his end of the bargain. Evercloud felt horrible. He wished that he could go back in time. *How can I go back to them now? But where would I go? I have to make this right.*

It was time to act. Evercloud knew his uncle had been right when he had said that there would be far more difficult trials than buffalo hunting. He had to prove that he would be ready for them. He had to kill a buffalo and show him that he could do it on his own. He turned around and headed back in the direction of Whiteclaw and Riverpaw, knowing what he had to do.

•••

"Should we go after him, Father?"

"No, Riverpaw. Evercloud has to return on his own. There is no other way."

Riverpaw nodded and sat upon the ground. Evening was coming and the sun began its descent over the plains. The world was silent and it was this silence that gave Riverpaw his greatest feeling of discomfort. The Kingdom had always been full of bears and sounds. Even the forests around Gray Mountain were filled with the sounds of birds and other animals, the wind through the trees and streams running over rocks and stones. The silence made him feel as if he had left the world. Not just that he had left the world he knew, but that he had gone somewhere that didn't exist at all. He was floating in nothing. Lost in nowhere.

The sun became red as it reached for the shelter of the horizon. Riverpaw watched it and as he did, he saw the silhouette of Evercloud coming back to them in the distance.

"He's coming back."

"I see him," said Whiteclaw. "Let him do the talking. I'm sure that there are a lot of things weighing on his mind."

By the time Evercloud had reached the bears, the sun had almost reached its respite. He sat down across from Whiteclaw with the big, red sun directly behind him, rendering him opaque against the blazing sky.

"I was wrong, Uncle, and I am ashamed of how I acted today. It won't happen again." Whiteclaw remained silent. "I don't ask for your forgiveness, Uncle. I realize that I have not earned it. I have earned nothing, so I will no longer ask for things that I do not deserve. I will not be a weight around your neck. What I do is for the Kingdom, and I shall keep that in my mind and heart." Evercloud stopped speaking and sat in silence, waiting for a response. None came. The sun descended below the horizon and left the group of travelers in darkness. "I will kill a buffalo tomorrow and I will do it alone," said Evercloud, no longer waiting for a response.

"We shall see, Evercloud. We shall see."

•••

Morning came with grumbling stomachs and Evercloud rubbing dirt all over his body.

"It's so they can't smell me," said Evercloud to the bears.

"I believe the herd moved off in this direction," pointed Whiteclaw. "Let's go." Whiteclaw led them onward, and before midday they came across the herd.

"How is it that you plan on doing this?" asked Riverpaw.

"Slowly," responded Evercloud.

Evercloud began crawling out on his stomach toward the herd. After Evercloud was about a hundred yards out, Riverpaw turned to his father.

"He can't be serious about this, can he?"

"Give him his chance."

Two hours passed and the herd had not been disturbed by anything. It had been sometime since they had lost sight of Evercloud. Riverpaw's stomach had been gnawing at him and he was beginning to grow impatient.

"Father, I think you should finish this job. I don't know what state we will be in if Evercloud fails."

"No, Riverpaw. We have to have faith in each other if we are going to survive out here. Evercloud needs to do this."

Just then, they heard a buffalo cry out. They looked out over the plains at the herd and saw a buffalo fall to the ground as the rest of the herd scattered.

"He did it," said Riverpaw, astounded. "I can't believe it."

"Are you going to stand there, gawking, or are you going to come get some food?" Whiteclaw smiled at his son and roared into the air as the two bears ran toward the kill.

16

Chapter 16: The Plan

"You don't fear humans, Riverpaw, because you have never had the misfortune of being hunted by them."

The group moved on westward. The day was cooler than many of the previous had been, allowing for easier travel and less irritable dispositions. It had been almost three weeks since they had departed on that promising morning. Evercloud felt like it could have been a lifetime.

"I still don't see why we should fear humans," Riverpaw shot back at his father. "We are bears. Humans fear us. So, if we make it known that we are friendly, they wouldn't want to anger us by being aggressive."

"There are things you are not taking into account, Riverpaw. For example, we don't speak to humans, do we?"

It was true. It was an unwritten law throughout the world that creatures that were not human did not speak to creatures that were human. All bears, as well as other creatures, had been told the stories from the time that they were young of the misfortunes that befell any animal that talked to a human. Riverpaw knew these stories and even Evercloud had heard them. It seemed that most humans had an insatiable curiosity to know everything, why and how. Unfortunately, when they were unable to figure something out, they would label it as evil and become aggressive against it. This was the overwhelming theme of most of the stories. Of course, the bears had hoped they might be able to change these circumstances with Evercloud as ambassador, but that plan had been tabled out of necessity.

"So pray tell, Riverpaw, how will we let the humans know that we are friendly when the very sight of us sends them into fits?"

"Evercloud will tell them."

"Of course," Whiteclaw said whimsically, feigning idiocy. "A man they have never seen before, filthy from travel and adorned in clothes they have never seen before, claiming that he can speak to bears, will convince the village that we are friendly. Why didn't I think of that?"

Evercloud couldn't help but to chuckle at Whiteclaw's sarcasm.

"Well fine," said Riverpaw. "Then how are we going to question villagers about rumors of the Ancients?"

"Don't worry," said Whiteclaw. "I have a plan. Let us wait until we reach a stream where we can rest and I will explain it to you."

•••

It was another half day before the travelers reached a stream. They dipped their heads into the cool water to refresh themselves and then drank their fill. The sun was well on its way to setting and they decided to rest on the bank until the next morning. They were all very tired from travel, but Riverpaw and Evercloud were far too curious to hear of the plan to just fall asleep. So they held Whiteclaw to his word, and as they relaxed under the cool night sky, Whiteclaw laid out his plan.

"In order to obtain any information from humans, we will need to blend into their world and not seem suspicious. And when I say we, I mean Evercloud. You and I, Riverpaw, should not allow ourselves to be seen with Evercloud. It would ruin any chance he has of seeming normal. Now, if I am correct in judging our location, we are a few miles south of a village called Yorebrook and possibly ten miles north of a village called Hendrick. In the morning, Evercloud, you are to bathe yourself in the stream and use your claw to cut off all of your hair. Try to shave the hair off as close to your scalp as possible. That should fit you with an acceptable style to the villagers, much more than the hair you have now, at least." This did not sit well with Evercloud. He had not cut his hair in a very long time. In fact, he couldn't remember having it cut at all. As his hair was now, it hung to his shoulders in dreaded clumps, pulled to the back and tied off with a leather strap. He really didn't like the idea of cutting it off, but he knew not to argue. It was necessary to blend in. "I will travel north to Yorebrook tonight and return with clothing for Evercloud to wear into the village. In fact, I should leave soon if I want to be back with enough time to rest before morning."

"What if you are caught?" asked Riverpaw. "Shouldn't we go with you?"

"I won't be. Don't worry. I want the two of you to be fully rested. We will head south for Hendrick tomorrow morning and we will have quite the day ahead of us. I must be leaving now." And with that, Whiteclaw ran off into the night.

"I'm starting to think that my father has a bit of a communication problem," Riverpaw said to Evercloud. Evercloud just shrugged his shoulders and then he stretched out and fell asleep.

•••

The night was still very dark when Whiteclaw returned to Riverpaw and Evercloud, who were fast asleep by the stream. Whiteclaw was panting heavily as he slowed his run and approached them.

"Get up!" he yelled, gasping for breath. "Wake up!" Whiteclaw nudged Riverpaw quite forcefully and yelled again. "Get up!"

Riverpaw rose quickly to his feet, eyes wide. "What is it? Did you get the clothes?"

"Yes, I have the clothes, but the plan has changed. We must move, now."

Evercloud was now on his feet. He couldn't see anything in the darkness and neither could the bears, but their senses were better than his. He tried to look around and heard Whiteclaw to his right.

"Evercloud, get on my back. We must run." The urgency in Whiteclaw's voice told Evercloud and Riverpaw to not ask questions. Evercloud promptly climbed onto his uncle's back. "Riverpaw," called Whiteclaw. "Cross the stream and run south. Do not stop until I tell you to. Do you understand me?"

"Yes, Father," answered Riverpaw.

Evercloud clung to the large bear's back as he crossed the stream. He wondered what had happened to cause an emergency exit like this. He couldn't see much with the exception of the moon as it reflected off the surface of the stream. He didn't dare ask any questions right now. As he put his head to the side, facing north, he saw what it was they were running from. Dotting the horizon from the north were the flaming torches of a mob. Whiteclaw had not gone unnoticed and now the citizens of Yorebrook were after them.

The bears had crossed the stream and now began to run south at a ferocious pace. Evercloud kept his body low, to cause as little wind resistance as he could, but he kept his eyes on the flames. If he could not aide in the escape, he could at least serve as a lookout, and alert the bears if they were losing ground. However valorous Evercloud's sentiments may have been, they were ultimately futile. These men had no chance against the speed of two full-grown bears and the travelers rapidly put distance between them and their pursuers.

The bears had almost run all the way to the village of Hendrick before Whiteclaw called for them to stop.

"Enough, Riverpaw. We must take cover."

It had been sometime since Evercloud could see the flames on the horizon. He assumed that the villagers had given up the chase. The sky had become a little lighter during their escape and Evercloud thought that he could now see large clumps of trees and brush. Whiteclaw found one particularly dense group of trees and led the party inside. Once again, the travelers were shrouded in complete darkness.

"Sleep," commanded Whiteclaw. "Make no sound. We will be safe."

Evercloud rolled off of his uncle's back and curled up upon the soft ground. They were all quite exhausted and no one had the least bit of trouble falling into a dreamless sleep.

•••

"Father?" whispered Riverpaw, his jaw agape. He stood, frozen, just feet from the mountainous bear as Evercloud woke. Whiteclaw stirred briefly and then yawned. The sun was now high in the sky and the party was no longer under the protection of darkness. Whiteclaw slowly rose to his feet, and as he did, Evercloud saw what had held his cousin petrified.

Whiteclaw's face was matted in blood and there was a deep wound where his left eye had been. Tears welled in Riverpaw's eyes as he stared, dumbstruck, at his father. Whiteclaw looked back at his son with sadness in his one eye.

"Do you now understand, my son, why men are to be feared?"

The tears that welled upon the eyelids of Riverpaw never fell, but instead burned off in the heat of the young bear's rage.

"They will pay with blood!" Riverpaw croaked. "I'll rip the flesh from their bones for what they've done! I'll crush their bodies to pulp! I'll-I'll–"

"Riverpaw," said Whiteclaw calmly. "They react in fear. I knew this before I went into the village."

"Why?" screamed Riverpaw. "Why? We have done nothing to them. We would have gladly bartered for clothes, were it not for their prejudices. We do nothing that they do not do themselves. We live our lives protecting our land and our families, no differently than they do, and yet they attack us without compassion as if we were monsters. Does a man lose his eye for theft? Does he? I hate them!"

Riverpaw ran at the nearest tree and swung at it with all of his frustration and rage. It splintered upon impact and fell to the ground. Evercloud sat, quiet as a mouse, wishing he could disappear. He knew that he hadn't caused Whiteclaw's wound and he knew that when Riverpaw spoke of men, he was not referring to him, but he was human and felt guilt. Whiteclaw walked over to his son and touched him with his paw.

"Channel your anger. We quest for change." Riverpaw looked at his father and the hatred melted from his eyes. "From the moment we left the Kingdom, everything that we do is for change. We quest for the knowledge and the power of the Ancients so that we can unite the beings of Ephanlarea under the knowledge of what is right. We quest for peace. We quest for our lives and our souls. Channel your anger, my son. Evercloud is our hope. We cannot fail."

Riverpaw's eyes, once again, filled with tears and this time they fell freely to the fur on his face. He swung his head over to Evercloud and Evercloud's heart stung with the reflection of pain that he could see in his cousin's face. Evercloud stood and walked over to the bears, resting each of his hands upon them.

"You are my family and your pain is mine. What must I do?"

Whiteclaw took a bag from around his neck and handed it to Evercloud. Evercloud looked inside and found clothing.

"The plan continues. Go to the stream," said Whiteclaw.

Evercloud did as he was told.

The water felt good on Evercloud's skin. Cool and crisp. Evercloud took a stone from the stream's bed and used it to scrub against himself, partially because he knew that the stone would help remove the dirt from his body, but he also scrubbed himself with the stone as a sort of penance. There was no logic for it, but he felt responsible for what had happened to Whiteclaw. He scrubbed his skin until it was red, grimacing as he dragged the stone across his body. It was sobering; it somehow made him feel better. When he finished, he waded back to the bank and unsheathed his claw. He began to cut the dreaded locks from his head. One by one, he sawed them loose and watched as they floated away downstream. It took him a few minutes to cut out all of the dreaded locks of his hair, but once he had, he set to shaving off what remained. He knew that he had to do a thorough job or it would not seem convincing. His mission was to blend in, to not be noticed. He was sure that men in the village didn't shave their heads by themselves in streams. He must not miss a spot. He dragged the blades of the claw across his scalp with precision, guiding them along with his fingers. Over and over, he dragged the blade until he was sure that he had gotten every bit. When he had finished, he ran his palm over his head, feeling the transformation. That is exactly how it felt, like a transformation. This was when everything needed to change. There could be no more failure. No more giving it your best shot. He dipped his bare head into the water and ran his hands over his smooth scalp. This was his metamorphosis.

He got out of the stream and shook what water he could off of his body. Then he reached for the bag that contained his new clothes and opened it. He pulled out a pair of leather trousers and stepped into them. As he pulled them up, he realized that they were a bit too big, but he drew the string that had been laced through the waist and tied them as tightly as he could. A pair of leather boots was also in the bag and thankfully, they fit well. Lastly, there was a brown shirt made of some rough fabric. It chafed Evercloud's skin as he put it on. He was not used to wearing shirts, especially in the heat. Thankfully, the shirt was armless. Evercloud looked at his reflection in the stream and did not seem as fearsome as he had felt after cutting his hair off. He wanted to look like a warrior, yet he looked rather common. *I suppose that's the point*, he thought to himself.

Evercloud returned to Whiteclaw and Riverpaw to find Whiteclaw drawing with his claw in the sand. Riverpaw was watching intently. When Whiteclaw saw Evercloud, he motioned for him to come over and sit next to him.

"I was going over the plan with Riverpaw while you were away. This is what we will need you to do." Evercloud sat down and pulled at his shirt as Whiteclaw detailed the plan. "Your main objective will be to enter the village and learn whatever you can from the villagers about any rumors of the Ancients. It is important for you to learn as much as you can without raising suspicions. Be careful of how you enter into conversations with people. Most humans worship the Holy and will not take kindly to talk of the Ancients. I have heard that in some villages it is prohibited by the law to do so. That is

108

where Riverpaw and myself will come in. When you enter the village, first go to the authorities and tell them that you are from Yorebrook and that you were assaulted by bandits just outside of the village. That should send them out of the village where Riverpaw and I will be waiting for them. This should free you to ask questions without being reported. After you have spoken to the authorities, I would suggest visiting a tavern. Humans have been known to be friendlier when imbibing ales. Also, make sure, before you leave the village, to visit a medic and purchase a salve for open wounds. My head wound should be treated and we may find the salve handy in the future. Here is some of the currency used by humans." Whiteclaw then looked sternly at Evercloud. "Only use it on purchasing the salve." Evercloud nodded and Whiteclaw continued. "Once the sun is roughly two hours from setting, leave the village and follow the stream south. Riverpaw and myself will catch up to you there. Have you got all that?"

"Yes, Uncle."

"Good, now go ahead. You'll need as much time as possible." Evercloud stood and began to walk toward the village. "Oh, and Evercloud," Whiteclaw called after him. "Make sure to use a human name. Don't use your real name."

"Yes, Uncle," Evercloud called out. *Well*, he thought, *this is it.*

109

17

Chapter 17: Poor Ale and A Fine Bear

Evercloud tried to keep his head down as he walked into the village. It was just about midday and the streets of Hendrick were full of people tending to their daily business. Evercloud had never seen so many humans before. He felt alien. Everything was so foreign about these people who looked just like he did. The way they dressed and the way that they walked and even their smell seemed so exotic. He was unable to keep his head down for very long and before he knew what he was doing, he began gawking at people as they passed him on the street.

"Whatchoo lookin' at?" said a man Evercloud was staring at. The man startled Evercloud. He wasn't aware that he had been doing anything wrong.

"Sorry," he uttered, turning his head back to the path in front of him and walking quickly away from the man. *They're going to figure you out,* thought Evercloud. He vowed to keep his head down until he reached the village authorities, but it wasn't long before his senses and curiosities betrayed him again. A woman with long, blonde hair and a violet dress was coming toward him as he walked. As she came closer, he noticed that she smelled of the most wonderful fragrance. He wondered what it might be. As she began to pass him, he turned his head toward her and sniffed at her, intoxicated by her fragrance.

"How rude," the woman said and slapped Evercloud on the cheek. Many villagers who had seen what happened began to point and laugh at Evercloud. His face turned bright red and he shuffled away from the scene as quickly as he could, enveloped in the heat of embarrassment.

The slap to the face had been enough to remind Evercloud to mind his business, and it wasn't long before he had found what seemed to be a village officer. The man was standing outside of the bakery, looking around at the crowds, doing everything that he could to seem imposing and important. Standing tall, arms folded, eyeing suspicious characters. He wore a little hat that had a star upon it. He reminded Evercloud of the castle guards back on Gray Mountain. The fellow was taller than most, but he was also rounder than most and had a funny, little growth of hair on his upper lip. Evercloud laughed to himself that this man was counted on to protect the villagers. He gathered himself and approached the man.

110

"Excuse me, Sir," said Evercloud. The officer looked at him and twitched his mustache, squinting his eyes.

"Yes. What is it?"

"Sir, I was traveling this morning from Yorebrook when just outside of your village, I was ambushed by a group of bandits. They stole everything I had, except for my clothes."

The officer squinted even more. "Yorebrook, eh. Well that explains why I don't recognize you. What's your name, lad?"

Evercloud searched his mind for a name. He'd forgotten to come up with one. *What is a man name?* he thought. Then he remembered that the game he and Riverpaw played so often, Johnball, was named for a man.

"John. My name is John. I'm from Yorebrook." Evercloud was beginning to sweat a little.

The officer tilted his head sideways and twitched his mustache again. "And your last name?"

Last name? thought Evercloud. *What's a last name?* Evercloud was beginning to panic now and blurted out the first thing he thought of.

"Ball."

"Did you say Ball? John Ball?" asked the officer.

Evercloud's head shrank back to his shoulders as he tentatively answered, "Yes?"

"Well why didn't you say so?" laughed the man and patted Evercloud on the shoulder. "Didn't know Old George had a boy. How's Old George doing these days?"

"He's…well," choked Evercloud.

"He won't be too happy to hear you've been robbed by bandits, now will he?"

"No, Sir."

"Well don't you worry, John," the man said, twitching his mustache and hefting up his girth. "We'll get those bandits. How many did you say there were?"

Evercloud tried to come up with a number that would get all the officers out of the village. "Ten?"

"Ten, you say? Well, this is serious. You done a good job coming to get me, boy. It'll take all the officers to get this job done. You stop by the jailhouse later, and we'll have 'em, you'll see."

"Thank you, Sir."

And with a final twitch of the mustache, the hefty man waddled away faster than Evercloud had thought anyone could waddle. Evercloud smiled, he couldn't believe his luck. *Johnball. Wait till Riverpaw hears this.*

Evercloud walked through the village trying to find a pub or a tavern where people were gathered. He felt a bit more confident after having successfully tricked the officer. The first tavern he came across took the name

111

of the village, Hendrick Tavern. He went inside and looked around. The tavern was rather dingy and there were not many windows. He wondered why anyone would want to come into such a morose place on such a nice day. There were a few groups of people sitting at tables, but they were seated facing each other, backs to the rest of the tavern. Evercloud thought that it might be difficult to engage them in conversation. Toward the back of the tavern, there was a bar where a few men were seated alongside each other. They seemed friendly and were in a conversation with the barkeep. Evercloud thought that this looked like a good opportunity. He walked up to the bar and took a seat to the left of the man sitting on the end of the group. The man briefly looked over as he sat down but then returned to his conversation. The barkeeper, however, stopped the conversation and came over to Evercloud.

"What'll it be?"

"I'll have an ale, please."

"Ain't you a bit young for ale?" asked the barkeeper.

"I'm served ale all the time," responded Evercloud, forgetting where he was.

"Oh, really?" said the barkeeper. "That's funny, cause I ain't seen you in here before." Now all the men at the bar had turned to look at Evercloud. He looked back at them, realizing that he might be too young to drink ale by human standards.

"Well, that's because I haven't been here before," said Evercloud, trying to recover from his slip. "I meant that they serve me in Yorebrook. My name is John, John Ball."

"From Yorebrook, eh?" said a man with a red beard, two seats down from Evercloud. "I got a sister in Yorebrook." Then the man turned to the barkeeper. "Give him an ale, Gene. It ain't gonna hurt him."

The barkeeper shrugged his shoulders and turned around to the tap. He poured Evercloud a mug of ale and placed it down in front of him. "That'll be three gold pieces, young man."

Evercloud thanked him and handed over the money.

"So," continued the man with the red beard. "Tell us news of Yorebrook, my boy. How goes it there?"

Evercloud took a sip of the ale and struggled to stop himself from spitting it out. *That's horrible,* he thought. Bear ale was much finer than that which was brewed by men. Evercloud swallowed and answered the man.

"All is well in Yorebrook," he said, nodding. "Nothing of any excitement to speak of…although," Evercloud saw this as his first opportunity. "There have been rumors of a return of the Ancients…have there been such rumors here in Hendrick?"

The tavern went dead silent and all of its inhabitants now had their eyes pinned down on Evercloud. A sinking feeling worked its way into his stomach and he wondered if it were the ale. The man with the red beard pushed his stool away from the bar and stood up. He walked over to Evercloud and put a heavy hand upon his shoulder. Evercloud looked up at the man, who now had a very stern look upon his face, and swallowed hard.

"I highly doubt," said the man with an edge in his voice, "that anyone in Yorebrook talks about Ancients, and I guarantee that no *good* person in this village does so either. So, friend from Yorebrook, why don't you just tell us who you really are and what unholy place it is that you come from?"

At this moment, Evercloud desperately wished that Whiteclaw and Riverpaw were there. He slowly moved his hand down his side and felt the golden claw that he had concealed inside his baggy trousers. He knew that revealing the claw would mean the end of his inquiries in this village and ultimately, failure of his objective, but he was no longer sure that he was going to have a choice in the matter.

"There he is," came a voice from across the tavern.

"I told you that waiting at the tavern was a good idea," came another.

Two men walked over to Evercloud and the red-bearded man, and stood directly between them. The first man was tall and thin, with an olive complexion and large, dark eyes. He placed a hand on Evercloud's shoulder. "There you are, cousin."

"Been drinking again, have we?" said the other man as he put his hand on Evercloud's other shoulder. He was of the same complexion as the taller man. In fact, they looked like brothers. However, this man was much shorter, had longer hair and had more handsome features. He turned to the red-bearded man. "Says some funny things when he drinks, doesn't he?"

"Very creative imagination," added the tall man. "Well, we better get you back to Uncle," he said, turning to Evercloud. "Don't want him to get angry."

"Scary man when he's angry," said the short man, shaking his head at the red-bearded man. And with that, the two men grabbed Evercloud under the shoulders and ushered him out of the tavern.

"Who are you?" asked Evercloud once they were outside of the tavern. The two men didn't stop walking and continued to usher Evercloud down the busy street.

"Keep your mouth shut and keep walking," said the tall man.

Just then, the man with the red beard burst out of the doors of the tavern and hollered after them as they walked away.

"I don't want to see him back here again!"

"Yes, Sir," called the short man brightly. "Have a lovely day." Then he muttered under his breath, "ugly bastard."

After walking quite a distance away from the tavern, the men turned down a narrow alley between two houses and entered a side door at the end of the alley. The room was very dark, as there were no windows, and it seemed

113

empty with the exception of a chair. However, there were a few candles lit that provided some light. The men sat Evercloud down in the chair and began asking him questions.

"All right," said the tall man. "Who are you and why are you here?"

"My name is John Ball and I'm from Yorebrook–"

"Don't play with me!" the tall man pointed his finger and shouted. "Do you think we're stupid? Your pants don't fit, you've recently shaved your head and you strike up conversation with strangers about things that could get a man killed. Another ten minutes and they would have had you up the stake as a heretic. Now, I'll only ask you one more time, who are you?"

Evercloud didn't know what to do. These men had seemingly helped him out of a precarious situation, but how could he be sure that he could trust them? He looked around the dark room. Only the tall man could be seen, hovering over him. He couldn't see the short man any longer. *What would Whiteclaw do?* he thought.

"Well," came the short man's voice out of the darkness. "We're waiting."

"How do I know that I can trust you?" asked Evercloud.

"We just saved your life," said the tall man.

The man was right. These men didn't know Evercloud, yet they had helped him. Besides, there wasn't much alternative unless Evercloud wanted to fight them.

"My name is Evercloud and I am from the Kingdom on Gray Mountain."

"You think this is funny, don't you?" The short man was beginning to become irritated. He stepped forward into the dim candlelight and Evercloud could now see the large knife that he held in his hand. "This is not a game."

Evercloud was now beginning to get frightened. He again placed his hand upon the claw concealed in his trousers and prepared himself for what he might have to do.

"Please," he said. "I'm not lying. I swear it. I come from the Kingdom on Gray Mountain."

"There is no Kingdom on Gray Mountain!" yelled the short man.

"There is!" pleaded Evercloud. "The Kingdom of Bears."

"You come from a kingdom of bears?" chuckled the tall man as he turned to the short man. "Maybe this one is a drunkard."

"I'm not drunk!" yelled Evercloud. "I was abandoned in the forests around Gray Mountain when I was a small child. The bears took me in and raised me as their own. I am now on a quest to find the Ancients and stop the Great Tyrant."

The short man paused and looked at Evercloud with a genuine curiosity. "Where did you learn of the Ancients and the Great Tyrant?"

"My family told me of them, just recently."

"So, when you say your family, you mean bears?"

"Yes," said Evercloud defiantly. "They are my family."

The short man shook his head and turned to the tall man who shrugged.

"Okay," said the short man. "You say that your uncle and cousin, who are bears, are on this quest with you. Then where are they?"

"They are waiting for me outside of the village."

"If that is true," said the tall man. "Then you will take us to them."

•••

Twenty armored men walked out of the village of Hendrick, holding wooden shields on one arm and spears in the other. They marched two by two as their leader called out cadence, as if they had been trained to put on a show rather than to fight. Whiteclaw and Riverpaw lay low to the ground, behind a group of trees, as the officers walked past.

"You remember the plan?"

"Yes, Father."

"We are only trying to keep them occupied. Do not kill unless it is completely necessary. Do you understand me?" Riverpaw did not answer. "Riverpaw, do you understand me?"

"Yes, Father."

"All right, on my mark, make the first pass."

Whiteclaw lifted his arm and Riverpaw prepared himself to run, waiting for the signal. He could feel his muscles tense in his anger. He could not so easily forget what men had done to his father. He was reminded every time that he looked at his face. The anger boiled inside of him and fueled him with adrenaline and determination. He clenched his jaw and waited.

Whiteclaw dropped his paw to the ground and Riverpaw was off. He circled behind the group of men and then came at them where they were blind. With all of their calls and clinking armor, the officers never heard the bear coming. Riverpaw barreled into the group, knocking six of them to the ground. Hearing the commotion, the rest of the group spun around to find Riverpaw having already retreated to a safe distance.

Just then, a booming roar came from the other direction. The officers turned back around to find that Whiteclaw had cut their path off to the north. They were caught in between the bears.

The men formed a tight circle and raised their shields and spears.

"All right, men," yelled a large man with a twitching mustache. "Grip your spears tight and prepare to defend yourselves."

Whiteclaw let out another roar and the bears began to circle the men, moving counterclockwise, keeping their distance.

"Hold tight, men!" yelled the mustache. "They are preparing to charge."

But they were not. They continued to circle the men, and every once in a while, Whiteclaw would roar and the bears would rest, holding their positions. Whiteclaw would roar again and the bears would begin to circle the

115

men, moving in the other direction. Things continued in this way for hours and then, one of the officers spoke up.

"Sir, I don't believe that the bears are going to charge."

The twitching mustache rolled his eyes. "Good work, officer. Your powers of observation are an unbelievable asset."

"What should we do now, Sir?"

"Do nothing. Allow them to make the first move. We have the advantage. They will most likely run away after a time."

"What if they are waiting for other bears, Sir?"

The twitching mustache hadn't thought of that. Was that possible? Could bears be that intelligent? The odds, right now, were well in his favor, ten men to each bear. But with each new bear that might show up, their odds would plummet drastically. Could they afford to wait around? He would have to make the first move.

"All right, men! Stay close to each other and begin moving slowly back toward the village. Stay on guard!"

Whiteclaw saw the men moving and knew that it was time for phase two. He reared up on his hind legs and roared into the air twice. Riverpaw took the cue and he and Whiteclaw ran from their positions back to the trees.

"Hold formation and move slowly!" cried the mustache. "They may return."

And return they did. The bears came running with a felled tree, balanced on the back of their necks. They stopped almost ten yards from the men and dropped the tree. Then, lifting it together, they reared on their hind legs and heaved the tree at the men. The men did not know how to react and the tree struck them, knocking them to the ground. Before they could move, the bears were upon them, not attacking the men, but attacking their weapons. Not an entire minute had passed and every spear that the men had carried lay shattered on the ground. Twenty men stood, huddled behind their shields, confused and afraid, as two large bears barred their way back to the village.

The men looked out at the bears that stood roughly twenty yards from them, wondering what this meant. Why were they not being attacked? One of the men whispered to the twitching mustache that was now twitching most nervously.

"What is happening?"

The mustache shook his head; beady eyes darting from one bear to the other. "I don't know. Just give me some time."

Time was exactly what the bears wanted and it continued to pass as the two groups stood in standoff. The sun crept across the sky and was now beginning to turn a vibrant orange as it headed for the horizon. *We've almost finished,* thought Whiteclaw. *This was easy.*

But the twitching mustache had been thinking and as he watched the sun begin to set, a panic had come over him. These were not normal bears. Maybe they weren't bears at all. Maybe they were witches, disguised as bears.

What did they want? Why had they destroyed their weapons but not killed them? The sun is setting and soon it will be dark. Maybe they are waiting for the dark?

The twitching mustache couldn't take it any longer. He picked up a broken spear and screamed, charging the bears with it in his hand. His men looked on in horror as the mustache got closer to the bears. Like a flash of lightning, Riverpaw knocked the man to the ground, pinning him under his giant paw.

"Riverpaw. It is time. Let us go," said Whiteclaw, but Riverpaw did not respond. He lowered his head to the twitching mustache and gnashed his teeth. The man cried out, terrified. "Riverpaw!" yelled Whiteclaw.

"Why is the bear talking?" whimpered the mustache, talking to himself.

Riverpaw removed his paw with one final snarl and ran off to his father. The bears ran along the stream, leaving the men alive but shaken, having to wonder for the rest of their lives, what in the world had happened to them.

"I thought you were going to kill that man," said Whiteclaw as he and Riverpaw ran.

"I refuse to become the monster that they think I am."

Whiteclaw grinned. "You're going to be a fine bear, Riverpaw."

18

Chapter 18: The Family Floyd

"You've got to be kidding me," said the tall man as he and the short man stood with Evercloud by the stream, watching two large bears come lumbering toward them.

"Put the knife on him," whispered the short man to the tall man.

The tall man grabbed Evercloud and held the knife to his throat. "You make the bears play nice and we'll play nice, got it?"

Whiteclaw and Riverpaw stopped just a few yards short of Evercloud and the men. They saw the knife, up to Evercloud's throat, and they both began to growl.

"It's okay," said Evercloud to the bears. "They just want to be sure that they can trust you. Speak to them." Whiteclaw shook his head very slightly at Evercloud, not wanting to give away that bears could speak or even understand speech. "Really, it's okay. They helped me in the village. They're just protecting themselves."

"Take the knife away from his throat or I'll crush your heads," said Riverpaw to the men.

Whiteclaw spun on his son. "What are you doing?"

For a moment, everything was silent. The two men were wide-eyed in amazement. Then they began to whisper to each other.

"The bears are talking, right?"

"Yes, the bears are talking."

"They're going to kill us."

"Say something to them, would you?"

"Um," started the tall man. "We mean you no harm...nor your friend here. Um...are we correct in assuming that you are friends to those who search for the Ancients and reject the Great Tyrant?"

This time Whiteclaw spoke, however reluctantly. "I don't know. Are we correct in assuming that you will not do anything that will force us to kill you?"

The short man came up behind the tall man and whispered into his ear. "Tell him yes."

The tall man spoke, "Yes."

"Then, yes," said Whiteclaw.

"So what do we do now?" asked the tall man, obviously unsettled by the events that were taking place.

"Well, first," said Whiteclaw. "I suggest that you remove the knife from Evercloud's neck and tell us who you are."

The tall man looked over at the knife he was holding to Evercloud's neck and this seemed to bring him back to his senses. "Oh, sorry," he said, lowering the knife. "We trust you'll understand that was just a precaution. Never really intended to…er…my name is Ben Floyd, and this," as he pointed to the short man, "is my brother, Tomas. Our family has been worshipping the Ancients for generations and has always harbored the belief that they have not left us. We have made it our mission to do what we can to find them."

"So that's why you helped me in the tavern," said Evercloud.

"Yes," said Tomas. "And we apologize for not believing your story, Evercloud, but you have to understand that we must be very careful. It is not safe to worship the Ancients in the world in which we live."

Evercloud nodded and then Whiteclaw began to speak. "I am Whiteclaw and this is my son, Riverpaw. We come from the Kingdom on Gray Mountain and we, along with Evercloud, have also accepted a mission to find the Ancients, if indeed they still exist."

"Oh, they exist," chimed Tomas.

"We have heard only rumors," said Whiteclaw. "Do you have any proof or do you speak from belief?"

"Well," said Ben, "I think it would be best if you followed us to our home. There is much we can explain."

"We appreciate the invitation, Ben Floyd, but my son and I cannot just walk into a village of men."

"Oh, we don't live in the village," said Tomas.

"Please," beckoned Ben, "follow me."

Ben and Tomas crossed the stream and began to lead the travelers into the dense forest that loomed on the other side. The sun was still up, but it would only be so for a little while longer. As it was already, the forest shut out most of the sun's light and made it very difficult to see.

"We should be there before the light is completely gone," Ben assured them.

"Evercloud," said Whiteclaw, "were you able to purchase the salve that I had asked for?"

Evercloud sighed and slumped his shoulders. "I'm sorry. That should have been the first thing I did."

"Don't worry," piped in Tomas, "we have all kinds of medicines back at home and you're welcome to them."

"Thank you," said Whiteclaw. Then, turning to Evercloud. "You still have all of the currency that I gave to you?"

"Well, not all of it."

"Evercloud, I told you to only purchase the salve."

"Yes, but you also told me to go to the tavern."

"And what did you purchase at the tavern?"

"A mug of ale."

"A mug of ale? Seriously, Evercloud?"

"Uncle, would you trust someone who entered a tavern, all alone, and didn't purchase a mug of ale?"

"Hmm," Whiteclaw pursed his lips. "I suppose you have a valid point."

"We're here," said Ben.

The party had reached the entrance to a cave and a faint light could be seen coming from inside. The entrance was not especially big, at least compared to the caves that Evercloud and the bears were used to.

"We'd better go inside first, so that Father and Sister aren't scared," said Tomas, and the brothers Floyd disappeared into the cave, reappearing only minutes later.

"Welcome to our home," said Ben, arms outstretched in welcome. The travelers entered the cave.

The cave was much larger on the inside, with a roomy common area and many rooms adjacent to it. There was a fire going directly in the middle of the common area and a large boiling pot sat upon it. The smell that came from it set Evercloud's mouth watering. He couldn't remember having eaten anything that day. Large, colorful carpets adorned the floor of the cave and scrolls and maps hung on the walls. The bears were fairly impressed.

"I suppose I'll do the introductions. This is Evercloud, Whiteclaw and Riverpaw," said Tomas, pointing to each of them in turn. The three travelers made their greetings politely. "And this is my father, Nikolas."

"Very nice to meet you," said the old man. He had lost the majority of his hair and it seemed as though a fair amount of his sight had abandoned him as well. When the man looked at the travelers, it seemed as if he were staring straight through them. "Bears that speak. Well, I never."

"And this," continued Tomas, "is our sister, Iolana."

"It is a pleasure to meet you," said Iolana and she bowed slightly. Evercloud could not take his eyes off of her. He had never seen a woman like her before. She was rather small and slender with long, red hair that fell in curls around her shoulders. Her skin was so pale that it almost seemed luminescent, and her blue eyes sparkled like a river in the moonlight. She smiled at him and he felt as if he might fall down. He put his hand out against the side of Riverpaw to steady himself.

"Are you all right?" asked Riverpaw.

"I'm really well. How are you?" said Evercloud.

Riverpaw wrinkled his nose and looked at Evercloud as if he were the strangest thing he had ever seen.

120

"Well," began Nikolas, "dinner is almost ready and then we can get to know each other a little better. The stew probably won't be enough for the two of you." The man gestured toward the bears. "But I have a couple of boars that were going to be for tomorrow. I'll think they'll do nicely."

"That would be most appreciated, thank you," nodded Whiteclaw.

"Whiteclaw," said Tomas, "if you would follow me, I can help you dress that wound." Whiteclaw again nodded and followed Tomas into an adjacent room.

When Whiteclaw and Tomas returned, everyone was finding a seat on a rug so that they could eat comfortably. Tomas had not only dressed Whiteclaw's wound but also found a thick, leather strap that fit nicely around the bear's head, in order to provide some protection. Evercloud thought it looked funny at first, though he never would have said so, but after a few minutes it took on more of an intimidating effect. Whiteclaw looked like a warrior, and in a strange way, Evercloud found himself moderately jealous.

Over dinner, Evercloud told the Floyds of how his father, Eveneye, had found him when he was very little, and then, of how he had become king. The family found the story very interesting. They seemed to want to know every detail of the Kingdom and how it operated. Evercloud was more than pleased to have an audience. He continued his story all the way up to their departure.

"So every bear in the Kingdom can speak?" asked Nikolas.

"All animals can speak if they wish you to hear them," said Evercloud.

"Well, I suppose I shouldn't be so surprised," Nikolas shook his head. "Why would the Ancients create creatures who cannot speak when they themselves have the ability to do so?"

"I agree with your statement, Old One," said Whiteclaw, swallowing a chunk of boar. "But for the sake of argument, how do we know that the Ancients could speak?"

"It is a good question," nodded Nikolas. "However, there are references in *The Book of The Holy* that suggest that they did."

"*The Book of The Holy?*" asked Evercloud.

"Yes, *The Book of The Holy*. It's the Tyrant's own account of how he came to power, mixed in with his teachings and codes and whatnot. Most men hold onto it as if it were the air they breathe. Rubbish, I say. Lies and propaganda. The Tyrant used this book to convince the human race that it was he who created the world, and that the Ancients were evil creatures intent upon destroying it."

"But you just said that this book is filled with lies and propaganda," said Evercloud. "How can we assume that any of it is true?"

"Your logic is sound, my boy. But all lies have some truth. I have my own reasons for belief."

"Would anyone like more?" asked Iolana, rising to her feet with a smile. Her voice ran through Evercloud's mind like a song. He found himself repeating her name in his head. *Iolana. Iolana.*

"No. Thank you, Iolana," said Evercloud, staring dumbly into her eyes.

Whiteclaw noticed his infatuation and turned to Riverpaw. "That didn't take long, did it?"

Riverpaw chuckled.

"What did you say?" asked Evercloud, shaking himself out of his trance and looking at Whiteclaw.

"Oh, nothing," said Whiteclaw, and then changing the subject, addressed the Floyds. "I think we have all had quite our fill and we thank your generosity and hospitality. You do a service to your entire race." Riverpaw nodded in agreement and thanked the Floyds as well.

Now Ben walked to the center of the circle and addressed the travelers. "You have told us of the rumors of the Ancients that have reached your kingdom and it's only fair that we now share what we know. The short of it is that we believe we know the general location of the Ancient, Tenturo." The three travelers looked at Ben in disbelief. "Allow me to explain. Firstly, my brother and I found the giant footprint that you spoke of. We found it in the Glass Desert that lies west of this forest. From there, my brother went to our cousin, Terrence, who lives in Yorebrook. He has sworn to the same mission that we have, and he spread the word among our supporters. I continued west, through the desert and into the White Mountains. It was there that I came across something that I think you should see for yourselves." Ben pointed to the entrance of a room, adjacent to the room they were in, that had a rug hanging to conceal it from sight. Everyone got to their feet, and following Ben, entered the room.

"By the Everflame," exclaimed Whiteclaw.

There, lying upon the floor of the room, was the largest white feather any of them had ever seen. It was so large that Evercloud thought it looked much like a bed he would quite like to fall asleep on.

"We believe that Tenturo is in the White Mountains," Ben said, looking at them as they stared in awe.

"Have you made any attempts to find him since finding this?" asked Riverpaw.

"No, we didn't believe that we had the force that might be necessary," added Tomas. "But now..." and he looked at his brother.

"What my brother is alluding to," said Ben, "is that with your help, we think we do have the necessary force."

"What exactly do you mean when you say *necessary force?*" asked Whiteclaw.

"Well," began Ben, "in *The Book of The Holy* it says–"

"You seem to derive a lot of your information from a book you claim is rubbish," interrupted the elder bear.

"Please," Ben pleaded, "hear me out. If this feather and the footprint in the desert are signs that Tenturo is out there, then why has he not returned to us? There must be a reason. Possibly, something keeping him. Let me read you a passage from this book and then you tell me yourselves." Ben went over to a shelf and picked up a copy of *The Book of The Holy* and opened it to a marked page. He then began to read:

"…And then the evil beast came at the Holy,
Cursing his name with its foul breath.
It came down from the sky and slashed with its claws
And it snapped with its beak.
But the Holy would not allow evil to win the day.
He conjured two magnificent steeds to combat the monster
And banish it from whence it came.

"Now, granted, we cannot take this book as truth, but something is keeping Tenturo away. It is only wise to prepare for all possibilities." Ben finished and stared at the travelers. "Will you help us?"

The bears looked at Evercloud and he looked back at them. It didn't take but a glance for him to see the concern in their eyes and only a second to realize why. Evercloud turned back to Ben.

"Almost all men worship the Great Tyrant and feel that the Ancients are evil. Why should we believe that you are different? Why should we believe that you would not use us to find the Ancients, only to harm them? We only ask these questions in protection of the Ancients."

Ben looked at the travelers with sadness in his eyes. "You haven't lived in our world to know why we feel the way we feel. So let me describe it for you. It is not a picture filled with harmony and happiness. It is not a picture of peaceful coexistence. It is a picture of fear and hatred and distrust. It is a picture of men at war with not only the world around them, but also with each other. And we have been told that this picture has been painted by a being that calls himself the Holy, a being that calls himself good, and kind, and all that is right. That doesn't seem to add up to us. So we call him the Great Tyrant and we choose to turn from him. We choose to do all that we can to bring about his end, however little that may be. We strive for a world that promotes trust and honor and peace, a world where children are not left to fend for themselves in the wilderness, a world where a man can believe what he chooses without fear of death, a world where I don't have to hold a knife to a man's throat before I can trust that he and his companions are good in nature. I see the Ancients as my only chance of such an existence. So what say you, travelers? Do we stand together?"

"Yes," said Whiteclaw. "We head for the desert in the morning."

19

Chapter 19: The Glass Desert

The next day, the group readied themselves for the journey.

"Here, take these, I've outgrown them. They're no use to me. Take them." Ben threw a pack at Evercloud. He opened it and found it contained some clothes. "And you can use the pack on the journey."

Evercloud took out a pair of trousers, a shirt, and a belt. He stepped into the trousers and pulled them up. They were a much better fit and were made of a much cooler material. The shirt was also a better fit and thankfully, made of very thin leather, rather than the rough material of the other shirt. This shirt was also sleeveless, which Evercloud felt, at this point, was necessary. He then strapped the belt on and found there was a holster that his claw hooked onto quite nicely. *Now I look like a warrior,* he thought, and strapped the pack onto his back.

Not all of the family was joining the quest. Old Nikolas was staying behind and much to the disappointment of Evercloud, so was Iolana. Once they had made sure that they had everything they needed, the group gave their goodbyes and thanks to Nikolas and Iolana. Evercloud couldn't help but linger in his goodbye to the beautiful woman.

"Thank you for your hospitality, Iolana…I hope that we will see each other again." Evercloud blushed slightly.

"I believe we will, Evercloud. Good luck to you." Iolana reached her hand out and touched Evercloud's, causing him to blush even more.

"All right," called Whiteclaw, "let's go."

Evercloud waved one final goodbye and the group began to make their way west. It was a beautiful morning to be walking through the forest. The sky was blue and the air was warm, a slight breeze moved through the trees and the world seemed to shimmer. Birds sang in the trees and Evercloud felt as if he could fly. He couldn't wait to find Tenturo. He thought of the feather and imagined the great beast, soaring high above the mountaintops, a bringer of peace and prosperity to all creatures. He imagined himself back at home on Gray Mountain, his mother and father so proud of him, and his uncle, aunt and cousin sharing in the happiness. They would all be around him, proud of him and loving him. They would all be there, and so would she.

The group had walked out of the forest, well before midday, and was now on a stretch of plains. Evercloud had been walking alone, silently, immersed in his fantasies, and ahead of the pack, as Ben caught up to him.

"So, Evercloud. Is this, in fact, the first time you have been around other humans?"

"Well, yes. I suppose it is."

"I think that you fit in just fine. The bears have raised you well. They are not so different from us as I used to believe. I mean, we both live in caves don't we." They both smiled at the joke. "I hope they feel the same way about us."

"I believe they will," said Evercloud. "That's really the point of all this, isn't it? To create a better world, restore a harmony."

"Yes, I suppose it is." Ben opened his canteen and took a sip, and then he offered it to Evercloud.

"No, thank you."

"Evercloud, I know that trust is something that builds over time, but I want you to know that you can trust me. You will meet many people who will not deserve your trust, so stay cautious, but remain open-minded. If there are any questions you have about our world, just ask."

"Thank you, Ben. I, as well as Riverpaw and Whiteclaw, are lucky to have found you."

Ben glanced back at the rest of the pack, the two bears walking alongside his brother. "So, you really are the only human that lives among the bears?"

"It's just me," said Evercloud nodding.

"Well don't worry, my friend, you will meet more men than I'm sure you care to before it is all over…as well as many other fair women." Ben patted Evercloud on the back and Evercloud smiled and nodded. Ben's words had seemed a bit odd to him though, after he had thought about it for a minute. *What did he mean by other fair women?* he wondered.

The five of them walked on through the day until the sun began to set, then they stopped by a stream.

"This is the last stream before we reach the desert," said Tomas. "We should make camp here for the night. I'll shoot some fish with my bow."

"Don't waste your time," said Riverpaw as he waded into the stream. Within seconds, he had already begun to throw fish onto the bank.

"Well, I suppose I'll make the fire then," said Tomas.

"What do you need to make a fire for?" asked Evercloud.

Tomas chuckled. "To cook the fish. Don't tell me that you eat them raw." Evercloud nodded. "Oh, well… we prefer them cooked. Besides, it's good to have fire going. It helps to keep the animals…away." Tomas realized what he was saying, just as the words slipped out of his mouth. He slowly turned his head toward Whiteclaw, horribly afraid that this was what Whiteclaw had been talking about when he had said, *not do anything that will force us to kill you.*

126

"Funny," huffed Whiteclaw with a stoic glare. "We don't start fires mostly to keep the humans away." Tomas began to shake faintly in the legs and stuttered, trying to apologize. Suddenly, Whiteclaw's lips cracked in a large bearish grin. "Calm down, little man. Where's your sense of humor?" Whiteclaw sat down and began to laugh heartily. "You looked like you thought I was going to eat you."

Riverpaw now began to laugh as he stood in the stream and even Evercloud and Ben began to smile.

"The bears are making fun of me," muttered Tomas to himself. "Wonderful."

It wasn't long before the fire had been built and everyone had eaten their fill. The sun had set and the group sat in the glow of the firelight.

"I should warn you, there are dangers in the desert," Ben began while he picked his teeth with a fishbone. "Apart from the danger of getting dehydrated, there are poisonous snakes and scorpions. Also, there are crabs."

"Crabs?" said Riverpaw. "Are they poisonous crabs?"

"Well, no," continued Ben. "But they're really big crabs."

"Oh," said Riverpaw with obvious cynicism in his voice.

"Anyway, I assume that the two of you defend yourselves without any weapons," Ben said, looking at Whiteclaw and Riverpaw. "My brother prefers the bow and I carry a sword. I noticed, Evercloud, that you don't carry a weapon, so I brought along a second sword."

"I have a weapon," said Evercloud.

"Oh, sorry, didn't see it," said Ben, confused. "Where do you keep it?"

Evercloud untied the piece of cloth at his waist and uncovered his claw. He walked over to Ben and held it in front of him. Ben's jaw dropped as he marveled at the golden weapon. It looked magical in the firelight, as if it held some ancient power.

"That's amazing," whispered Ben.

"My father gave it to me," said Evercloud.

"Well, anyway," said Ben, snapping himself out of the weapon's trance. "We'll want to have our weapons on us at all times, once we enter the desert. My brother and I know the safest routes, so we should be fine. The desert can make for quite the trek though, so I suggest everyone get a good night's sleep."

"That sounds like a good plan," said Whiteclaw and he rolled onto his side. The rest of the group made their sleeping arrangements and sped quickly off into a world of slumber.

•••

Morning came with another meal of fish from the stream. After eating, they put out the fire and began drinking their fill of water.

"Drink till your bellies hurt," called Ben.

127

After that, they began filling skins with water. The brothers Floyd had brought many with them, knowing every drop of water that they could carry would be precious. Evercloud strapped his claw on tightly, wondering how long it would be before he had to use it. The sun had not yet risen above the horizon and the brothers Floyd wanted to begin the journey before it had.

"Let's move," said Tomas. "We want to have covered a good bit of ground before the sun gets too hot."

And so they set out. It wasn't fifteen minutes of walking before the grass started fading away, and within a half hour of their departure they were in the Glass Desert. As Evercloud looked out along the horizon, he understood why it was called the Glass Desert. All the paintings he had seen of deserts and the stories he had heard of them suggested that desert sand was colored anywhere from yellow to orange to red. The sand in this desert was a dark color of blue that made it look like they were walking upon a frozen ocean. Evercloud bent down and scooped up a handful of the sand, letting it fall between his fingers. It looked like tiny crystals of glass.

"She's beautiful, isn't she?" said Tomas. Evercloud nodded. "She's just as deadly. Make sure the three of you follow the path that Ben and I make. We'll walk up ahead to make sure we're taking a safe path, but don't fall too far behind us."

They all agreed and that was how they made their way through the desert. For the first time in a while, Evercloud and the bears were able to speak freely to each other.

"Do you trust them, Father?" asked Riverpaw.

"I think so, but don't become too comfortable with them. Take care with what you say and the things in which you reveal."

"I noticed," added Evercloud, "that they made no mention of the powers that the Ancients once bestowed to man."

"We told you, Evercloud, that much knowledge of the Ancients has been lost to man. You saw how much they depended upon that book. Honestly, I'm surprised to find out that they know as much as they do. However, it would be wise to keep that information from them. If they thought that there might be power to gain in this quest, things might become very different. Though I must admit, they do seem to act under a higher purpose."

"That feather was amazing," said Riverpaw. "It must be Tenturo's. I mean, what else could it be?"

"I can't believe this is real," said Evercloud. "We're going to find one of the Ancients."

The wind had picked up and Evercloud looked into the sky. As the wind came across the desert, it made noises that Evercloud had never heard wind make. It almost sounded as if it were chittering. *There must be millions of little things like this that I've never experienced before,* Evercloud thought. He suddenly wished

128

that he knew what all those things were. He felt so fresh and new to the world, as if everything were happening for the first time. The sun was very hot now and Evercloud took a large gulp from one of the water skins he was carrying. The sun was blinding as he tilted his head back, so he closed his eyes. His listened to the wind chittering as the cool liquid glided down his throat. He momentarily thought that he heard something else on the wind. It sounded like yelling.

"What are they doing?" asked Riverpaw.

Evercloud opened his eyes and looked ahead. The brothers Floyd had gone ahead of them by about one hundred yards and were now turned back, waving their arms and yelling.

"Can either of you hear them?" asked Whiteclaw.

"It sounds like they are yelling *back*," guessed Evercloud. "Maybe they want us to turn back."

"No," said Riverpaw, shaking his head. "They're yelling *crab*. They must have found one of those really big crabs they said were so dangerous."

"Oh, I hope they wait for us to get there. I was kind of hoping for an easy target to practice some battle skills on," said Evercloud.

"They sure are making a fuss, aren't they?" said Riverpaw. The chittering wind had seemed to get a bit louder and suddenly, the world became much cooler, as if someone had turned the sun off. Riverpaw looked up to find it and was met by a horrifying pair of giant eyestalks. "CRAAAB!!" he roared.

The other two looked up, just in time to see a giant claw swinging toward them. They all dived to the desert floor, the claw narrowly missing them. The brothers Floyd were running at them, full speed, with weapons drawn.

"Attack the legs!" they yelled. "Attack the legs!"

Whiteclaw was the first into action, charging the giant, blue crab. The crab swung its mighty claw at him, missing again. Whiteclaw darted underneath the crab and barreled into one of its back legs, breaking it at the joint. The crab swayed momentarily but regained its footing. It shot its smaller claw at Whiteclaw and grabbed one of his hind legs, preventing him from retreating. The brothers Floyd had reached the crab now, and before it could do any damage to Whiteclaw, Tomas unleashed an arrow straight at the creature, striking one of its protruding eyes. The crab released its hold on Whiteclaw as it reeled in pain.

"That thing is huge!" yelled Riverpaw.

"I told you it was really big!" Ben shouted back.

"That is much bigger than really big!" Riverpaw looked back up at the creature and saw that it was preparing to charge them.

Now it was Evercloud's turn. He ran toward the crab and just before he reached it he slid, feet first in the sand. Then, with his claw, he reached out and sliced at the creature's leg, severing it fully. Ben held his two swords and made to charge the crab before Riverpaw stopped him.

"Get on my back!" Riverpaw yelled at him.

Ben jumped on and Riverpaw ran for the underside of the crab while it was still stunned by Evercloud's attack. Just as he ran underneath the crab's body, Ben rose up and plunged both of his blades deep into the crab's underside. The creature stumbled and swayed, swooning as its life faded away. The group retreated and made ready for another attack, but it wouldn't be necessary. The giant, blue crab fell into the side of a large dune and never rose again. The group fell to the ground, out of breath and sick on adrenaline.

"How…did we…not see…that thing coming?" gasped Riverpaw in between deep breaths.

"They are camouflaged to the sand and impossible to see at a distance. The only way to know that they're coming is their chittering," responded Tomas.

Ben walked over to the dead body of the crab and retrieved his blades from the monster's underside. As he yanked them out, he noticed that the crab had punched a hole into the side of the dune.

"Hey," he called to the group. "Come see this."

20

Chapter 20: Who Is Your Leader?

"It's a hole," said Riverpaw, not fully understanding why Ben found it necessary to show everyone.

"Yes. A hole," said Ben, not fully understanding why Riverpaw couldn't see the significance. "In a sand dune…it's a giant pile of sand, and it's hollow."

Riverpaw shook his head. "Nope. Still not impressed."

Ben threw his arms into the air and turned his head to the sky. Tomas crawled over to the hole and stuck his head inside to look around.

"I can't see anything," he said as he pulled his head back out of the hole.

The hole was rather large, large enough for Whiteclaw to fit through easily. However, it seemed as though the hollow beyond the hole went down instead of across, and despite the bright, desert sun, there was not enough light to see how deep it was.

"I believe I can be of some service," said Whiteclaw, stepping forward. "If we had something that we could burn, we could throw it into the hole to see how deep it is."

Tomas pulled a tinderbox from his pack and lit a long strip of cloth that he tore off of his shirt.

"Let's see if this works," he said. Tomas threw the wadded cloth into the darkness and watched as it fell.

"That was a good idea," said Ben.

"I saw it done somewhere," replied Whiteclaw.

"It's working," came Tomas' voice from the darkness of the hole. "It stopped about twenty feet down, and-and there's a…leg! Yeah, a leg! Wait, I can't see anything anymore. The fire is out. I can't see anythAAAAHHH!!"

A rope flew out of the darkness and looped itself around Tomas' neck. As it tightened, it ripped him from his perch on the lip of the hole, pulling him deep into the darkness.

"Tomas!!" yelled Ben and stuck his head into the hole. "TOMAS!!!" Ben could hear Tomas screaming in the darkness but his cries were getting further and further away, until they disappeared altogether. "We have to get him!" Ben yelled, turning to Evercloud and the bears. They stared blankly at Ben, in shock. "We have to save him!" he pleaded.

"Evercloud," began Riverpaw. "I'm going to hang my body down into that hole. Then you can climb down my back and try to reach the bottom. Tomas said it was about twenty feet. We should be able to reach that."

Evercloud nodded and Riverpaw began to lower himself into the hole. He moved slowly and dug his claws as deep into the sand as he could to have a sure hold. Once he gave the signal to Evercloud, Evercloud began to crawl down Riverpaw's back. He put his arms around Riverpaw's neck and then walked his feet down to Riverpaw's hips.

"All right, Riverpaw, I'm going to drop to your legs."

Riverpaw again dug his claws as deep into the sand as he could. "Go ahead."

Evercloud leaned back slightly and dropped the top half of his body down to touch his feet. He held onto Riverpaw at the hipbones, where his feet had been resting, and slid his feet off. His legs now hung freely in the air below Riverpaw, dangling in the darkness.

"Can you reach the bottom?" Ben yelled into the hole.

"Not yet," called Evercloud. "Hold on." He then released his grip upon one of Riverpaw's hips and dangled from just one arm. He tried to stretch out his leg, but still could feel nothing. "Nothing yet, but I must be close. I'm going to drop."

"No, Evercloud!" came Whiteclaw's voice, booming into the darkness. "That's too dangerous. We don't know what is on the floor."

But before Evercloud had heard the end of Whiteclaw's sentence, he had released his hold on Riverpaw and fallen to the floor, only a few feet below.

"It's okay," Evercloud cried. "I'm all right. It's not that fa–"

"Don't move a muscle," came a gravely voice from the darkness. "I've already killed your friend, so don't try any funny stuff."

"What's going on?" called Riverpaw. "Is it okay for me to drop?"

"No!" yelled Evercloud. "Don't come down."

"Tell your friends to get down here and move slowly, or I'll kill all of you," said the gravely voice.

"What do you want?" asked Evercloud calmly.

"I don't want anything."

"Then why do you want us down here?"

"So you can fix the hole you made in my roof," said the voice in the darkness.

"If that is all that you want, then why did you kill our friend?"

The voice huffed and sighed. "I didn't kill your friend. I just don't want any funny business."

"Where is he?" asked Evercloud.

"In the other room."

"And you'll let him go if we fix the roof?"

132

"Yes."

"Can I see him?"

"After you fix the roof," huffed the voice. Then, Evercloud felt objects being thrown in the direction of his legs and then he heard a door slam somewhere behind him.

"What's going on down there?" yelled Ben from above.

"Come down here," Evercloud yelled back at him. "We have to patch the hole."

As the others were making their way down to the floor of what seemed to be some sort of cave, Evercloud began sifting through the materials that had been thrown at his feet. There seemed to be a bag of candles, along with a box of matches, a hammer and some nails. *Is this it?* thought Evercloud.

"What happened?" asked Ben once he had reached the floor of the cave.

"We've disturbed whoever lives here. He's got your brother in another room and he'll only let him go if we patch up the roof."

"How are we supposed to do that?" asked Riverpaw.

"He left us a few things," said Evercloud. "Matches, candles, nails and a hammer, but nothing else."

"Well, first thing is first," said Whiteclaw. "Light the candles so that we can see where we are."

They lit the candles and looked around. There was not much in the room with the exception of a couple of torches and a large mattress upon the floor.

"This must be his bedroom," said Evercloud.

They lit the torches that were in the room and now they could see quite well. The room was still very sparse, however the walls were painted quite extravagantly with murals. The travelers marveled at the artistry with which the murals were painted.

"I've seen these before," said Ben. "But they're different." He grabbed a candle and moved closer to one of the scenes. "These are pictures of the Ancients being banished from the world. I've seen these before in churches of the Holy. These are different though. You see here." Ben pointed at the shape of a large griffin. "This is Tenturo. In this picture he is painted white. In the church's version, he is red. Also, in the church's version, there are two white stallions driving Tenturo away. I don't know what these are." Ben pointed at two black beasts painted upon the wall. "These pictures seem to suggest what we've been believing all along."

"That the Ancients were not so evil after all." The group spun around to see a stout, little man in the doorway, wearing a gray robe and a bashful grin. "Your friend has just told me of your quest. Please, follow me."

"What about the hole?" asked Evercloud.

"This is more important," said the man.

The group walked into another room and found Tomas, sitting at a wooden table, stuffing his face with bread, cheese and some sort of meat.

133

"It's crab," he said cheerfully with his mouth full. "It's delicious."

"You hunt the crab?" Ben asked the squat, little man, in disbelief.

"More like trap. Lucky for me, the creatures have far more flavor than they have brains. Please, help yourselves."

The group sat around the table, but not all began to eat.

"I apologize for my rudeness," said Whiteclaw, addressing the little man. "But who are you?"

"Oh, forgive me," said the man, wiping crabmeat from his face. "I am Padre Esteban, retired explorer, current aide to the great Tenturo."

"You have seen Tenturo?" asked Ben.

"Yes."

"So you know where we can find him?"

"Well, we'll get to that. First, eat."

"Excuse me again, Padre," began Whiteclaw. "But how is it that you trust us so easily? What if we, in fact, meant to harm Tenturo?"

"You?" laughed the Padre. "Harm Tenturo? That's a good one."

"Even still," added Ben. "How do you know that our intentions are good?"

"I don't. But we will get to that. Eat."

So they did. The travelers, along with the Padre, ate until they were full, finding the crabmeat quite succulent. At one point, Riverpaw turned to Tomas.

"How were you not hurt in the fall?"

"Landed on the bed," Tomas said with a cheese-filled grin.

The Padre poured them mugs of wine to wet their mouths as they finished eating. "Now," he said, "I have a story I would like to tell you that I think you will find most interesting. Then, if things go accordingly, I may find it necessary to administer a test."

"A test about the story?" asked Evercloud.

"No, I don't think so. Though that is a good idea… anyway, here's the story."

And so, Padre Esteban began. "When the world was young, and quite boring I might add, four ancient beings gathered together to create creatures to inhabit Earth. Many creatures did they create, some big, some small, some intelligent," and the Padre nodded at the bears, "and some not so," and he nodded at the empty plate of crabmeat. "However, they had yet to create a creature with their combined forces and they very much wished to do so. So one day, they gathered together and set about the task of creating a creature together, and they would call this creature, man. They argued over how it should be done and in the end, it was decided that Tenturo and Bahknar would create the body of fire and wind and Densa and Chera would give it life with earth and water."

"That's not how it happened," interrupted Riverpaw.

"Don't interrupt," said the Padre sternly. "Now where was I? Oh, yes. And thusly, they had created man. Yet, something was wrong. The body of man could not interact with the world around it. A body made of fire and wind was terrible to gaze upon and the other creatures of the world fled from man. And rightly so, as man's very touch would burn and rip their flesh. Even the vegetation of earth could not withstand man's touch. Everything man came in contact with perished before him. He was a cursed and damned creature, forced into isolation by his very nature. The Ancients had failed in their first combined attempt. Man, as they had created him, was not fit for the earth.

"So, the Ancients discussed their failure, long and hard, and finally, sadly, they agreed to destroy it. They killed their creation and buried it at the bottom of the deepest chasm they could find, in the deepest abyss, in the deepest sea, to forget about it forever.

"The Ancients, unable to deal with their failure, tried again to create man. On only their second attempt, they were successful. Earth and water made a much more pleasant exterior. Man was their pride and glory and the world existed harmoniously for quite some time. Unfortunately, there was one thing that the four Ancients had not accounted for, or should I say *someone* they had not accounted for.

"No one knows when time began and no one knows how many ancient beings there are or how many worlds there are across the scope of existence. But on that day that the four Ancients created man, they forgot to include one specifically important ancient being, quite possibly the most important ancient being of all, Earth."

"You mean to tell us that the very ground that we walk upon is an ancient being?" asked Ben.

"Sort of," answered the Padre. "I assume that you know Densa was the Ancient who controlled the element of earth. But if you will, imagine that the trees and rocks and dirt are but the outer covering of the ancient being that *is* the Earth; the core. And it has all the thoughts, feelings and jealousies of any other being. And jealous Earth was. Tenturo, Bahknar, Densa and Chera had done much creating without consideration for Earth. That was their greatest folly.

"In Earth's jealousy, it retrieved the body of the fallen creation and again, gave it life. Not only did Earth reanimate the creature, but also bestowed upon it a power only known to Earth itself. Thusly, the Great Tyrant was unleashed upon the world. The four Ancients were no match for the Tyrant's new power, and subsequently, were forced away. I assume that you know the rest."

The group was stunned. The Earth itself was an ancient being. How was this possible?

"You'll have to excuse me, Padre Esteban," began Ben. "I'm finding this a little difficult to swallow. Do you have any proof to back this story up?"

"I don't need proof, my boy. That's the funny thing about truth. Give it enough time and it'll see its own way through."

135

"Our quest is futile then. If we are to believe you," said Whiteclaw. "If what you are telling us is that the very earth that sustains our life willed the Great Tyrant forward. How can we fight that? *Should* we even fight that?"

"Don't be so negative," chided Padre Esteban. "We don't know what the Earth intended, and we don't know how the Earth feels now. Sometimes our actions can be quite like an avalanche, one little action can create an unstoppable force that we never intended. Who's to say that the Great Tyrant is not just something that got out of control? The Earth could be on our side, for all that we know."

"So what should we do?" asked Ben.

"Don't know," shrugged Esteban. "But I'm sure Tenturo has an idea."

"So you'll take us to him?" asked Whiteclaw.

"If one of you can pass the test."

"Just one of us?"

"Just one."

"Then let us begin this test, Padre Esteban." Ben stood up from the table. "I believe we are all eager to know what it is."

"It's very simple," began Esteban. "You are all to go back into the room where you entered my home and wait. I will call you out, one by one, and administer the test."

"But what will we be doing?" asked Tomas.

"You'll see," smiled the squat, little man.

So the group walked into the room in which they had first entered Padre Esteban's home, and waited underneath the hole in the roof. Riverpaw was the first to be called out and Padre Esteban led him down the hallway, past the kitchen where they had eaten, into a small room at the far end of the hallway. The room was lit well with candles and there were benches along the wall. Riverpaw and the Padre sat down on the floor, in the middle of the room, facing each other.

"What is this place?" asked Riverpaw.

"Merely where I come to gather my thoughts," said the Padre. "Now, Riverpaw, I will ask you one question. You will answer it as honestly as you can. That is the test. Are you ready?"

Riverpaw shifted uncomfortably. "Uh. I think so."

"Who is your leader?"

That's it? thought Riverpaw. It seemed like such a simple question. There must be more to it. However, maybe that was the trick. *Don't overthink*, he said to himself, *just be honest.*

"My father, Whiteclaw."

"Good. Thank you. Please go into the kitchen and wait for the others."

"Did I pass?"

"I will reveal that after all of the answers."

Riverpaw made his way to the kitchen and Padre Esteban retrieved Tomas from the room.

"Well, honestly. I think Evercloud is probably the leader," began Tomas. "I mean, he's the reason why my brother and I are on a quest with a couple of bears. He's sort of the bridge."

"Thank you. Please go into the kitchen and wait for the others."

Then it was Ben's turn.

"I don't mean to sound conceited, but I'm the leader. We wouldn't be trekking through this desert if it weren't for my actions. My brother is the only other one who knows the desert and I am the elder. So, yes, I would have to say that I am the leader."

Next came Whiteclaw and the answer was quick.

"I follow the King of Gray Mountain, Eveneye."

"Thank you," said Esteban.

Finally, it was Evercloud's turn. As he followed the Padre down the hall, he looked into the kitchen and saw the others. Riverpaw shrugged at him, signaling that they yet knew nothing. Evercloud swallowed hard and continued to walk.

"Who is your leader?"

The first thing Evercloud thought to say was Whiteclaw. *That's too simple,* he thought. *There must be a trick, a deeper meaning to the question. Maybe the answer is the Ancients. No, anyone would say that. It must be specific to our group so that no one could cheat.* Whiteclaw was the strongest and eldest, but Ben and Tomas knew the desert. They wouldn't have gotten this far without them. However, the party never would have met them if it weren't for Evercloud. *Could I be the answer?* he wondered. *To be fair, Riverpaw had done his share as well. Hadn't it been his idea and action that had dealt the final blow to the giant crab, ultimately opening the hole to Padre Esteban. It could be any of us, really,* he realized.

"I need an answer, Evercloud."

I hope one of the others gave the right answer. Evercloud grimaced and sighed.

"Well," he began. "I guess if I'm being forced to name a leader…I would have to say…Whiteclaw…and Riverpaw, and Ben, and Tomas, and also myself…is that all right to answer the question that way?"

"It is your answer, Evercloud. You may give it in whatever way you like. Now, let us join the others."

Padre Esteban and Evercloud made their way into the kitchen and joined the group. Once again, everyone sat around the table. All eyes were on the Padre now, waiting expectantly for the results of the test.

"I received some interesting answers to my question," began the Padre. "Very interesting indeed. None of which were ultimately wrong," he paused and

137

the expectant eyes around him began to twinkle with hope, "and none of which were ultimately correct." The twinkle left the eyes of the travelers and they began to hang their heads, unable to believe that they had all failed. "However, for the purposes of this specific test, one of you gave an acceptable answer."

"You mean we passed?" said Evercloud brightly.

"Yes, you passed the test."

The group jumped from their seats and began to celebrate, throwing their arms into the air and congratulating each other. Riverpaw grabbed Evercloud in his arms and rubbed his shaved head like a proud older brother.

"Wait," said Tomas, "who was it? Who gave the right answer?"

Padre Esteban looked around at all of them. "Do you all wish to know who it was?" The group nodded collectively. "Evercloud. It was Evercloud who gave the acceptable answer."

The group turned to Evercloud and began to cheer him. He couldn't believe that his answer had been right, or acceptable, as Padre Esteban had put it.

"What answer did you give?" asked Riverpaw.

"I-I said all of us. All five of us."

"Well done, Evercloud," beamed Whiteclaw.

The travelers continued to praise Evercloud and celebrate their victory, when the Padre interrupted.

"So, I expect that you would like to be on your way then? Or would you like to rest here a while?"

"On our way?" asked Ben absently.

"To see Tenturo," added Esteban. The group's eyes widened as they remembered what prize they had won. They gathered themselves and answered yes, enthusiastically. "Then follow me."

Esteban led them back into the room with the hole in the roof.

"We should fix the hole before we leave," said Whiteclaw, gesturing toward the roof.

"What hole?" asked Padre Esteban. The group, confused, turned their gaze up to where the hole in the roof had been, just a second before, and found that it was gone. They looked back at the Padre with a new reverence. "Well, don't look at me like that," said the Padre. "I'm not the one seeing holes that don't exist." The Padre shook his head and walked over to the mural on the wall in which Tenturo was being chased by the black beasts. He then took, from around his neck, a chain that had a small, white stone hanging from it and pressed the stone against the mural. All at once, the mural seemed to melt away from the wall and a passageway opened up. "Follow this passage and it will lead you to Tenturo."

The group thanked Padre Esteban and moved their way into the dark passageway. Evercloud was the last to enter the passageway and before he did, he stopped to ask the Padre a question.

138

"Padre, you said my answer was acceptable, but not ultimately correct. What did you mean?"

"My boy, your answer was acceptable because it mirrored the sentiment of the true answer. The truth is that every creature in this world leads itself. Or should I say, every creature in this world *should* lead itself. Remember that, Evercloud."

"Thank you, Padre."

And with that, Evercloud disappeared into the darkness.

WATER

21

Chapter 21: Between the Earth and the Sky

There was absolutely no light inside of the passageway, so travel was slow. It proved especially difficult for Whiteclaw. He had not yet become adept at navigating with only one eye. The small, dark space he was in made the weakness glaring. He found himself bumping into the wall of the passageway. On one occasion, he stumbled to the floor. Evercloud had been walking behind Whiteclaw and moved in front of him as the bear picked himself back up.

"Follow my lead, Uncle."

Evercloud stayed directly in front of the bear as they continued down the passageway, walking close enough that Whiteclaw could sense him.

"Thank you, Evercloud. I guess I haven't gotten my bearings back just yet."

"Don't worry, Uncle, you will. The darkness makes it difficult for even those of us with both eyes. Once we get back into the light, everything will be better."

"I've always admired your optimism. It's a good thing to have on these long journeys."

"Well, I'll take what I can, I suppose."

"You know, Evercloud, sometimes we bears don't always say the things we are thinking, even if we have thought it many times before. Sadly, it's usually the good things that are left unsaid. I'm saying this now because I want you to know that you have succeeded. Whether by the standards of man or by the standards of bear, you have become a good person. You are just and kind and brave and you should be proud of that. I am proud of you...and if your father could see you now, I know that he would be too. I just want you to know that."

"Thank you, Uncle."

The group continued down the passageway for a long time. More than once did they question if there might have been a fork in the tunnel that they had missed. However, every time the question was raised, it brought about the same conclusion. It did not matter, they wouldn't be able to find it in the darkness, keep moving. They had no idea for how long they had been walking or even what time of day it was. All that they knew was that they were tired and they wouldn't be able to continue much longer without rest. They walked and walked for what felt like hours and finally, Ben called for a halt.

"We need to rest. We have no idea how much further this goes. We should sleep."

Nobody argued with Ben. They were all tired. As they lay down, Evercloud remembered something he had been meaning to tell the bears. He took his opportunity now, figuring a little levity may help their sleep.

"Uncle, do you remember when you told me to use a human name while in the village?"

"Yes," said Whiteclaw.

"Well, the name I chose was John. John Ball."

The bears began to laugh heartily, the echo carrying down the passageway.

"I don't understand," whispered Tomas to Ben. "The Balls are a very nice family."

"I assume, Tomas, that there are some things that we are better off not knowing," replied Ben. "Have a good sleep."

Once the laughter died down, everyone fell happily to sleep.

•••

No light came to wake the weary travelers. Riverpaw was the first to rise. He had no idea what time it was or for how long he had been asleep. One hour? Possibly ten? His body was a little sore, but he felt ready to continue, so he called to the others.

"Breakfast time. Get up and get your food."

The rest of the party lazily opened their eyes. Tomas lifted his head up.

"I'm starving," he said. "What's for breakfast?"

Riverpaw chuckled. "Nothing. I just knew that would get you up."

"That's a lousy joke," whined Tomas. He rubbed his belly and pouted in the darkness, not understanding why all of the jokes seemed to be confusing or at his expense.

They all took out some stale bread that they had in their packs and munched on it, washing it down with water from their skins.

"Ugh. I think that Esteban's delicious food and drink may have spoiled us," said Ben, choking down his bread.

After they had eaten, they wasted no time in continuing the journey.

"Pray for light, everyone," called Ben.

"Pray it doesn't blind us when we finally see it again," muttered Tomas.

The fates seemed to be shining on them this day, for it wasn't long before they saw a dull light in the distance. They now moved forward more rapidly, eager to see the end of the passageway.

"There are two torches," said Ben. "Looks like they are on the walls. They must be in front of a door. We're almost there."

Able to see more and more with every step, the travelers rushed forward in excitement. But as they reached the torches, shoulders and spirits fell once again.

"Some great sign these torches turned out to be," said Riverpaw.

There was no door in front of the torches, no break in the passageway at all. Merely a change in direction as the path turned into a flight of stairs, going up as far as they could see.

"Do you think we've reached the mountains?" asked Evercloud.

"Only one way to find out," said Ben, and the group began to climb the staircase.

Their path was no longer impeded by darkness, as torches lined the walls intermittently. This gave the group hope that they were close and morale rose a little higher. Tomas figured he'd break the monotonous silence with a song:

"Oh, there once was a girl who enchanted my world,
And her eyes were as bright as the sea.
If I could've, I swear, I'd have married her there.
But her waves, they weren't crashing on me."

At this point, Ben decided to join in for the chorus:

"Oh Delilah, Delilah, what can I do?
I'm lost in the ocean alone.
And I pray for the waves, that one of these days,
Will deliver me onto your shore."

Riverpaw turned to Evercloud. "Want to dance?"

Evercloud shook his head. "Between their depressing songs and your bad jokes, I think I may have been better off staying at the cave with Iolana." Evercloud's face went red. *Why did I say that?* he thought. The brothers Floyd had stopped singing now, and Evercloud hoped that it didn't have to do with what he had said. He looked over to find Riverpaw, laughing quietly. Evercloud hit Riverpaw on the shoulder. "Stop laughing at me," he whispered.

"Then stop making a fool of yourself," replied Riverpaw.

Evercloud frowned and continued to climb the endless staircase.

Hours went by and still the travelers climbed. Short breaks were taken far more often as the climb was proving to be quite arduous. The bears and Evercloud were doing far better than the brothers Floyd, having lived on a mountain and having dealt with inclines. However, no one was finding the climb to be pleasant.

"We have to be close," said Ben, breathing heavily. "The desert is not that large. Even walking through the sand, we would have been well into the White Mountains hours ago."

As if on cue, Tomas looked up. "I think I see the end of the stairs."

And indeed he did. The party had reached the top of the staircase and it had brought them to a short corridor with large red double doors at its end. Everyone smiled as their spirits soared, though smiling was all they had the energy to do. They reached the doors and Ben knocked upon them.

Slowly, the doors began to open away from them. Orange light poured over their faces and it seemed as if it was the brightest light any of them had seen in their lives. It was the light of the sun. They walked into a large room with a table placed in its center. Many ornate chairs lined the sides of the table and it seemed quite awkward, alone in such a large room. As their eyes adjusted to the light, they looked toward where it came from and noticed that the room they were in was open to the sky at one end, as if an entire wall had been forgotten in the planning. The sun played along the line of the mountain range, glowing in its heavenly perch. They had, in fact, been climbing through a mountain as Evercloud had guessed. Now, they stood in some sort of room, dug out of the side of a mountain, looking out upon the range. The scene in front of them was inspiring and the air was crisp and fresh, filling their weary muscles with renewed energy.

"This must be higher than Gray Mountain," said Riverpaw, in awe of the beautiful vista.

"I believe it is," added Whiteclaw. He turned away from the orange glow of the sun to gaze at the rest of the room. It was a very long room, with little decoration, save for the table and chairs. Though at the other end of the room seemed to be the statue of a man. Whiteclaw began to walk across the room toward it. The others noticed his departure and began to follow him.

The party reached the statue and looked upon it. It wasn't especially large for a statue, no bigger than a normal sized man. It seemed to be cast in some polished metal that no one could recognize. The statue stood at attention with its eyes fixed upon the horizon. The group looked around at the rest of the room, hoping to find a clue, but there was nothing.

"What are we supposed to do now?" asked Riverpaw, rhetorically.

Suddenly, the eyes of the statue began to glow red and a voice emanated from its metal frame.

"Who has passed the test?" asked the voice.

The group looked at Evercloud. He stepped forward, in front of the statue and answered, "I have."

The statue made a whirring sound and the red glow of the eyes changed to a deep blue. Then a small click was heard and the voice returned.

"Take the parchment and candle. Good luck to you."

The door of a small compartment in the torso of the statue swung open slowly. Evercloud looked inside to find a small piece of parchment and a candle. He took them out and turned them over in his hands. The candle was plain enough, yellow, roughly the length of his hand and not even two fingers thick. The parchment was ordinary as well, yet it was weathered and folded in upon itself. He unfolded it and saw a message had been written in ink. He read it aloud:

Whoever has passed the test must be brave and strong and true,
To travel down to Oldham's Bog and retrieve these items two.
An apple from the tree of death, none ever seen so red,
To poison both the guardians and free the wind again.
Next the hammer she hath made from oak and steel and bone,
Nestled tightly underneath the witch's cursed throne.
Use the candle for passage quick to the bog and back,
Two may go and two may come but must stay close at hand.
The world is old and full of lies but also full of truth,
And here between the earth and sky the questions fall to you.

"So we have to travel to a bog?" asked Tomas.

"*We* won't be doing anything," said Whiteclaw. "Evercloud passed the test. It is he who must travel to Oldham's Bog."

"Well it sounds like I can take someone with me. The parchment says that the candle can take two there and bring two back." Evercloud looked at everyone. "So who should I take?"

"That is your decision," answered Whiteclaw. "We cannot choose for you."

Evercloud looked around. Who to choose? Should he choose whom he wanted to choose, or whom it made the most sense to choose? As he pondered his decision, Riverpaw stepped forward.

"I don't care if it is your decision," he said to Evercloud. "If you think you're going to leave me here with that creepy statue while you're off having all the fun, then you've lost your mind."

Evercloud smiled at his cousin. "Well, since you asked so nicely."

"So, what are we supposed to do?" asked Tomas. He walked over to the table and had himself a seat. As soon as he sat down, the table was covered with food and drink. His eyes widened as he gazed at the sumptuous dishes before him.

"We eat," said Ben, his mouth watering.

Evercloud filled his pack with some of the food and then looked at the candle. "I guess this must work once it's lit."

"Yes," said Whiteclaw, "but the parchment seems to suggest that you and Riverpaw must remain in physical contact while it works."

"Fair enough," said Evercloud and hoisted himself onto Riverpaw's back.

"Make sure you two return to us," said Whiteclaw. "Even if you have not completed the task. We can always try it again. Do not be foolish."

Riverpaw and Evercloud nodded.

"Here," said Tomas, handing a lit match to Evercloud. "I took it from the Padre's place."

Evercloud took the match in one hand and held the candle out in his other and then looked down at Riverpaw.

"You ready for this?"

"I've been waiting my whole life for something like this," Riverpaw replied with a grin.

Evercloud lit the candle and with a flash, they were gone, without a trace.

22

Chapter 22: Biding Time

The little tavern along the road from Kreskin to Gable wasn't seeing the business that it used to. This was due to the feud that had been going on, for years now, between the two most powerful families in each village: the Laughlin family of Gable and the Montgomery family of Kreskin. It had all started with a rumor that Lady Montgomery and Lord Laughlin had been having a secret affair. Rumors being what they were, it spread like a plague upon the two villages, reaching the most esteemed doorsteps of the Montgomery's and Laughlin's respective estates. Lord Montgomery, being none too pleased with what he was hearing, questioned his wife on the matter. Without hesitation, the Lady denied the accusations and called for retribution against whoever started such a nasty rumor. The tales of her husband's infidelity also shook Lady Laughlin. In his defense, Lord Laughlin swore that he would find the vile perpetrator.

So, the search began. The villagers of Kreskin and Gable were all interviewed on the matter, mostly by thugs, working under the command of the effected lords. These thugs, being what they were, were very adept at extracting information from the villagers. However, under the pressures of certain "tactics" used by the thugs, the information being given was not always reliable.

In the end, every person in both villages had been implicated by someone. Everyone, with the exception for a man by the name of Derrick Kane of Kreskin. After much deliberation, the two lords decided that Derrick Kane of Kreskin was, indeed, the perpetrator, and had, in fact, scared all of the villagers into giving any name but his own. It was decided that Derrick Kane would be hung in Kreskin Square. Derrick Kane's last words, as he stood with a noose around his neck, were still remembered in both villages to this day.

"All right," he had said. "Quit pullin' my leg."

A few months later, it had been discovered that Lady Montgomery and Lord Laughlin had, indeed, been having a secret affair. Ever since that time, it had become very common to say, when things of a tragic and unjust nature had occurred, 'There they go, pulling Old Derrick's leg again.'

After the adulterers had been outed, the feud had begun. All trade and general niceties had been cut off between the two villages, which had drastically cut down on traffic passing the little tavern. A few years after the feud had begun, the owner of the tavern decided to rename the tavern, Derrick's Leg, as a tribute to the man whose fate the tavern shared.

This night, as smoke poured from the chimney into the chilling air, a conversation about recent happenings sprung up between the patrons of Derrick's Leg.

"I say it's not true," said a man named Jensen as the barkeeper poured him a small glass of strong-smelling stuff. "Too grotesque. Can't be real."

This wasn't Jensen's first glass of the night and he was beginning to give off a stronger smell of alcohol than the drinks themselves. His gray, wispy hair, which he usually combed over his bald dome, was now waving in the air, giving the impression that Jensen was a drunkard. Jensen *was* a drunkard.

"I don't know," said Bing, a fat man, sitting at a table behind Jensen. "I travel all over Ephanlarea, and I'm starting to hear these stories everywhere." Bing's black hair was slicked back and he constantly eyed a pocket watch that he had set on the table next to his mug of ale. "What do you think, Bart?"

The barkeeper, Bart, was rubbing a glass with a rag he kept behind the counter. The rag was dirty and so was the glass, but Bart kept on rubbing as if friction alone would be enough to get the glass clean.

"Don't know," he grimaced. "I hear a lot of stories and rumors, but you know what they say about rumors."

"See," Jensen barked. "People are gettin' all worked up for nothin'." He put his fist around the glass on the bar and shot its contents back into his throat. He wiped his mouth on his sleeve and continued. "Listen to this one I heard. So this guy, this…Messenger, I guess they're callin' him. One night, he just walks into this young couple's house while they're eatin' dinner. He sits down at the table and starts eatin' their food and talkin' to them like he knows them. The young man asks him who he is, and this guy tells him that he's a messenger. Real sense of humor this guy has. Then he turns to the young lady and tells her that her husband is a thief, and he stole all the food that she was eatin'. So the husband gets upset and tells the guy that he don't know who he is or why he's here but he better leave or else. And this guy's shovin' his finger into the Messenger's face. Now listen to this, this is where it gets good. The Messenger gets up from his seat and grabs the guy's finger. He tells the guy to tell his wife the truth or he'll break it. So this guy starts cryin' and he tells his wife that he's a professional thief and everything they have was bought with dirty gold and whatnot. The guy's wife starts cryin' and yellin' at him. The guy tells his wife he's sorry and asks for forgiveness. Next thing you know the Messenger breaks this guy's finger and then strangles him to death. The wife runs out of the house screamin' and when she returns with the authorities, they find the dead guy sitting at the dinner table and the word thief is written on the walls in blood. And guess what? The Messenger is nowhere to be found."

Jensen shrugged his shoulders smugly as he finished his story. "Now you tell me that doesn't sound fake."

The barkeeper nodded, but Bing shook his head.

"I'm not saying this Messenger fellow isn't a little off his rocker. But where there is smoke, there is usually fire, and there is smoke all over this land. Listen to this story I heard from a man claiming to have seen the Messenger, all the way down in Cerano. This fellow who said he saw the Messenger describes him as a large man, bigger than he'd ever seen. He also said that his hands glow with light."

"Oh, I see," laughed Jensen. "Ten feet tall and shoots lightnin' out of his bum. I can see where this story's goin'."

"Just listen," said Bing. "I ain't making it up." Bing shook his head and stole a look at his timepiece, then continued. "So this guy says he was riding his horse through the forest near Cerano, when he saw funny lights in the darkness. It was late and he thought he might be seeing things, but in the end, he decides to check it out. He rode through the brush where he had seen the lights and came upon a dead body. He looks at the body and there's no head. So he panics and rides his horse as fast as he can into the village to alert the authorities. But when he gets there, he finds the officers outside of the jailhouse looking at something on the ground. Turns out it's the head of the dead body in the forest, and the head's got a piece of paper in its mouth. One of the officers pulls it out and sees that it's a note. 'I was selling your children as slaves' is what it said. Turns out, kids had been disappearing in Cerano for about a year. So this guy tells the officers that he found the body out in the forest. So they all go out there to retrieve the body, but when they get out there, they find the Messenger waiting for them. He's got a big hood over his face and his hands are glowing with blue light. They're all so scared they can't move a muscle. The Messenger tells all of them that what happened to the slave trader is what will happen to all who are evil. Then the Messenger disappears. The scary thing is," added Bing, "that this guy who told me the story was a doctor, and he said that the head of the slave trader wasn't cut clean. He said it looked like the head had been ripped off."

Bart the barkeeper swallowed hard and ran his hand over his neck.

"Rubbish," said Jensen. "Biggest pile o' rubbish I ever heard. Glowing, blue hands. Please."

"I'm telling you, Jensen," argued Bing. "I've heard a story about that Messenger from all corners of this land, and every one talks about those glowing hands. I've heard rumors before and the stories never match; the fundamentals change. All these stories match. This man, if he's even a man at all, is out there, and he's punishing those who do wrong." Jensen waved an arm dismissively at Bing. "I even heard one account," continued Bing, "of a guy who says he'd seen under the Messenger's hood. He said he's got no eyes."

149

"Now I've heard it all," said Jensen, throwing his arms into the air.

"Well, you know. It's funny you should say that about the eyes," said Bart, still rubbing the dirty rag against the dirty glass like a bad habit. "I just recently heard a story of this Messenger and the eyes came up. But this fellow told me that the Messenger was blind."

"Really?" said Bing with a curious tone. "Let's hear the story."

"Well it wasn't so much a story, I guess, as just a conversation."

"Well, go on anyway," said Jensen, becoming more inebriated by the minute. He eyed his empty glass. "I'll take another drink as well."

"You sure you want more?" asked Bart. "You don't look so good."

"I'm ffffine," slurred Jensen.

Bart poured the man more alcohol and began to tell them what he had heard. "So, like I said, I was told the Messenger is blind. Well, sort of. The guy said that the Messenger sees through the grace of the Holy, but he can't see like we can. He told me that the Messenger works for the Holy and that's why he punishes evil. He told me that the world needs to change."

"Well," said Bing. "Sounds like that guy has spoken to the messenger himself."

"Don't know," said Bart. "Didn't want to pry. But you can ask him yourself if you want. He's right over there."

Bart pointed across the tavern at a large man in a white robe, slumped across a table in the corner, sleeping.

"Oho," started Jensen. "Didn't even see him over there. Thought it was just the three of us tonight."

"Came in around supper time and ordered some water and potatoes," said the barkeeper. "Talked to him briefly while he ate. He was the only customer in here. He kept that hood on the whole time though. Thought that was kinda weird. He fell asleep when he finished eating and I figured I'd just let him sleep. Must've needed it pretty bad."

"You know, maybe we should just let him sleep," said Bing tentatively.

"Nonsense," said Jensen, stumbling off of his stool. "I'm starting to like these stories. Good entertainment. I want to hear what this fellow has to say." Jensen tried with difficulty to walk in a straight line over to the man. When he finally reached him, he tapped him on the shoulder. "Hello," he called. "Hello in there. Anybody home?" The stranger raised his head from the table and looked toward Jensen, his large, white hood shading his eyes. "There you are," continued Jensen. "My friends and I were just telling tales of this myth that's been going around the land, and we were wondering if you might have any stories to add. Have you any tales to tell of the Messenger?"

The stranger grabbed the glass of water that he had not finished and poured the rest of the liquid down his throat.

"I'm sorry," he said from under the hood. "I have no stories to tell. But I do have a question for Mr. Bing."

Jensen turned his face to Bing with wide eyes and a foolish smile. "Bing, this man says he knows you."

"Oh, uh, really?" said Bing nervously, his eyes darting to the watch on the table. "You must have misheard him, Jensen."

"Why do you keep checking your watch, Bing?" asked the stranger with a louder and clearer voice.

"I-I-I don't know w-what you're talking about," Bing stammered and slid his watch into an open pocket.

"Waiting for something?" asked the stranger.

"I th-think you have me confused f-for someone else."

The stranger turned to Jensen. "I'm sorry, Mr. Jensen, but it would seem as though you're going to have to die."

"What are you talking about?" exclaimed Jensen.

"What I am talking about, Mr. Jensen, is the poison that Mr. Bing put in your drink when you left to relieve yourself. He continues to check his watch so that he knows when it will be a good time to leave the tavern and steal your horse. Probably about the same time that you, Mr. Jensen, lose the ability to breath. Am I right, Mr. Bing?"

Bing shot out of his chair and began to head for the door. "This is preposterous. I never. I'm not going to sit around and listen to–"

The stranger raised a hand and suddenly, the tavern was bathed in blue light. Bing stood, frozen, unable to move.

"I'm sorry, Mr. Bing, but I just wouldn't feel right with you leaving. At least not until we've seen eye to eye." The stranger stood from his seat, hands glowing blue, and pulled his hood back from his head. He walked over to the petrified Mr. Bing and looked into his eyes. Behind him, Mr. Jensen clutched at his throat and fell to the floor. "As you can see, Mr. Bing, I do, indeed, have eyes."

As Bing stared into the milky-white orbs that bore down upon him, he knew that the stories were true and that now, he would be added to their tome. The Messenger placed a hand upon Bing's back and the other upon his chest and began to press.

"I-I'm sorry," muttered Bing. "I'm s-so s-sorry."

"I forgive you."

Bing felt the Messenger's hand digging into his chest and gasped in pain as his ribs cracked. Sharp pain seared his chest and warm blood poured down the front of his shirt. The Messenger closed his hand around Bing's frantically beating heart and then darkness enveloped Mr. Bing forever.

"Hmm," groaned the Messenger. "I thought it would be black."

He dropped Bing's heart to the tavern floor and walked away, scattering a pile of blood-soaked, gold coins along the bar as he exited the tavern. Bart stood alone, behind the bar, rubbing a dirty rag against a dirty glass, muttering prayers with every breath he took.

23

Chapter 23: Hearing Voices

He had become a shadow in a world of darkness, walking across the land like a true creature of the night, smoothly, stealthily, unnoticed. He thought of the conversation in the tavern. One of them had called him a myth. He laughed inside of his head, *a myth. Let them think that I am a myth. Soon, I will become a legend.*

He walked through the blue smoke of his world as it whirled and bent itself to form the trees that surrounded him. Fluttering sounds came from above and he knew that they were bats; predators of the night, surveying the world below for food. The bats were killers, not murderers. *We have so much in common*, he thought. Murder was evil; killing was natural, and necessary. *Only men murder,* he thought. *How have we become so flawed? How have we strayed so far?*

He raised his hand and looked at it, framed in blue smoke, tiny wisps playing upon his fingertips. He could smell that evil man's sickening blood still on his hand. He rubbed his fingers together. He felt dirty and he needed to be clean. He walked south until he came to a river and once he had disrobed, he waded in. The water was freezing to his skin, but it didn't matter, he needed to be clean.

As the water rushed around his body, he watched it moving through his ethereal vision. This was one thing, he thought, that he would never get used to. The feeling was so familiar, yet the vision of this new water, rushing around his body, was so alien. It was like millions of snakes, slithering past him, against him, under him, over and through each other. He tried to stop them, but they always found their way around his reach. Slipping past as if they were on their way to something of far more importance, as if he didn't even exist. He closed his eyes to stop the vision. It was beginning to make him feel nauseated. There were times, in the beginning, when his constantly moving world had made him sick. He had gotten over it. Now, only the water still held that sway over him.

He looked into the air, into the blackness. He saw no stars, no moon. The smoke didn't travel that far. The sky was always a reminder of the limits of his new vision. He couldn't complain though. The gifts the Holy had bestowed upon him were great, greater than he had ever imagined, and he found new limits to their potential with each new day.

The blue light that emanated from his hands came as a pleasant surprise. Reaching out one night, in pursuit of an escaping target, he had found that he had the power to stop people in their tracks. And the strength. He could run faster and jump higher than any man alive. He could bend steel and splinter wood. He didn't even carry a weapon. Why should he? He *was* a weapon. He could put his fist straight through a man, and had. The first time he had done it, it had scared him. He had looked down at his arm in horror, his mind unable to grasp what his senses were transmitting. But he had gotten used to it. He had gotten used to a lot of things.

He finished washing himself and left the water. He put his clothes back on and continued his path west. West was where he needed to go. He just knew it. Communication with the Holy had not been at all like the experience he had had during that first encounter. It now came to him as more of an intuition, or often times, as a voice in his head. Though he heard it less now than in the beginning.

Closer to the beginning, he would spend large periods of time in conversation with the Holy. He had been very curious and eager to learn. Once, he had asked the Holy why there was so much evil in the world? *It is the work of the Ancient Evils*, replied the Holy, *the creatures that I had banished so long ago.* He asked why, if they were gone, did they still have the power to pollute the world? *Their memory pollutes the minds of men*, was the answer. *We must erase their memory.* How can we do this? he had asked. *By showing people what happens to those with evil in their hearts, and by ensuring that the Ancient Evils can never come back.* They can come back? How is this possible? *It is not possible, as long as we continue to lead the world away from darkness.* It had all seemed so easy, yet so complicated.

A deer walked out into his path. It did not notice him at all. *I wonder*, he thought. It was again time to test his skills, as he so often did, in an attempt to find the limits of his power. He picked a twig off of the ground and held it in his hands. Then, he snapped it. The sound of the breaking twig spooked the deer and it ran from him. He watched it momentarily, unmoving, and then began his pursuit. The chase didn't last long and the challenge turned out to be a remedial one. He ran alongside the deer and slapped it on the back to alert it of his presence. The deer tried to change direction, but he was too fast and cut it off. The deer darted in another direction, but he cut that path off as well. This continued for a short time until finally, the deer gave in, it could not escape. The deer stared at him and he gazed back into the creature's eyes. *Why do you fear me? I can see it in your eyes.*

He didn't expect an answer, the question was to himself. He turned and walked away from the deer. He was wasting time, he must continue west. There was something to be done west.

•••

He had walked all night and now the heat of the sun touched his face and the pangs of hunger stabbed his stomach. *Food,* he thought. *Must I hunt? Is there a village near?* There was no village near and he knew that he would have to hunt. The western path had stayed along the river in which he had bathed. Fish came to mind as something that would make for a nice meal. He walked south to meet the river and wondered to himself, *when was the last time I fed on fish? Fed,* he thought. *When did I begin to call eating, feeding?*

He found the river's edge, disrobed, and again entered into the water. *I should have done this last night,* he thought. *Wasting time.* Within seconds, he had caught a fish and without moving to shore, he began to devour it, all of it. *Has no taste, this fish. Wonder why?* He caught another fish and began to eat it in the same manner. The second fish held no flavor for him either. He threw it, half eaten, back into the water. *Not hungry anymore.*

Intuition told him that it was time to head south, and in order to do so, he would have to cross the river. So cross the river he did. First, he grabbed his clothes from the shore and tied them around his waist. Then, he reentered the water and began to swim across the surface. If someone had seen him from a distance, they might have thought he was a small rowboat. His strokes were powerful and he propelled himself forward quite quickly. When at last he had crossed the river, he knew that he had expended a lot of energy and he would need to rest. So he lay down on the southern shore of the river and went to sleep, his soaking clothes still tied around his waist.

He woke to the jostling and clinking of a caravan, passing not far from where he slept. It was kicking up dust as it moved across the flat land, the driver showing no signs of having seen him sleeping by the river. He stood up and stretched his body. He was expecting to have to work out some sore muscles after his exertions, but that would also be something he would have to get used to. He was never sore. He brushed the dirt off of his body and dressed himself in his clothes that were still slightly damp. He wondered if he might purchase food from the caravan. He decided he would pursue it.

•••

I hate drivin' this caravan, thought Morduk. The land stretched out before him, for what seemed like forever, in all directions. He had good horses and they pulled the wagons quickly, but not quickly enough for Morduk. *Shoulda gotten bigger horses*, he thought as he swigged water from his canteen. His mind began to wander as he looked into the sky. *I could probably take a nap, sittin' right here, and still be on track when I wake,* he thought, staring into the sun. His leg began to itch and he slapped at it. He turned his head to see if it were a fly that had caused the itch. Suddenly, there was someone standing right in the caravan's path. Morduk pulled back on the reins until the horses came to a stop.

155

"Wot d'you think you're doing?" yelled Morduk, taking off his large, brimmed hat and slamming it on the seat next to him. Morduk climbed down from his perch and began to walk out to the man. Morduk was a tiny man; only about as big as a child, but his bushy, red beard and mustache left no question to the fact that he was full-grown. He yelled again as he walked out to meet the stranger that was blocking his path. "You got a death wish, do ya?"

As Morduk approached, the stranger held out his hands in a sign of peace.

"My apologies. I had hoped that I might be able to purchase some food from your caravan."

Morduk looked up at the stranger suspiciously and then looked all around as if looking for someone else to show up.

"You all alone out here?"

"Yes, I am a traveler."

"What happened to your face?" Morduk was so small that the white hood the stranger used to shield his identity had little to no effect. He, in fact, could see right under it.

"Childhood accident," replied the stranger.

"I suppose I could sell you some food," said Morduk. "Wait here." Morduk walked off to the caravan and rummaged around inside. After a minute, he returned with a hunk of bread and two sausage links. Morduk knew that no man in his right mind would pay any more than three gold pieces for the food, but Morduk was not the type to pass up an opportunity to swindle someone. "Ten gold pieces," he said to the stranger, expecting some sort of argument. Although he knew that he held the leverage, out here in the middle of nowhere.

"Hold out your hand," said the stranger. Without going into a pocket, he held his closed hand over Morduk's empty palm and dropped exactly ten gold pieces into it.

"What did you say your name was again?" asked Morduk.

"I didn't," answered the stranger.

Morduk eyed the man suspiciously and nodded his head. "A man after my own heart, I can respect that." Morduk ran his stubby fingers through his beard. "You seemed to come up with those ten pieces right quick. Almost out of the air. You some sort of magician?"

"No magician, I assure you," replied the stranger.

"Where you headed off to then?" Morduk squinted his eyes. "What's yer business?"

A voice crept inside the head of the stranger, whispering a message of one word. *Hendrick.*

"My business is my own. But I travel to the village of Hendrick, if you must know."

"Well, well," said Morduk grinning. "That be the way I'm headed. I'll give you transport for twenty more gold pieces." Morduk held his palm out

156

and again, the stranger, without reaching into his pocket, dropped twenty gold coins from his hand. *I've got a magician here, surely,* thought Morduk. *Can't let him get away.* Morduk pocketed the gold and extended his arm. "Right this way, my friend. You'll find the back of the caravan most comfortable, I think." The stranger climbed into the back of the caravan and Morduk rubbed his greedy little hands together. He walked back to the front of the caravan and climbed up to his seat. "Next stop, Hendrick," he called out and then slapped the reins down on the horses' backs. Morduk began to hum a tune as the horses took off, his beady eyes twinkling in the sun.

It was a rough ride in the back of the caravan. The wagon was being pulled at such a speed that every little bump was throwing the stranger into the air. He sat, his knees tucked into his chest, and began to meditate. He had been given a location and now he needed a name.

Images swam through the stranger's mind as he sat, huddled, eyes closed. Not the smoke images that he saw through his milky eyes, but images like he used to see; images just like everyone else sees. He saw images of bears and of a cave. He saw images of a giant feather and of a stout man in a gray robe. He saw images of a blue crab and of a golden-bladed weapon. Then he saw the images of two distinct faces, hovering in his consciousness and the voice came back into his mind. *Floyd*, the voice whispered, *Ben Floyd*. The stranger repeated the name in his head. *Tomas Floyd*, the voice continued. *Two targets. Brothers. These two men are evil, violent and depraved. They fight to endanger the soul of every person on the earth. As we speak, they come closer and closer to returning an Ancient Evil to power. They must be stopped at all costs.*

The stranger opened his eyes as the voice in his head faded away. *At all costs.*

•••

Hours later, the caravan came to a stop. *We must have arrived*, the stranger thought to himself. He waited a few minutes to see if it was just a momentary break. Once he had decided that enough time had passed, he put his legs out the back of the wagon and lowered himself down to the ground.

"Turn around very slowly," said a voice from behind, once the stranger had fully exited the caravan. He turned to find Morduk standing with a long knife pointed at him. "You see, I never introduced myself proper-like," said Morduk maliciously. "Morduk's the name and your gold be my game. And I don't lose, stranger. I saw with my own eyes as you conjured gold from the air, magician, and if you'd like to be leaving with your life today, you'll be making it a third time. And Old Morduk thinks it better be to the tune of five hundred gold pieces."

The stranger watched blue tendrils of smoke snake across the scarred surface of the little man's face. "You're a bandit," he said.

"And a darn good one, I'd wager. Now stop stallin', magician." The stranger clenched his fists and they began to glow. "That's it, magician, get my gold."

Before Morduk knew what had happened, the stranger's leg had darted out from under his robe and kicked the knife out of the short man's hand. The stranger then shot his arm out and grasped Morduk by the throat, lifting the man so that their eyes were level. Morduk's eyes bulged as he struggled for air.

"I don't like bandits," said the stranger, and with that he snapped Morduk's neck. He dropped the body and faced south. *No sign of the village. No matter,* he thought and began walking south.

Why did you kill that man? came the voice in his head.

"What? That man was a bandit," he said aloud in confusion. "He was evil."

Did I ask you to kill that man? asked the voice.

He shook his head. "No, but was that man not evil?"

Who are you to decide what is good and what is evil? Who are you to judge fate?

His mistake became clear to him. "I am sorry, my Holy. Never again will I assume to know your will. Please forgive me, my Holy." He dropped to his knees and bowed his head.

Let this be a lesson to you. I will not be so forgiving in the future. Never forget that it is I who has shaped, and will forever shape this world and all that walk upon it. I choose to work through you.

"Yes, my Holy."

He stood and continued to walk south, knowing without being told that he would never be entering the village of Hendrick. He saw images in his head of the entrance to a cave and his feet knew how to take him there.

The Floyds, he thought. *I must kill the Floyds.*

24

Chapter 24: Taken

"I didn't think that a place like this could be real," said Riverpaw.

He and Evercloud stood, shin-deep, besieged in bog water. A chill climbed Evercloud's back. He looked off into the distance, which wasn't far given all of the fog, and what he could see wasn't encouraging. The fog that hung in the air all around them was an ill color of green and smelled like old vegetables. Dead trees intermittently dotted the landscape, their jet-black bark matching the muddy water that the travelers stood in. Neon-green moss grew upon the trees like a disease and protruded randomly throughout the surface of the bog water. This world felt hollow.

"Should it be this cold?" asked Evercloud as he fought phantom shivers.

"This place is evil," answered Riverpaw. "It's sucking the warmth away from us."

A vulture screeched high above them from its gnarly, wooden perch. Evercloud looked up at the vulture, bobbing its head in the tree, thinking that it looked like it was laughing at them.

"Did you say something?" asked Riverpaw.

"No. That was the vulture."

"Not the vulture. I heard whispers." Riverpaw watched the fog in suspense. "Listen."

Evercloud focused his hearing out into the surrounding bog. He couldn't hear anything. But just as he was about to tell Riverpaw that he couldn't hear anything, the noises began to reach his ear. Quiet at first, like the breeze moving through the leaves in the trees. But there was no breeze and the trees bore no leaves.

"What is it?" asked Evercloud.

"Shhh," warned Riverpaw.

The sounds were growing, swelling and rolling like barely-breaking waves; the beginnings of what could be voices. Small whispers, coming at them from all directions. They swore they could make out the words. *Come this way*, whispered the voices. *Look out behind you*, they teased. *She'll make soup out of your bones.*

"Who's there?" called Riverpaw.

"Shut up," whispered Evercloud. "I don't think we should announce our presence."

"But the voices," said Riverpaw.

"Probably don't want to help us. I don't have a reason for it, but I don't think that we should listen to them."

"Well, I suppose we should start moving."

Evercloud looked around with his arms extended. "Take your pick."

"The way we're facing?" shrugged Riverpaw.

"Looks as good as any other direction."

And with that, they began to move through Oldham's Bog.

Plodding on, one soggy step at a time, the travelers scanned their surroundings for some sort of clue, but the bog didn't change. The sickly fog hung thick in the air and the dead, black trees, with their skeleton branches, reached for the sky like the hands of drowning men. At one point, Evercloud slipped on a patch of moss and tumbled into the water. He came back up, soaking and gasping for air, his body revolting against the freezing liquid. Riverpaw helped him to his feet and picked some moss off of his shoulder.

"It's freezing," breathed Evercloud.

Riverpaw looked at him empathetically. He didn't really know what to say. "Walking might warm you up."

Evercloud shivered as he nodded and they continued on their search. As they walked, the whispers continued. *Don't come any closer. Please, stay away. She will set your flesh on fire.* Another vulture screeched far behind them. Evercloud continued to shiver.

"How are we supposed to find anything in this place?" asked Riverpaw. "The only things out here are those creepy voices. Maybe we should try talking to them."

"I don't think so," disagreed Evercloud. "There's got to be something we're missing. Maybe we should start inspecting the trees."

So as they walked on, they began to inspect the trees they came across. A couple of times, Evercloud stood upon Riverpaw's back to get a closer look at the branches, and a few times, Riverpaw tore a good deal of bark off of the trunk. Still they found no clues. They had been walking for what seemed like hours, but there was no change in either the temperature of the air or of the lightness of the fog-filled sky. They came close to the next tree in their path and it left their jaws hung wide. Bark had been torn from the trunk and Riverpaw recognized, very distinctly, his own claw marks.

"We're walking in circles," he shook his head. "I can't believe we're walking in circles."

Evercloud sat down upon a mound of green moss and put his head down between his knees. "We need to sleep, Riverpaw. We need fresh minds and bodies to figure out this puzzle."

"Where? In the cold water?"

"Well we can't hope to continue like this," said Evercloud, raising his voice.

Riverpaw huffed in frustration and leaned his weary body against the tree trunk. It shook from the impact of his weight and the mossy lump that Evercloud sat upon rose slightly into the air. Evercloud turned, wide-eyed, to Riverpaw whose face reflected the same sentiment.

"Are you thinking what I'm thinking?" asked Evercloud.

Riverpaw didn't even answer the question. He turned his head and galloped about twenty feet away from the tree. Evercloud knew what was coming and quickly got himself out of the way. Riverpaw dug his legs down, deep into the muddy water, and without warning, began to charge the tree. He barreled into the tree, hitting it with as much force as he could. Bark flew from the tree trunk and dead branches fell to the ground. He continued to put pressure on the tree and Evercloud watched as it slowly came splashing to the bog below.

"There," said Riverpaw. "It's not much, but it'll have to do."

"It's more than I could hope for." Evercloud smiled for the first time since they had entered Oldham's Bog. The two weary travelers sprawled out on the tree, more than ready to hide inside the refuge of slumber. *She'll kill you in your sleep*, said the whispers in the fog.

"Let her try," muttered Riverpaw.

Evercloud yawned. "Yeah, let her try." And with that shared fortitude, they fell into a deep sleep.

•••

Riverpaw and Evercloud woke after a lengthy rest to find everything exactly as they had left it. Evercloud stretched and looked around, shaking his head.

"Well?" asked Riverpaw.

"Well, I don't think that we should just continue walking around randomly. That got us, literally, nowhere. We need a plan."

They sat down on the dead tree and tried to think of a plan of action.

"You know," said Riverpaw. "I was having a pretty good dream. It was a shame to have to wake up to all of this."

"Oh yeah?"

"Yeah. I was dreaming that we were back in the Kingdom. We were heroes. We had returned after finding the Ancients and defeating the Great Tyrant. We were in the arena being presented with a feast. You should have seen it." Riverpaw licked his lips. "Fresh breads and puddings, cakes and plates of fruit. Watermelon, Evercloud. Do you know how long it's been since I've eaten watermelon?"

"You do like your watermelon."

"Aww. I must have had three big ones to myself. And the fish." Riverpaw shook his head. "I can't even begin to describe it."

161

"Yeah," agreed Evercloud. "This is a pretty sore sight to wake up to, after a good dream."

"How about you?" asked Riverpaw. "Good dreams?"

"Yeah," nodded Evercloud.

"Well, out with it."

"I'd rather not."

Riverpaw furrowed his brow. "Here we are, out in…well we don't even know where we are, risking our lives together and you're gonna bottle up. Are you joking?"

"Fine, fine. But I don't want to hear any goofy remarks out of you. Got it?" Riverpaw shrugged in agreement. "I was dreaming about…Iolana."

"Ahhh," said Riverpaw. "That's why you didn't want to tell me."

"I can't seem to get her out of my mind."

"Now, don't jump down my throat," warned Riverpaw, "but I think maybe you were going to feel this way about the first woman you saw, no matter what."

"She's not the first woman I saw."

"First one you talked to?" asked Riverpaw.

"Maybe," said Evercloud, lowering his gaze to his feet. "But it's more than that. There's something there. I feel some sort of deep connection with her. I can't explain it."

"Am I the only one you've told this to?"

"Yes, but I think that Ben knows. He made some comment about there being plenty of *other* women."

"Well, you can only expect as much. She is his sister. Do you remember when I told Shiningsun that I found his sister attractive? He hasn't talked to me since."

"Yeah, I suppose," said Evercloud, and then changing the subject. "So anyway, there's still the issue of this bog."

"You had to bring that back up, didn't you?"

"It's not going anywhere."

"And you still don't want to talk to the whispers?"

"I don't know, maybe we should give it a try."

"No, don't talk to them," came a small voice. "They've got nothing good to say; very negative."

Evercloud and Riverpaw spun their heads to see a small, white mouse, sitting upon a root of the fallen tree.

"Are you?" began Evercloud.

"Yes, I am," said the mouse. "And no, you are not." Evercloud and Riverpaw looked at each other in confusion. The mouse scurried from the tree root and came to a stop on Evercloud's lap. The mouse sighed in frustration. "I am," he continued, "the same mouse that you met in the

162

woods. And no, you are not doing a very good job of getting what needs to be gotten."

"Can you help us?" asked Riverpaw.

"And what do you think that I am doing right now?"

"So you'll show us the way then, to find the apple and the hammer?" asked Evercloud.

The mouse left Evercloud's lap and ran up Riverpaw's arm, finally stopping on the top of his head. "Where are your brains?" asked the mouse, rapping his tiny mouse fist against Riverpaw's skull. "Hello, anybody in there?"

Riverpaw frowned. "Are you going to help us or insult us?"

"I believe," said the mouse with an air of superiority, "that I am currently doing both."

Evercloud stood up from the tree and looked at the mouse. "All right, mouse, where is the Tree of Death and the Witch's Throne?"

"How should I know?" said the mouse indignantly. "I don't live in this filthy place."

"No one lives in this filthy place," muttered Evercloud.

"That," said the mouse, "is not true."

A vulture screeched in the distance and the mouse perked his ears. "Well, it's time that I be off or it's time that I be dinner. Glad to see that you're not dead yet, and good luck, you're going to need it." And with that, the mouse scurried into a hole in the dead tree and disappeared.

"You know," said Riverpaw, turning to Evercloud, "I don't really like that mouse."

But Evercloud was not paying attention to him. He was deep in thought. Then, suddenly, his eyes brightened. "That's it. I can't believe we didn't think of this."

"What?" said Riverpaw.

"I'm a human and you're a bear and we talk to each other, right?"

"Yeah."

"And that mouse can talk to us, right?"

"Yeah," said Riverpaw, squinting his eyes, not really knowing where Evercloud was going with his point.

"So, we should be able to talk to any other creature with the brains to do so."

"Yes, yes," hurried Riverpaw. "But what's your point?"

"The vulture," said Evercloud.

Comprehension broke across Riverpaw's face. "The vulture."

Without another word, they began walking in the direction of the last heard screech, hoping they had figured out the puzzle of Oldham's Bog.

•••

"Hey," called Riverpaw. "You there. Vulture." The vulture stuck his

163

wrinkly neck out and peered down at Riverpaw and Evercloud. He looked from one of them to the other and ruffled his feathers, retracting his neck and deciding to ignore them. "I said, hey, you," continued Riverpaw. "We want to talk to you."

The vulture turned his gaze to Riverpaw, and again made no reply. He then looked at Evercloud with a raised brow and called out, "Human, your bear is talking. Why is your bear talking?"

"He can do that," answered Evercloud.

"He can?" returned the bird.

"Yes, I can," answered Riverpaw.

"Wow," said the bird. "That's a new one."

"I can also rip your stupid head off," Riverpaw muttered under his breath.

Evercloud called back up to the bird. "We would like to ask you a few questions."

"Go ahead, I'm not going anywhere."

"We wanted to know if you could tell us how to find the Tree of Death?"

The large black bird flew down from its perch, high in the dead tree and landed on a branch, just above Riverpaw's head.

"I knew it. I knew it," said the vulture, shaking its head. "The moment I saw you, I knew you looked like one of those fools, searching for the Tree of Death. I was laughing to myself and thinking that. You know why they call it the Tree of Death, don't you?"

"Because its fruit is poisonous," said Evercloud.

"Yeeesss," replied the bird. "So why in the world would you want to find it?"

"That's not your business," shot Riverpaw. "Now can you tell us how to get there or not?"

"Look here, bear," said the vulture. "Up until a few minutes ago, you didn't even know how to talk. So don't get chippy with me."

Riverpaw growled at the bird.

"Please," began Evercloud, trying to keep the conversation on track. "It's very important that we find it. Will you help us?"

"I don't see why not," said the bird. "But what's in it for me?"

Evercloud turned to Riverpaw at a loss. They didn't have much of anything to offer the bird. They only carried with them the bare essentials for their survival. Evercloud took his pack off and began to rummage through it, but just as he expected, there was nothing that they could afford to give up. Evercloud turned back to the bird empty handed.

"I'm sorry," he said. "We have nothing to give."

"Everyone's got *something* to give," said the bird. "How about a story. It gets pretty lonely out here, you know. I'd enjoy a good story if you've got one."

So Evercloud began to tell the only story that he knew, his own. He told the vulture of the Kingdom, and the Ancients and the Great Tyrant, and then he began with the quest. He told the vulture of buffalo hunting and his trip into the village of Hendrick. At that point, Riverpaw added in an account of the standoff with the village officers. Evercloud told of the Floyd family, with no short description of the beautiful Iolana. He told of the battle with the giant, blue crab and of Padre Esteban and the test, and then of the dark passageway and the metal statue. Once he had worked his way up to the present, he began to make up the rest of the story. He told of the noble vulture, who had helped Evercloud and Riverpaw find the items that they needed, and how they retuned to the White Mountains to free Tenturo. He told of how they had killed the evil guardians with the apple from the Tree of Death and everyone lived happily ever after. And of course, in the end, Evercloud got the girl.

"What a story," said the vulture, once Evercloud had finished. "However, it seems to me that the noble vulture was the real hero. He should have got the girl in the end."

"Uh, yeah," said Evercloud. "I'll be sure to change that part in future telling."

"Well then," smiled the vulture. "I suppose I owe you my help. I'll show you to the Tree of Death. I'll fly up in the sky and you just follow me on the ground. We'll be there in no time."

"Thank you," said Evercloud.

The vulture turned around on his branch and spread his wings, preparing to take flight. "Oh and by the way," he said, "you may also want to consider changing that Riverpaw character. He came off like a real dolt." With that, the bird leapt into the air.

Riverpaw turned to Evercloud. "Let me kill him, Evercloud. Please, let me kill him."

"We need him."

"Fine," grumbled Riverpaw, and the two travelers began to follow the vulture as he soared above their heads.

They walked for no more than fifteen minutes before they started noticing changes in the bog. The fog began to clear and they were soon able to see further than they had since entering Oldham's Bog. In fact, it cleared so much that they were able to see the night sky and all the stars that filled it. Not only were they able to see the clear sky, but also the bog itself seemed to benefit, and they began to see trees that were alive. No longer was their bark black, but instead a light-tan color. The neon-green moss still clung to everything, but it was no longer the only green to be seen. The living trees had leaves, just as vivid, and they rustled lightly in the breeze.

"This is almost pleasant," observed Riverpaw.

It was now difficult to see the vulture against the stars, but every once in a while he would give a screech so they knew where he was. Evercloud even noticed that the trees they were passing were starting to bare fruit.

"It's a good thing we have a guide," he said. "We'd never know which one of these apple trees was the right one."

"Actually," said Riverpaw, and gestured for Evercloud to look ahead. "I don't think there would have been any doubt."

Evercloud scanned the horizon and saw the most beautiful apple tree he had ever seen in his life. It radiated ahead of them as if it were made of light. As they got closer to it, they noticed that its leaves seemed to tinkle brightly in the wind as if they were made of glass or metal. The tree was so bright that they couldn't believe it was real. Evercloud walked up and plucked an apple from the branches. It was warm to the touch as if it were alive in his hand. Evercloud felt more as if he were holding a heart than a piece of fruit.

"I never would have thought that a tree of death would look more like a tree of life," said Riverpaw.

"That's what it wants you to think," said the vulture, landing on the ground next to the two travelers. "But believe me when I say that one bite out of that apple and you'll be dead before it falls to the ground."

Evercloud opened his pack and stuffed the apple deep inside.

"Well, I suppose that you'll be leaving now, eh," the vulture said sullenly.

"Actually," said Evercloud. "We would like to ask another favor of you." The vulture's eyes lit up, happy to be able to retain his company for a while longer. "We need to be taken to the Witch's Throne."

The vulture's beak dropped and he began to shake his head violently. "No, no, no, no, no. I won't do that. Don't ask for *that*. What is wrong with the two of you? Taken to the Witch's Throne." The vulture spat on the ground in disgust.

"Please," begged Evercloud. "You must. We'll do whatever you ask of us."

"All I want is to not do that."

"Please. We have to. It's our mission."

"I can't. I can't." Now the vulture was begging Evercloud. "You don't know what you're asking. You *can't* know what you're asking."

Evercloud bent down to look at the creature. "Do you remember that story I told you, with the noble vulture?" The vulture nodded his head. "Sometimes we have to do things that are frightening, but we have to be brave, or else there will never be a happy ending. We must be taken to the Witch's Throne. It is the only way. Can you be brave, vulture? Can you do this for us?"

The vulture bowed his head to the ground. "All right," he said. "If that's really what you want."

"It is."

166

The vulture turned around and spread his wings. "And I was just beginning to like the two of you." The vulture flew into the air and Riverpaw and Evercloud watched him, ready to follow once again. But suddenly, the vulture stopped at about twenty feet in the air and began screaming.

"INTRUDERS!" he screamed into the air. "THE BEAR! THE HUMAN! INTRUDERS! GET THEM!"

The ground began to quake and Evercloud and Riverpaw almost lost their balance. Evercloud looked at Riverpaw with panic in his eyes. "What have we done?"

"Quickly, get on my back," said Riverpaw.

As Evercloud climbed aboard, long, fibrous tendrils began to reach out of the bog. Thick and vinelike, they wove along the surface of the water toward them.

"RUN!" screamed Evercloud.

Riverpaw splashed through the bog as fast as his legs could carry them. As if commanded by some forgotten evil, the vines came closer to them, green with moss and bloated with bog water. They lashed out, narrowly missing Riverpaw's heels as he flew by in panic.

"I told you!" cried the vulture. "I told you I didn't want to do it! You stupid creatures! I told you!"

More and more giant vines rose from the wet blackness. Riverpaw ran with every ounce of energy he had, but it was of no use. The vines closed around them, wrapping around their extremities, and closing around their throats. They struggled with madness to free themselves, but the vines held tight, dragging them down until they disappeared underneath the freezing waters of Oldham's Bog.

25

Chapter 25: Leverage

The forest was dark by the time he had reached the path that led to the Floyd's cave. He preferred the night. There always seemed to be less interference at night. *What deviants must these be, to live inside of a cave,* he thought, *so afraid that the world might see the evil inside of them.* He shook his head. Disappointment did not begin to describe his feelings. It had been disappointment for a while, near the beginning, when he had felt a yearning to help or change people. That had been very naive of him, very naive indeed. There was no changing these people, who had allowed evil to soil and corrupt their hearts. The only help that he could provide them was to end them; to destroy them. In that way, disappointment had turned to pity, had turned to monotony, had turned to frustration, had turned to disgust. As he walked along the forest path toward inevitability, that was the predominant feeling. Total revulsion.

•••

Nikolas Floyd hovered over the bubbling cauldron of stew, letting the steam hit him full in the face. He inhaled the wonderful smell of boiling meat and vegetables, savoring it like a precious thing. He exhaled and smiled.

"It's the simple things," he said. "The older I get, the better they are. Simple things." His mouth watered and he dipped the ladle in, drawing out a chunk of boar and carrot with the broth. He blew upon it to cool it, and then he sipped the broth. "Delicious." He dumped the rest of the contents of the ladle into his mouth and chewed. He lifted an eyebrow as he did so, his curiosity taking hold. "You sure this is boar meat?" he asked Iolana as she sat, sewing up a ripped shirt.

"Yes," she replied.

Nikolas tilted his head slightly and continued to chew. "Something's not normal. Different."

"That's nice," said Iolana.

Nikolas looked at her, realizing that she was not paying attention to anything that he had been saying. "Thinking about them again, aren't ya?"

"Sorry," said Iolana, putting down the needle. "I'm just worried, that's all."

"Don't worry," said Nikolas, putting the ladle down. "They are the ones." He walked over and sat down next to Iolana, placing a fatherly arm around her shoulders. "Do you have doubts?"

"No," said Iolana. "I know they are the ones. I could see it when I looked into Evercloud's eyes."

"Then what's the worry?"

"What if they find out, Father? What if they figure out that the footprint was a lie and that the feather is a fake? They will leave, won't they? Their faith will be broken."

"Iolana," said Nikolas in a calming voice. "The only way they will ever figure that out is if they really do find Tenturo. And then what will it matter? The lies will have been a means to an end, and the end will be good. Like tricking a child into taking its medicine. Ben and Tomas will never tell them, unless they find the Ancient."

"I know. I shouldn't worry."

"Oh, you should worry," came the voice of a man who had suddenly appeared in the room. "You should worry your little heart out."

Nikolas and Iolana got up as quickly as they could and Nikolas put his frail body between Iolana and the intruder.

"What do you want? Who are you?" yelled Nikolas.

"I'm looking for Ben Floyd and Tomas Floyd. Where are they?"

"I don't know what you're talking about," shot Nikolas. "I've never heard of them."

The intruder took a step toward Nikolas and Iolana. "Do not lie to me, old man. I do not appreciate it. Lie to me again and I will kill you in the most inefficient way that I can." The intruder frowned. "And I hate inefficiency."

"Leave us alone, you evil man," yelled Iolana.

"How dare you call *me* evil." The intruder clenched his jaw and continued to close in upon them. "Tell me where they are," he said through his teeth.

"Never," cried Iolana.

The intruder grabbed at Nikolas, catching him by the shoulder. He ripped the old man away from Iolana and put his hands around Nikolas' throat.

"Tell me or he dies."

"Run, Iolana," choked Nikolas, clutching at the hands around his throat.

Iolana did as she was told and ran out of the cave and into the forest as fast as she could. A voice crept inside of the intruder's head and whispered to him. *Kill the old man. Retrieve the girl.* The intruder lifted Nikolas off of his feet and threw him at the wall of the cave. His head thudded loudly as it impacted against the rock and he fell to the floor, dead. Without a moment of hesitation, the intruder ran after Iolana. *Take the girl,* said the voice. *We'll use her as leverage.*

Iolana ran through the forest as fast as she could, thorns and brush tearing at her legs. Tears streamed from her eyes and blurred her vision. *Father,* she thought.

Her heart ached as she pictured that man's hands around her father's throat. She hated herself for running. She hated every step that she took away from him, but she didn't stop running. She couldn't stop running. They had been over this, time after time, Ben and Tomas and her father, warning her that something like this might happen, warning her that if the wrong people found out about their mission that they would try to stop them. Every time, they had told her the same thing. Run, no matter what, Run. So she did what they had asked, even though it killed her inside.

The intruder watched her as she ran through the forest, stumbling over herself. He shook his head. This was no challenge. *Stop wasting time*, said the voice impatiently. The intruder took off and within seconds, he had cut off Iolana's path.

"You can't escape," he said simply.

She flew into him, kicking and punching with every bit of energy and anger she had. It did nothing to him. He didn't even bother to shield himself from her attack. She backed away, bruised and broken of spirit, tears rolling down her porcelain face.

"What kind of monster are you?" she cried. "What do you want?"

"I only wish to make the world a better place," said the intruder. "And to do that, I need to find your brothers."

Iolana wiped the tears from her eyes and looked at the man. He was much bigger than her, there was no way that she could escape him. His hood was pulled back and she looked upon his face.

"What happened to your eyes?" she said.

"Childhood tragedy," replied the man. "The doctor said I'd never see again."

"You're blind?"

"I do not see in the way you mean, but I would like to think that I see things much more clearly than most."

"How can you do this if you cannot see?" asked Iolana.

"Let's just say things have a way of speaking to me."

Iolana continued to look at the man who killed her father and noticed that he carried no weapon.

"You have no weapon."

"Yes."

"I will take you to my bothers," said Iolana with venom in her voice. "And I will watch them kill you."

"That is very unlikely," said the man.

Iolana turned around and began to walk toward the Glass Desert. *We will avenge you, Father.*

The intruder followed behind her, fully understanding why this woman led him to her brothers. She deemed him incapable of harming them. *That's fine*, he thought. *You will see your error in the end.*

•••

The sun was ablaze above the Glass Desert, but the wind helped to cool their heads. Iolana had never wished ill upon another creature in her life, but she relished in the possible ways this man might die. She wanted it so much, she didn't even care for her life. *If I die of thirst,* she thought, *so then will he. If a poisonous snake kills me, he will die as well.*

"How do you live with yourself?" she asked him. "A murderer of innocent men."

"I have never harmed anyone who is innocent," he replied.

"My father was innocent," Iolana said through her teeth.

"Your father was guilty of heresy against the Holy."

"You are mad," she said, hoping to anger him. "You are a fool, and your Holy is a tyrant."

"The Holy is the only good thing this miserable world has ever known. You should repent to him and throw yourself upon his mercy now, before you end up like your pathetic father."

Iolana spun around and spit in the man's face. "I will never bow to a tyrant. Never."

The man wiped the spit away from his face and then grabbed Iolana, throwing her to the ground just as a gigantic claw came groping over a dune. The man grabbed hold of it and held on tightly as it carried him through the air. He let go of the claw as the crab raised him over its body, and he fell onto the giant creature's shell. Iolana rolled over on the desert floor to see the man hanging onto the crab's shell. The man held on with one arm and began to pound at the shell with the other. The creature spun wildly, trying to shake him loose, but he would not release his grip. Finally, after minutes of pounding at the shell, it gave way and the crab fell to the ground, broken. The man got up from the carcass and regained his bearing. Iolana looked at him in horror.

"How did you do that?" she asked.

"Keep walking," said the man. Iolana looked around, unsure of which direction to head in. "You don't know where you are."

"I don't know where my brothers are," she admitted. "I just knew that they were coming this way."

"Then it is no longer necessary for you to lead. Follow me."

The incident with the crab had renewed Iolana's fear in the man and she was no longer sure that she wanted him to find her brothers.

"Who are you?" she asked.

"I'm a messenger."

"And who do you carry a message from?"

Tell her nothing, said the voice.

"Keep walking," said the man.

"No," said Iolana. "You've killed my father and search for my brothers,

171

most likely with the intention to kill them. I won't follow you. Kill me if you will, but I won't follow you."

"Have it your way," the man raised his hand and a cool, blue light came forth from his palm. Iolana tried to avert her eyes, but too late, found herself unable to move. The man walked over to her and picked her up at the waist, throwing her over his shoulder like a child. The man walked on as images flew through his mind of another giant crab, a hole, a small man and a dark passageway. *You must hurry*, said the voice in his head.

An hour passed and the man came upon the carcass of a different giant crab. Large birds sat upon its carapace, picking strips of its flesh out from the cracks in its shell. The man shooed the birds away and walked to where the crab's shell met the dune. He sat Iolana, still paralyzed, onto the sand and began to dig at the side of the dune.

He's going to bury me alive, thought Iolana. She struggled to free herself from her invisible prison, but it was no use, she couldn't move a muscle.

The man dug for a while and after he had made a sizable hole, he began to throw punches at the bottom of it. Iolana could see into the hole from where he had left her, and after a couple of swings, the man had punched the bottom of the hole out, revealing empty blackness. He began to widen the gap he had made, and after a minute, Iolana realized that she wouldn't be the only one going down there.

"Hello," came a voice from deep inside the blackness. "Did you forget about the passageway? Did you find Tenturo?"

"Yes, Padre," said the man, smiling. "Why don't you come out and say hello?"

26

Chapter 26: The Witch's Nightmare

If one could fly high enough and somehow get rid of all the fog, they would see that Oldham's Bog was located inside a great maze. The most harmless place in the maze, being the outer ring, was the place where Riverpaw and Evercloud had begun. Some didn't even consider the outer ring to be part of the maze, given its docile nature and the fact that it was impossible to move further into the maze unless one knew exactly how. The inner portion of the maze, however, had a much different reputation.

In villages around Ephanlarea, nasty, old men would scare children with tales of what they called the "Witch's Nightmare." *Mind yer elders*, they would say, *or the witch'll getcha and putcha in her nightmare.* They'd make up stories of trolls and goblins and any other nasty things that they could think of to scare the children. The truth was that no one who had ever entered the Witch's Nightmare had ever returned to tell the tale, so no one really knew what horrors lied in wait.

It was also said by the nasty, old men of Ephanlarea, that the witch herself lived at the center of the maze. The old men would tell of a large, black castle, covered with the slime of the bog. They told of how it towered into the sky, blotting out the light of the moon, creating a darkness that none could escape. Even the evil creatures that inhabited the Nightmare dared not go near it. They said that the witch was a tall, thin woman, with fingers like razors and eyes like ice, quick as lightning and just as harsh. She sat upon a grotesquely decorated throne, a tyrant over the souls of children who had misbehaved. Unfortunately for Evercloud and Riverpaw, these fairy tale descriptions paled in comparison to the cold truth.

It was inside the Witch's Nightmare that Riverpaw and Evercloud had found the Tree of Death, and it was also there that they had suffered such a tragic miscommunication with their guide, the vulture. When the fingers of the bog had reached out and captured them, they were brought to the witch's home. Black, covered in slime, oozing and dark were the walls, ceilings and floors of the witch's den. The den was at the center of the maze, but it was no grand castle, reaching into the clouds. It was a pit, reaching instead into the bowels of the earth. Far below the waters of

Oldham's Bog, Riverpaw and Evercloud lied upon the floor of an oozing cage, trapped.

Evercloud scrabbled on the floor in the darkness, searching for Riverpaw, but everything that he touched was cold, wet and slick.

"Riverpaw," whispered Evercloud. "Where are you?"

"I'm over here," Riverpaw answered. "I can't move."

Evercloud crawled in the direction of the voice and finally, he found Riverpaw's fur. "Are you hurt?"

"No, I think that I've been bound."

Evercloud continued feeling around, and sure enough, he felt slimy vines around Riverpaw's legs. Evercloud used his claw and began to cut away the vines.

"Don't move," he said. "I'll cut you out."

Evercloud freed Riverpaw and they got to their feet, only to bump their heads upon a slimy ceiling. They crouched back down on the floor and tried to move forward. It didn't take them long to realize that they were in some sort of cage. The cage was made of the same vines as Riverpaw's bindings, so the two of them began to cut their way out. Something screamed in the distance. It was sharp and brutal and only came once, then silence.

"What was that?" whispered Riverpaw.

"I don't want to find out," said Evercloud. "Keep cutting."

Finally, they freed themselves from the cage and crawled outside of it. They were still in total blackness, so they stood with caution. This time, they were able to stand completely.

"What do we do now?" asked Riverpaw.

"Feel for a wall. Maybe we can follow it out of here."

They groped for a wall and when they found one, they began to move along it slowly. The wall was smooth and slimy, like everything else. Something dripped upon Evercloud's head and he jumped.

"What?" said Riverpaw.

"I don't know. Something dripped on me." Evercloud's heart was beating furiously. Scared, he had flattened himself against the wall, and as his heart rate came back down, he tried to move back away from the wall to find that he was stuck. The blades of his claw had punctured the wall. He wrenched them out and noticed that a faint light came from the holes he had made.

"Riverpaw, look."

Riverpaw saw the light and started clawing at the holes, trying to make them larger. They widened with ease, seemingly made out of the same vinelike stuff that everything in the cage was made of. He ripped a hole large enough for them to move through and they moved out into the light.

They found themselves along the wall of a large pit that descended, in steps, down to a center. They stood on the top ledge. Above them, the wall shot straight up a great distance. It was still very dark, but the pit was open to the sky, allowing moonlight into its depths. They looked up at the moon far above, neither of them ever having seen it seem so small.

"Do you think we could climb out?" asked Riverpaw.

Another scream came and they looked across the great pit. Far on the other side was what looked like a giant, green starfish, writhing against the wall. The creature was at the top ledge, just as they were.

"That thing has got to be ten times bigger than you," Evercloud whispered to Riverpaw.

They stood motionless and watched it as it moved against the wall of the chamber.

"Wait," said Riverpaw, "it looks like it's moving away from the wall."

"We need to go back into the tear we made in the wall, Riverpaw." The giant starfish pulled further away from its place along the pit wall. "Get back into the wall."

They rushed back into the darkness and watched the giant thing from the rip they had made. It wasn't a starfish at all, and what they had seen of it were just its legs. It was the witch.

The pit walls were filled with smaller areas, "cages," just like the one Riverpaw and Evercloud were in now. These cages within the walls were all filled with the unfortunate creatures that the bog had taken prisoner. The screams that they had been hearing were the cries of those creatures that the giant witch had chosen as her next meal.

They watched from the darkness as the witch slithered down to the center of the pit. Her giant tentacle-legs that had looked like a starfish, carried her gelatinous body down the steps. She was a terror to see. The flabby torso of her body sat atop the tentacles, covered in arms that would have been considered human, if there had only been two of them. Her face might be considered human as well, but her mouth was gaping like the snare of a Venus flytrap, or like the hem of a garment that someone forgot to sew shut. However, what stood out most upon this ghastly monster was her hair, if it could even be called that, as upon her head sat a nest of fire that lit the pit walls red. The very sight of her made both Evercloud and Riverpaw tremble. As she slithered to the bottom of the pit, she sang rhymes only the blackest souls could ever know.

The hammer cracks, the hammer breaks,
The hammer splits 'em narrow.
The bones of legs and arms and head,
For sweet and tasty marrow.

The witch reached the bottom of the pit and stood upon a bone-covered

175

platform. With her serpentine legs, she reached underneath it and pulled out a hammer that, in comparison to her size, was tiny.

"That must be the hammer we need," said Evercloud.

The witch stopped singing and stood still. "I hear voices and whisperses." The witch's voice was both low and high in pitch, discordant and petrifying to hear. She turned her massive head around, scanning the walls. Riverpaw and Evercloud tried to close the rip as much as they could, hoping she wouldn't notice them. Holding their breath, they peered out of the crack that was left. They had apparently gone unnoticed and the witch began humming again and moving up the steps of the pit. She returned to the hole in which she came from and inserted her grotesque body back inside, again creating the appearance of a giant starfish upon the wall.

"How are we going to get the hammer?" asked Evercloud.

"We watch and wait, and hope that we're not next," answered Riverpaw.

In no time at all, the witch began to pull away from the wall again and Evercloud and Riverpaw tried to close the rip and hide. The witch moved back down the steps as the frightened travelers watched her every move. She reached her platform and placed the hammer back underneath it. She then laid herself down and began to fall asleep.

Riverpaw and Evercloud watched her silently, unwilling to do anything that might interrupt her slumber. After a few minutes, Riverpaw looked at Evercloud with a look that suggested he might say something, but Evercloud shook his head violently and Riverpaw understood. They were trapped and too frightened to move, so they did the only thing that they could, they waited.

Time moved so slowly that it felt like torture, and every time the witch moved an inch, their hearts jolted with shock. They had been so scared for so long that their bodies were becoming exhausted and their minds were becoming paranoid. Evercloud's mind began to tell him that they were going to starve to death, and even if they got the chance to escape, their bodies wouldn't have the energy they needed to be successful. As slowly as he could, he began to take off his pack and open it. Riverpaw looked at him in horror, trying to will him into silence. Smoothly and silently, Evercloud produced some cheese and bread from the pack. He broke the cheese and handed the majority of it to Riverpaw. Riverpaw took it in his mouth, chewed and swallowed it, never making a sound. Evercloud did the same with the small amount of cheese that he had kept for himself. They both looked at the bread. Evercloud reached for it. Riverpaw shook his head. No, he mouthed. But Evercloud wasn't looking. He picked up the bread and began to tear it. The crust cracked and Riverpaw cringed. They looked out at the witch, but there was no movement. Evercloud handed the large piece to Riverpaw and he ate it whole, afraid to make noise chewing. Evercloud chewed his carefully and slowly. They had eaten without incident, and silently breathed a sigh of relief.

176

However, it's always the one thing that we never take into account that ends up being the most important thing of all. Unfortunately, for Riverpaw and Evercloud, their stomachs didn't understand the importance of silence in this situation. Their stomachs had again felt what it was to digest after long fasting, and they voiced their opinions for it to continue. The two travelers looked at each other, wide-eyed and terrified, as their stomachs began to gurgle for more food.

The witch stirred and opened her eyes. "Time for more foods."

Riverpaw and Evercloud stared, motionless and with bated breath. The witch slithered off the platform and began to climb the steps, thankfully, away from them. She reached the wall across the pit and tore into it, directly next to where she had been before. Again, screams blasted the air.

"She didn't take the hammer," said Riverpaw. "This is the only chance we'll have."

They slid out of the tear in the wall and began to descend the stairs without caution. Across the pit, the witch writhed in the darkness. They moved as quickly as they possibly could down the giant stairs, trying to be quiet, but speed was the priority. Nothing mattered but the hammer. They reached the platform and Evercloud turned to Riverpaw.

"Get the hammer," he whispered. "I have to find the candle and the matches in my pack. When you get back up here, we can light the candle."

Riverpaw nodded and dove under the platform. Evercloud began to dig through his pack. It was making a lot of noise, but he couldn't help it and he didn't care. He felt the candle at the bottom of the pack and took it out. Now he had to find the matches. Riverpaw poked his head up above the platform with the hammer in his mouth. He climbed up to where Evercloud searched.

"Let's go," said Riverpaw, with the hammer still in his mouth.

"I'm trying, I'm trying," said Evercloud. "They're not in here. I can't find them."

"No. No," said Riverpaw, grimacing as if he was in pain.

"I never had the matches," said Evercloud, realizing why Riverpaw grimaced. He stood up from the pack, dumbstruck. "Tomas had them."

Suddenly, the walls of the pit glowed red, their damp and oozing surface reflecting the light of a fiery nightmare. The witch had come out of the wall.

"What's it doing on our throne?" yelled the witch, her voice shaking the platform and piercing their ears. "The foods is out of its cage." The two travelers cowered in fear as the giant witch's tentacles carried her toward them. "It thinks it can have our hammer!" she yelled. "We'll bites it apart!"

The witch opened her mouth wide to reveal rows and rows of razor-sharp teeth, coming at them like stars falling out of the sky.

"Come on! We have to run!" yelled Riverpaw.

"We won't make it!" Evercloud yelled back. "Just hold on to me! Whatever you do, don't let go of me!"

The witch was upon them and she bent down to take them in her mouth. Evercloud could see his reflection in each of her gigantic eyes. He raised his fist into the air, holding the candle as high as he could as he felt her fire come down upon him.

27

Chapter 27: An Unlikely Pair

"So, anybody got any good stories?" Tomas looked at Ben but he was sitting at the table with his arms folded, deep in thought. He looked half angry and half scared, as if something important were weighing on his mind. Tomas looked over at Whiteclaw. He was sitting by the opening, looking out over the night sky. Tomas walked over and sat down, joining him at his watch. "What are you looking for?"

Whiteclaw looked over at Tomas, just realizing that he was there. "Oh, I'm not looking for anything. Just thinking."

"Thinking about Riverpaw and Evercloud?"

"Yes, Tomas." Whiteclaw looked back out at the stars in the sky. "It is a difficult thing to send your son and your nephew off to complete what is sure to be a dangerous task. I swore to protect them. I made an oath to the Everflame."

"What's the Everflame?" asked Tomas.

"It's the soul of our Kingdom, Tomas. It sits atop Gray Mountain and burns forever, as a sign of all that we are and all that we believe. To swear upon it is to swear upon your life. More than your life, really. Your life, and the memory of you after you pass."

"I think I sort of know how you feel," replied Tomas. "I've never sworn on anything like the Everflame, but I swore to keep my father and sister safe from harm, and I don't even know how they're doing. Sometimes, I let myself think about it too much, and it makes my skin crawl with worry."

"Then you do know how I feel, Tomas."

"I wish that we had something like the Everflame," said Tomas.

"The Everflame is a symbol, Tomas. It has no power. It's just a reminder of something we all have, our spirit. And it is to this spirit that we are accountable, not to an all-powerful tyrant, not even to ancient creators, simply to ourselves. By making an oath to the Everflame, I am merely making an oath to all that I am. If I break that oath, it is I who suffer the greatest loss, and nothing can change that. All these men who barter with their Holy for forgiveness should ask themselves, first, for this forgiveness. They would not find it so easy to come by. We all have the ability to judge our own hearts, and we should all have the courage to do so."

"Then I think that I have sworn on the Everflame. I think all of us Floyds have." Tomas turned around and looked at his brother. He knew that Ben could hear what they were saying. He wasn't far enough away not to. But Ben still had an absence to him. He was somewhere else right now. Tomas turned back to the night sky and to Whiteclaw. "Do you regret not going with Evercloud?"

"Would I have felt better if I were the one to go? Yes. But I don't regret it. It was the right decision. We bears have a saying, 'a tree will not grow tall in the shadows.' This was Evercloud and Riverpaw's time to grow tall." Tomas nodded, silently staring out into the distance. It seemed as though all of his questions had finally run out. "Maybe it would be better to get some rest than to stay up, wondering." Whiteclaw stood up and walked toward the inside of the room. Tomas followed and took a seat at the table. Whiteclaw looked and Ben, now noticing the man's conflicted visage. "Ben," he said. "Stop worrying yourself and get some sleep." Whiteclaw continued walking to the back of the room, where he planned on curling up in a corner.

"Whiteclaw."

Whiteclaw turned back around to see Ben, standing from his chair and staring at him with what seemed to be shame in his eyes.

"Yes?" Whiteclaw said with a hint of concern.

"There is something that I," and then he looked at his brother, "that we, need to tell you." Tomas looked at his brother, wide-eyed. "It has been tearing me apart, knowing that there are things we are keeping from you, things that we have sworn to keep from you, and anyone else. But I cannot do it any longer, because I don't believe that it is right to keep it from you. Especially now."

"Ben," said Tomas. "I don't–"

"Please, Tomas. It will be easier if I do this."

Whiteclaw looked at the two men very sternly, worried what surprises this conversation would hold. Just then, a flash of light enveloped the room. Whiteclaw, Ben and Tomas spun around to see Riverpaw and Evercloud, covered from head to toe in some sort of black goo, clinging to each other.

They looked around and realized that they had made it back. They looked down at themselves and began feeling their bodies to make sure that all of their parts were still there. Riverpaw, still holding the hammer in his mouth, dropped it to the floor and looked at Evercloud.

"We did it. We made it."

The two cousins flung themselves at each other in exhilaration and relief, barely noticing the others in the room. But it wasn't long before those others made their presence known. Whiteclaw barreled into the two of them, knocking them to the floor. Unable to contain his excitement at their return, he began laughing and pawing at them. They all laughed and then got back to their feet.

"We did it," said Evercloud. "The apple and the hammer."

Now Ben and Tomas were there to meet them with handshakes that quickly turned into embraces. No one was able to contain their elation.

"Tell us everything," said Ben. "All of the details."

So they all sat down at the table and Evercloud began to relate the story of their time in Oldham's Bog while Riverpaw stuffed himself with food and drink. After a while, Riverpaw took the telling of the story over and Evercloud was free to gorge himself.

"I would have killed that vulture," said Tomas.

"I wanted to," replied Riverpaw.

Everyone took turns asking questions, and Evercloud and Riverpaw answered them all in full, relishing the role of heroes, now that they had returned safe.

"Who do you think it was, whispering in the fog?" asked Tomas.

"Probably the souls of the people who never found their way out," said Evercloud.

"You must have been petrified," said Ben.

"Of course not," said Riverpaw. "We had a job to do, didn't we?"

Once they had all finished asking their questions, Evercloud put the apple and the hammer on the table for everyone to see. The hammer looked rather ordinary, with the exception of the head being made of what looked like bone. From what creature it had been derived, it was impossible to tell. What really captured everyone's attention was the apple. They all took turns holding it, mesmerized by its glow.

"One taste will kill you," said Riverpaw.

"I'm just happy to see you two back, safe," said Whiteclaw. "Wasn't the same without you."

The two cousins beamed.

"Did anything interesting happen here?" asked Evercloud.

The room became dreadfully silent and it was apparent that something had. Ben looked into his brother's eyes.

"Let me do this, Tomas." Ben stared Tomas down until he agreed and then Ben addressed Whiteclaw, Riverpaw and Evercloud. "I actually feel better about this, now that you two are back. I feared that Whiteclaw may kill me while you were gone." Ben tried to smile, indicating his joke, but it quickly faded in the face of cold gazes. "Before I say what I need to say, the three of you need to understand that our intentions have always been good. Our mission, like yours, has always been to find the Ancients. It has been passed down in our family for more generations than we know. We never lied to you about that. But when this mission was passed down, a prophecy came along with it. It was a simple prophecy, really. It basically says that 'an unlikely pair' will free the Ancients and defeat the Great Tyrant. We think that Evercloud and Riverpaw are that unlikely pair."

"Why don't you tell us what this prophecy says, exactly?" said Whiteclaw. Ben thought about it, trying to recollect the exact words. When he seemed to have got them, he began:

"In the world's most desperate hour of need,
Earthly elements shall be set free.
And evil tyrants should beware,
The coming of an unlikely pair.

"So, like I said, we believe that Riverpaw and Evercloud are the unlikely pair."

"That seems like a very small amount of information to go upon," said Whiteclaw.

"Well, yes," said Ben, "I understand what you're saying. But when you also take into consideration the fact that you were the first to answer the call, then–"

"What call?" asked Whiteclaw.

"This is the part that was slightly underhanded on our part. I don't really know how to say this–"

"Out with it," growled Whiteclaw.

"It has been our family's mission to find the Ancients. Given what the prophecy says, we saw that it was also our mission to find the unlikely pair. So we did things that would entice the pair to find us."

"The footprint?" asked Whiteclaw.

"A lie," said Ben.

"The feather?" asked Evercloud.

"A fake," said Ben.

Whiteclaw stood up and roared at Ben. "I should tear you limb from limb, you stupid man."

Ben stammered as he backed away. "B-But the mouse. T-The mouse was real. And you've seen it twice now. A-And the statue, and the Padre-"

"Could all be liars like you," roared Whiteclaw.

Evercloud stepped between Ben and his uncle, and Whiteclaw stopped growling. "We saw him, Uncle. You and Riverpaw and I. We saw him in the sky. We acted to stop him. Ben and Tomas want to help us. They didn't need to tell us what they just did, but they wanted to. They wanted to make it right. They are on our side."

Whiteclaw backed off, seeing the truth in what Evercloud said, but as he did, he said to Ben, "Next time there is danger, it better be you risking your neck, Ben Floyd."

"I think we should all get some rest," said Riverpaw. "This has been a day I'd very much like to forget."

They all found a place to lie down. Riverpaw and Evercloud fell asleep first, obviously exhausted, and Whiteclaw was not very far behind. The brothers Floyd, however, did not sleep so easily, having just narrowly missed a bear attack. They both hoped they had not irreparably damaged Whiteclaw's trust.

Tomas leaned over to Ben and whispered, "Shouldn't we also tell them about–"

"No," Ben cut him off harshly. "No, we should not. Now go to sleep."

28

Chapter 28: Light in the Darkness

There wasn't a lot of talking when they had all woken up in the morning. They avoided each other almost completely, each taking their meal at the table when nobody else happened to be there. Even Riverpaw and Evercloud didn't say much to each other, both feeling that any conversation started would only bring the issues of the previous night back into focus. Riverpaw looked over at his father who was sitting near the open end of the room, observing the sky. *He's worried*, thought Riverpaw. *He's always worried when he sky gazes.* Riverpaw wanted to go over to his father, but he knew that pairing off now could permanently damage the overall group. There were some unwritten rules in life, and Riverpaw understood that the only people who could fix this problem were his father and Ben, no one else.

Ben sat at the table, but he barely ate anything, nerves sapping his appetite. If he had jeopardized his family's quest because of his scruples, he wouldn't be able to forgive himself. Ben looked at his brother who was across the room. *Have I failed us?* He tore a small chunk of bread from a loaf and poked it into his mouth. He wanted to say something to Whiteclaw, anything to break the tension, but he thought better of it. *What could I say? We lied, and we still have secrets.*

Tomas hadn't exactly been last night's target, but Whiteclaw's reaction had put enough fear into him that he was keeping his mouth shut. He sat on the floor, up against a wall, and picked at an orange that he had taken from the table. He hadn't wanted Ben to tell their secrets, but now that he had, he wondered how it was right to divulge some secrets but not all. He was starting to feel the weight of conscience that Ben had been dealing with last night, and he didn't like it at all. *I know what's right,* he thought. *It's right to protect the ones we love.*

Whiteclaw was struggling with his own inner turmoil. Was it more important to keep his guard up, ultimately protecting his family and himself, or was it necessary to have allies, even though trust brought risk. He weighed the benefits and disadvantages in his mind, and as he did so, he began to notice something sobering. Weren't Ben and Tomas doing the very same thing that he was, protecting the ones that they love, while still trying to gain alliances?

He would have never divulged family secrets without first establishing trust. This new revelation softened Whiteclaw, and in a strange way, he almost felt that he could trust Ben and Tomas more because of their loyalty to their family. Not so unlike himself.

Whiteclaw got up and walked over to the table, sitting near Ben. The man looked up at the bear, prepared for the worst, but tried not to show his fear.

"I cannot blame you for acting in the best interest of your family," said Whiteclaw. "It is no different from what I would do. I should not have overreacted."

Ben began to respond but found his throat dry. He coughed and grabbed for a cup of water. Then, again, he tried to respond.

"I am sorry that things had to be the way that they were. I appreciate that you understand why we made the decisions that we did."

"We are much alike, Ben. Hoping for a better future, yet so stubborn in holding on to the ways of the past."

"But we're learning, aren't we?"

"I suppose we are."

Tomas heard the conversation and walked over to the table, standing next to Whiteclaw. "So we're okay?"

"We're okay," Whiteclaw confirmed.

Tomas nodded and tried to smile, but it still felt awkward and forced. Riverpaw and Evercloud came over and sat at the table with the rest of the group. Evercloud placed the hammer and the apple on the table and raised his eyebrows.

"So, what do we do now?"

"We know from what the parchment says that we need to use the apple to poison the two guardians," said Riverpaw. "Though where we can find the two guardians is still a mystery."

"And we still don't know what the hammer is for," added Evercloud.

"Well, as far as the apple is concerned," said Whiteclaw, "it would seem to be a disadvantage that we have only one apple for two guardians."

"We can cut it in halves, right?" asked Ben.

"I don't know," said Whiteclaw. "We can touch it, so I assume that it is only the juice that is deadly, but I wouldn't dare have that juice touch my flesh. Cutting that apple could put us in severe danger."

Evercloud and Riverpaw had never considered that possibility while in the bog.

"I suppose it would have been smart to take two apples," said Evercloud.

"No," disagreed Riverpaw. "The parchment said 'two items,' the apple and the hammer. For all we know, the tree may not have let us take two apples. It may have been a mistake to deviate from what the parchment said."

"You should probably talk to the statue again," said Tomas to Evercloud.

"Oh," said Evercloud. "Yeah. Of course."

185

He got up from the table and picked up the apple and the hammer and walked over to stand in front of the statue. Its eyes no longer glowed as they had before Evercloud and Riverpaw had left for the bog, but the small compartment door in the statue's torso was still open. Evercloud looked the statue over to see if it made any reaction as he approached, but it did not. He held the two items out in front of him and spoke to the statue.

"Uh, hello." Evercloud cleared his throat. "It is I, um, the one who had passed the test. I have returned with the items. The two…items." He paused and waited for some sort of reaction from the statue, but again, there was no response. Evercloud looked back into the compartment and found that it was still empty. The others now joined Evercloud around the statue, too eager and curious to stay back.

"Maybe something will happen if you put the items into the compartment," suggested Tomas.

"I don't think the hammer will fit, but maybe…" Evercloud put the apple into the compartment and it fit just fine. He closed the compartment door and stood back.

Without delay, the eyes of the statue began to glow. Riverpaw and Evercloud shivered as the eyes turned a sickly, green color that reminded them, far too much, of the moss in Oldham's Bog. Something inside the statue began to whir, and this noise continued for a few minutes. The group waited patiently, never taking their eyes off of the statue. Then, without any warning, a second compartment door popped open at the back of the statue. Evercloud opened it and reached inside. When he pulled his hand back out, it came with two glass vials of a yellowish liquid.

"The juice?" guessed Ben.

"It must be," said Riverpaw. "I suppose all that whirring was the statue juicing the apple. We can't touch the juice, but it can."

Evercloud pocketed the vials and turned back to the statue.

"That still doesn't help us find the guardians. There must be someplace to fit the hammer."

"Why not the hands?" asked Whiteclaw.

The hands of the statue were closed, but not all the way. There were gaps, possibly large enough to rest the hammer in. Evercloud tried to fit the handle of the hammer into the left hand of the statue but the hole was too small. So Evercloud tried the right hand. At first, it also seemed too small, but Evercloud was persistent and eventually, the hammer fit.

Once again, the eyes of the statue glowed and everyone knew that the hands had been the right place. Violet was the color of the light on this occasion, and again, the statue began to produce whirring sounds. This time, the statue was also beginning to move. It started with just the arms, bending forward and back, in jerking motions. Soon, the jerking motions spread to

186

the rest of the statue's body. The travelers stepped back a few paces, just to be safe. They continued their watch as the statue gained full animation. The movements were becoming less jerky and more fluid with each second, looking like a man stretching his muscles loose. Suddenly, all the movement stopped and the statue addressed them.

"Hello," it said without moving its mouth. "My name is Tomaton. Thank you for waking me."

"Hello, Tomaton," began Whiteclaw. "I am Whi–"

Tomaton was not listening. He turned himself around, toward the back wall, and began walking toward it. Once he had reached the wall, he cocked his arm back and raised the hammer. Then, in one swift motion, he swung the hammer at the wall with great force. A loud boom echoed through the room and a large slab of the wall crumbled to the ground. When the dust settled, the travelers could see that a passageway had been opened, revealing a staircase that led up, further into the mountain.

"Of course, more stairs," grumbled Riverpaw. "Why not a nice slide going down?"

Tomaton turned back to the travelers and stood, motionless. "Please, let me know when you are ready to continue," he said.

The travelers all looked at each other.

"I think that we've come to the point where we need to be ready for anything," said Ben.

Everyone nodded in agreement and then turned to where they had their things, lying in wait. Riverpaw and Whiteclaw had no packs, and hadn't needed to carry water since the desert. Being bears, they also carried no weapons. In all respects, they were ready. The three men filled their packs and secured them tightly to their backs, taking care that they were neither bulky nor restricting of movement. Ben grabbed his blades and swung them through the air, stretching his arms and making sure he was comfortable with the weight of the blades. Tomas strung his bow and knocked an arrow, pointing it out the open end of the room, and checking his sights. Evercloud strapped his claw on, making sure that it was tight but comfortable. He walked over to Ben and handed him one of the vials.

"Here," he said. "One person shouldn't carry both of them."

Ben nodded and placed the vial into his pocket. The men returned to the two bears and they all nodded that they were ready. Whiteclaw began to speak.

"We don't know that the guardians will be waiting for us up those stairs, but now is not the time to hope for the best. We must prepare for the worst. Do not throw those vials for any reason. For all we know, they are the only weapons that will kill the guardians. Losing those vials could, very well, mean our death. Most importantly, stay together. These guardians have the power to keep the Ancients at bay. To think that one of us could harm them on our own is ludicrous. Be smart first and brave second." Whiteclaw looked all of them in the eye to make sure that they understood what he was saying. "Do any of you have any questions or confusions?" No one spoke. Whiteclaw nodded. "All right," he continued, raising himself up to his full height. "Now you must remember what it is that we fight for. We fight to bring peace to this world, to free the Ancients, to stop the Great Tyrant. Remember your mothers, your fathers, your sisters, and your brothers. Remember all those who have loved you, and remained close to your heart. For it is that love that has seen us through the darkness of this world. It is that love that has been a light. See that light. Feel its heat. Now become that light. For it is now we who must banish the darkness for those who have done the same for us, and by everything that I am, every thread of my being, I swear that I will not fail! By the Everflame!" he roared.

"By the Everflame!" the others shouted in unison.

Whiteclaw turned to the statue, poised in the doorway.

"We are ready to continue."

29

Chapter 29: Into the Blinding White Light

Tomaton led the way up the staircase at a constant pace, never slowing, never stopping for a break, his violet eyes floating through the darkness. Hammer in hand, he moved forward, metal feet clinking against the rock. No one spoke; speech was unnecessary and only distracting from the objective. Tomaton's violet eyes lit the way, giving them a vague idea of what was in front of them. His clunking feet urged them on like the beat of a battle drum. They had been travelers, hunters, adventurers, and searchers, and now they prepared themselves to be warriors, unrelenting, efficient, hardened and invincible.

Whiteclaw had stirred something in them. Possibly something they didn't know existed, something instinctual, primal, animal. Philosophers of the day might find it curious to see such anger born from a speech concerning love. Strange are the ways of the mind, and stranger is the fuel of emotion. Each one of them had found that 'one thing' during Whiteclaw's speech, during that sobering moment that only times of true passion can evoke. That moment when a being reveals to itself the things that it already knows. That moment that we see, within the mirror of our souls, the reason that we choose to live each day. And we do, though we may forget, choose to live each day.

For Ben, that one thing was truth. He anguished in a world full of gray muddiness and confusion. He yearned for life to be black and white, once and for all, right and wrong. No more masks, no more compromising, simplicity and purity.

For Tomas it was peace. Not in the sense of a world without violence, but in the sense of personal serenity, stability, tranquility. No man can be a pacifist in a world that no longer affords him the quiet moments of his own mind.

For Whiteclaw, it was his son, his student, and the legacy he would leave to him. He could not leave this world knowing that he had allowed what is wrong to live on without fighting for what was right. He fought for change. He fought for the future.

Riverpaw was driven on by his desire to win the hearts of his Kingdom. Every bone in his body ached to show that he could be great. Showing them that he could protect them from danger. He would be a rock by which they could shelter themselves from any storm. He would be their champion.

Evercloud wanted the world. Most men did. But most wanted it for greed or power, reasons that were evil and base, reasons that were for the benefit of the individual and the detriment of all else. Not Evercloud. Evercloud wanted the world because he saw within in it light and beauty, and he wanted every other creature on this planet to see what he saw, feel what he felt. He wanted to show everyone that life and living were a gift and not a cruel tragedy, and he knew that he could be the one to show them the way.

It was these things that drove them up the staircase. It was these things that were moving them, so resolutely, onward. These things that were all that they were. These things that were their own definitions, the reason that they fought for every single life-giving breath they took. Their hearts. Their souls. Their Everflame.

They could see the end of the passageway, a flat circle of white light that grew larger and larger with each step forward. It was a light at the end of the tunnel, as if they were making their way into the arms of salvation. The hot stagnant air of being enclosed in rock was now being replaced by crisp, fresh air. They moved ever closer to the light and the air became colder, slightly chilling. The silent passageway, once filled with only the sound of Tomaton's plodding steps, now howled as the wind blew against the exit, like breath over a bottle top. They were only feet away from the exit now and could see that the last stairs were covered with snow. They were now being hit in the face with flakes, gone maverick from the storm outside.

They emerged from the passageway into blinding whiteness, biting winds and a flurry of snow. They were upon the peak of the mountain, or at least very close to it. Tomaton continued to trudge on, leading the party down a path that cut between two sheer, rock walls, creating an alley. The alley was easily one hundred feet wide and the path was flat, as if some ancient architect had made it that way. Down the alley they walked, heads turned from the wind, doing all they could to shield themselves from the relentless elements. Suddenly, Tomaton stopped walking and turned to face the travelers.

"Destroy the guardians," he said.

Tomaton turned back along his path, and they watched him move forward, now noticing the gigantic statue before them. Easily thirty feet tall, if not more, stood a statue of Tenturo the griffin. The statue looked over them with a noble, yet menacing, stare. His wings were folded against his body his and ears were pointed back, he seemed as if he were about to pounce on them. The toes of his massive paws were as high as Evercloud's waist. They stood in awe, wondering if the real Tenturo were just as big. He must be close now, and if Tomaton's words had been any indication, so were the guardians.

The group felt invincible at the feet of the statue. They would soon be in the presence of an ancient being, fighting alongside a mythical power, bent on defeating the darkness. They readied themselves to attack, adrenaline warming their bodies and spirits. They remained attentive and searched for Tomaton so they could follow his lead.

As they looked back upon him, however, they noticed that he had stopped at the foot of the great statue. Tomaton climbed up on one of the mammoth paws and cocked his arm back, raising the hammer just as he had done to uncover the passageway. He struck the statue and a gonging sound echoed over the mountain. A crack appeared upon the leg of the statue and Tomaton raised the hammer to deal another blow.

Then, they heard it, high in the sky, a sound to dominate all sounds, the cries of a beast. But no ordinary beast could make this sound, only a terrible beast, a tortured beast. The cry came again, chilling their blood, locking their joints like a nightmare. Their eyes searched the sky and finally, they found them. Two black shapes glided through the blizzard above the travelers. They flew closer and closer, the party now able to see their gigantic, black wings. Tomaton continued to pound at the statue, sending cracks all along the body, but the group could no longer watch Tomaton and his hammer, for behind them had landed the guardians.

Two horses, each as big as the statue of Tenturo, landed and closed wings that looked like they belonged to a giant raven. The black beasts released their terrible cries at the travelers. They dragged their hooves in the snow, dipping their heads, indicating they meant to charge. They shook their manes wildly and the group could now see that their necks were not covered in hair, like the creatures of the earth. Instead, they were covered with writhing serpents, like the fell things that only the blackness can know. One of the creatures reared upon its hind legs and blew a jet of fire, high into the air. These beasts were created to bring death.

"Retreat behind the statue!" yelled Whiteclaw, and the party ran through the snow, the guardians charging behind them.

They ducked behind the statue as a jet of flame narrowly missed Ben. Tomas spun and unleashed an arrow at one of the beasts. It flew through the air and met the guardian directly in the throat. The arrow lodged itself deep in the hide of the beast, but caused no effect.

"The juice!" called Ben, the wind howling as if trying to silence him. "Put the tip of your arrow in the juice!"

Ben took the vial out of his pocket and emptied some of the contents onto the tip of Tomas' arrow. Tomas spun, ready to release the arrow into one of the beasts, but they were gone. Suddenly, a cry came behind them and the guardians landed on the side of the statue where the group had taken cover. One of the creatures kicked Riverpaw, sending him flying into the rock wall. Tomas wheeled himself around and unleashed his arrow, burying it deep into the flesh of one of the guardians' chest. The great thing reeled and fell to the ground. In shock, the other guardian took off, disappearing into the sky. The wounded beast lay upon its side, unmoving, yet still breathing.

"It's not finished!" said Ben. He poured the rest of the vial onto one of his blades and ran at the beast. He climbed upon the creature, aiming to get at its head. Giant serpents struck at Ben as he walked upon the beast. Swinging his blades, he cut them down before they reached their mark. Ben reached the head and the beast's black eye stared at him.

"Tell your maker, the Ancients shall return."

Ben plunged his blade into the creature's eye, all the way to the hilt. The great beast shook and Ben was thrown from it, into the snow. They watched as its massive body convulsed and slowly disintegrated into the air, leaving no trace of its existence.

Evercloud ran to Riverpaw who was just pulling himself back up. Riverpaw was all right, with the exception of cuts and bruises.

"Where did the other one go?" he asked.

"Don't know," said Evercloud. "But I'm sure it won't be gone long."

They returned to the group, keeping their eyes to the sky. Tomaton continued to pound away at the statue, which was now cracked over its entirety.

"What is Tomaton doing?" asked Tomas.

"It doesn't matter," said Whiteclaw. "We don't have time to guess why he destroys that statue and it doesn't seem as though Tenturo is coming. That thing will be back soon and we have to be ready for it. Tomas, your arrow worked beautifully. Evercloud, pour a bit of your vial over his arrow. We should be able to wait for the creature, under the cover of this statue, until it returns and decides to land."

A cry came from the sky. The second guardian reappeared and flew high above their heads, shrieking in anger. However, the creature would not land. They waited and waited, and all the time, the shrieks never came closer.

"The blasted thing won't land," said Ben.

"Then we'll have to bait it," said Whiteclaw.

"Bait it?" said Tomas. "With what?"

Whiteclaw answered, "With me."

"No!" yelled Riverpaw. "What are you saying?"

"Tomas," said Whiteclaw, ignoring his son's protests, "I'm going to walk out there. When that thing comes for me, release your arrow."

"It'll kill you!" cried Riverpaw. "You can't! Let me go instead!"

Whiteclaw walked over to his son and pressed his forehead against his son's. "Everything will be all right. I must do this." Whiteclaw backed away from a stunned Riverpaw and walked out into the snow, alone. Instantly, the guardian took the bait. The beast shrieked in the sky and dove at Whiteclaw, blasting fire from its evil maw. Whiteclaw looked into the sky and whispered at the beast. "Come for your death."

The guardian came closer and closer to him, falling like a meteor from the sky.

"Shoot it!" Riverpaw screamed at Tomas.

"It's not close enough. The arrow won't reach it."

"It'll kill him! Do it! Shoot it!"

The creature was almost upon Whiteclaw now and he raised himself up on his hind legs to meet it and roared, "COME FOR YOUR DEATH!"

"NOOO!"

Tomas released his arrow and it sped toward the guardian as the beast descended upon Whiteclaw. All eyes were upon the arrow as it flew to meet its mark, as if they were willing it to stay true. The arrow met the beast in the throat and it fell, crashing down upon Whiteclaw.

"FATHER!" screamed Riverpaw as he ran out to him.

Evercloud poured the rest of the vial upon his golden claw and sprinted out toward the beast as it lay paralyzed on top of his uncle. He reached it and slashed at its throat as tears stung his eyes. Over and over, he sent his blades tearing through the creature's flesh. He raged in the agony of loss until the guardian disappeared to join its twin in the nothingness.

Riverpaw bent down and looked at his father. "You're going to be all right," he said. "You are."

"You," said Whiteclaw, licking his son's face, "are going to be just fine." And with that, Whiteclaw's eye grew still and he passed, forever into the blinding white light.

30

Chapter 30: The Gift of The Wind

The wind had stopped. The snow had stopped as well, and only the last few flakes were left hanging in the cold air like the seeds of a dandelion, looking for a new home. But there was no refuge on the mountain, and there were no words either, no touch, no sight, no smell, nothing. All was loss. They knelt around the body of Whiteclaw, wondering how the world leaves us so quickly, so finally. Kneeling there, staring at him, it seemed as though they had died in his place, even as they drew in one shallow breath after another.

Something nudged Riverpaw from behind, but he paid it no mind. His muscles weren't feeling up to turning his body around to see something that, most likely, didn't matter.

"Who was he?" asked a softly rumbling voice.

"His name was Whiteclaw," Riverpaw said almost inaudibly. "He was my father."

"The memory of Whiteclaw shall live as long as my own," said the voice. "For I am forever in his debt, as I am, also, to the four of you."

Finally, the weary heads of the travelers turned to see where these words of kindness came from. The sun broke through the clouds as their heads turned, giving warmth to their chilled expressions. Their eyes adjusted to the light and then, they saw the very thing for which they had been searching. Before them stood the Ancient, Tenturo, master of the wind, the great griffin. The Ancient arched his sprawling back and opened his silver-tipped wings as the last pieces of rock fell from his body.

"Tenturo?" asked Evercloud.

The griffin blinked his large, glassy eyes. "I am."

The travelers looked for the statue, but it was gone. Tomaton now stood in its place, once again inanimate, behaving as a proper statue should.

"You were trapped in the statue," said Evercloud.

"I was," said the Ancient. "No doubt you knew that from your time with Padre Esteban."

"Actually," said Ben. "We may have seemed in a bit of a rush and did not receive all the information the Padre had. We have been told the Great

Tyrant's story, but we are not aware of how the Ancients, I mean you, were driven away."

"I see. I suppose it would only be fair of me to fill you in on that bit." Tenturo lowered himself to the ground, the way a lion might rest itself while it watched the savannah. "Well, firstly, the Tyrant had the element of surprise on his side. We didn't really know what was going on until it was far too late. Also, he was smart enough to ambush us each separately, diminishing the power we held as a group. Unfortunately, for that very reason, I do not know exactly what happened to the others. But in his vast arrogance, the Tyrant told me things that gave me clues as to what he did with the others. I was the last that he attacked, and he taunted me while I was trapped in stone."

"You mean you were awake in there?" said Tomas.

"Oh, yes," replied Tenturo. "We'll get to that. The Tyrant drove me here with those two foul beasts that you dispatched. I know not where they came from or how they came to be in the Tyrant's service, but when they drove me here, the Tyrant was waiting for me. He had received a power from the Earth that we were all powerless against. In appearance, it was very much like lightning, but he controlled it with his hands. He used that power to melt the rock of this mountain, and then, cast me in it, choosing to leave me as a statue. I am immortal, so I stayed conscious inside a prison of stone.

"It was then that he began to taunt me and give me clues to his actions. He told me that I was the last, that he had already driven the others away. He told me that he would make sure that this world remembered us as evil, destructive beings, and by the time he had finished, the world wouldn't remember us at all. He told me that he had cast Chera into a sea of fog, to remain there for all eternity. There is no sea of fog in this world that I am aware of, but he did tell me that he ambushed her in the land of Felaqua that lies south, across the sea. Chera had always been fond of Felaqua. He then told me that he had trapped the great dragon, Bahknar, just as he had trapped me. He gave no evidence of where he had trapped him, though he did say that Bahknar didn't share the monumental dwelling that he had given me. Regretfully, the Tyrant did not give any real clues as to the fate that befell Densa. However, the Tyrant gained an edge in his voice when he spoke of Densa, merely saying, 'he will know my pain.' It is a mystery, what he meant by that. He continued taunting me a while longer, with nothing that was of any use, and then he left me, never returning. For ages upon ages of this world, I lived in that statue. I so deeply regretted what we had done to the Tyrant. After all, I was partly to blame for what he had become. I couldn't feel sad for myself during my time trapped in stone. I only felt sadness for the world.

"But then, after ages of solitude, a man found me. He came up to the statue I was enclosed in and spoke to me, not with words, but with his mind. I asked him how he knew that I was there and he responded that he could feel my presence. We spoke at great length and shared our stories with each other. To this day, he still visits me regularly. A wonderful man, that Esteban. It was his plot that brought you here. He came up with the test that gave you passage to this mountain, and it was also he that knew we could use the items found in Oldham's Bog to free me. He even made little Tomaton over there, an ingenious invention." Tenturo looked at the group and he could see that they were only half listening to him, their minds being occupied with something else. "Loss is difficult," he said. "I would assume that this bear is from the Kingdom on Gray Mountain."

"Yes," said Riverpaw.

"Then, before I return to my home in the Green Mountains, I shall take him back to his home and oversee his burial. All in his kingdom should know of his sacrifice and herald him as a champion. I owe him that much."

"Thank you, Tenturo," said Riverpaw.

Then Tenturo began again. "It is of my nature to reward the four of you for the service that you have provided me. A gift, if you will. Ask of me anything."

"Anything?" asked Tomas.

"Yes," replied the griffin.

Ben stood up eagerly and addressed the Ancient. "Great Tenturo, my name is Ben Floyd and it has been mine and my family's mission, for ages, to find the Ancients and return them to power. All that I would ask of you is help in completing this mission. Transportation to the land of Felaqua, Tenturo, so that I may gain clues in how to free the great Chera."

"Your request is quite noble, Ben Floyd. It does me well to know that I am not alone in this endeavor. I will grant your request, happily. Travel south, to the village of Cerano, and find a Captain by the name of Nesbitt. Speak freely and honestly to him and you shall receive what you need."

"Thank you, Tenturo," said Ben as he bowed.

Next, Tomas stood and spoke. "Tenturo, my name is Tomas Floyd. Ben is my brother and we share the same mission. I also ask for help in that mission. Today, I failed those who depended upon me. My bow was not strong enough and my aim was not accurate enough. I do not want to fail anyone in these areas ever again." Tomas lowered his head in shame.

"Tomas Floyd," said the Ancient, "step forward." Tomas did as he was told and stood before Tenturo, merely feet from the massive being. "Present to me your bow." Tomas took his bow and placed it upon the ground, in front of Tenturo. The griffin stared at it, and as he did, the dark, wooden bow began to change its color to a leafy green. "Now look into my eyes, Tomas."

Tomas stared up at the Ancient, slightly trembling and gazed into the creature's eyes. Suddenly, there was a blinding flash of light. The group rubbed their eyes and readjusted them upon Tomas and Tenturo. "Now, Tomas, take

196

your bow and shoot that bird from the sky." Tenturo looked upward and Tomas followed his gaze. So did the others, but as Evercloud, Riverpaw and Ben looked into the sky, they were unable to see any bird. Tomas, however, took his bow in his hands and shot an arrow straight up into the air, so far and fast that it disappeared from their sight. Moments later, a large condor began to fall from the heavens. When it landed near them, upon the snowy mountain, the bird disappeared as if it had not existed at all.

"That's amazing," said Tomas. "It's as if I can see forever. Thank you, Tenturo." Tomas bowed to the griffin and returned to the group.

Then Evercloud stood. "My name is Evercloud, son of Eveneye, and I am from the Kingdom on Gray Mountain."

"You live among the bears by choice?" asked Tenturo.

"Well, yes and no," replied Evercloud. "I was abandoned by my human guardians when I was too small to remember. The bears took me in, and have raised me as their own. They do not keep me against my will, they are my family."

"Interesting," said Tenturo.

Evercloud continued. "I, like the brothers Floyd, am also on a mission to find and free those who created the creatures of this world. However, my mission varies in some regards. I have been told stories, by the bears upon Gray Mountain, that long ago, there were powers bestowed upon man so that he could act as a protector of peace for the world. I wish to reclaim those gifts, once given to men, so that I may work to unite the creatures of this world harmoniously."

"Looks like we're not the only ones with secrets," Tomas whispered to his brother.

"That is quite a request, Evercloud, son of Eveneye." Tenturo gazed down at the young man as if his eyes could see through him.

"Even so, great Tenturo, I have seen that creatures of different kind can exist together, and I see it as my responsibility to promote that for the betterment of the world."

Tenturo nodded. "Is that the only reason you wish to reclaim these powers, Evercloud?"

Evercloud considered saying yes, but something inside of him told him that it would be a mistake to lie to the Ancient. Something made him feel that Tenturo could see into his heart.

"No," said Evercloud, "there is another reason that I wish to have these powers. I also wish to rid this world of the Great Tyrant. I want to use these powers to defeat him."

This statement came as a shock to everyone in the group, even Riverpaw, but if it had surprised the Ancient at all, he did not show it.

"And what if you fail?" asked Tenturo.

197

"I have sworn to myself that I will not."

Tenturo hummed, thinking. "And would you swear to me?"

Evercloud's response came quick. "No, Tenturo, I would not. I do this for my own motivations and it would be a lie to pretend that I act in your interest alone, or in your service alone."

The jaws of the other three travelers dropped wide, in horror, sure that Evercloud had just made a fatal error in judgment.

But Tenturo smiled. "Maybe there is hope for this world yet." The travelers stared at Evercloud and Tenturo in wonder. "I shall grant your request, Evercloud. Please come forward."

Evercloud stood in front of the great Tenturo, alone in the cold air. The Ancient closed his eyes, deep in concentration, and then, Evercloud was enveloped in a silvery light. His body tingled all over as he felt the power surrounding him, the hair on his arms standing up. A mighty wind came and lifted Evercloud off of his feet, suspending him in the air. It swirled all around him, brushing against his arms and his face like gentle hands. Evercloud opened his mouth in surprise, and as he did, the light rushed inside of him, filling him with its power. His eyes grew wide as he could feel strength surging through every fiber of his body. His senses became acute, as if fear had filled his body with adrenaline, but there was no fear, only joy. Unimaginable happiness and serenity washed over Evercloud and then, the wind ceased and Evercloud's feet returned to the ground.

"What was that?" asked Evercloud.

"You have been given the power of the wind, Evercloud. It is the only power that I can give to you. In order to obtain the others, you will have to find the other Ancients."

Evercloud stood up from the ground. "I feel amazing," he said. "I feel strong."

He walked over to Tomas and picked him up with ease, hoisting him above his head.

"Hey!" yelled Tomas. "Try your power on somebody else."

"I feel strange," said Evercloud, setting Tomas back onto the ground. "I feel like running." Suddenly, he took off like a bolt across the snow, moving so fast that he seemed to be a blur. He came to a stop in front of Tenturo and bowed to the griffin. "Thank you."

"I do not give this gift to you lightly, Evercloud. I fully expect that you will fulfill your oath. You have been given great power because you wanted great responsibility. Do not forget that."

"Yes, Tenturo." Again Evercloud bowed and then returned to the group.

Now Riverpaw stood in front of the Ancient. He looked hollow and broken, like the ghost of a bear, but he stood resolutely in front of Tenturo with swollen eyes and asked for the only thing in the world that he wanted.

"My name is Riverpaw, son of Whiteclaw, and I want you to bring my father back." Riverpaw stared at the ancient creator, unyielding, desperately afraid that any sign of weakness might cause Tenturo to reject his request.

Tenturo looked down at the bear and slowly blinked his eyes. In all of the ages of his existence, through that vast expanse of time, he had never felt the wrenching pain upon his heart that he felt now. He bowed his head and accepted the fate of this sobering moment, and then he gave his answer to Riverpaw.

"I am sorry, Riverpaw. I cannot."

"That is not true," said Riverpaw, no longer able to stop the emotion from cracking his voice. "The Earth gave new life to the Tyrant. It has been done."

Tenturo softly shook his head. "It is not an existence that you would ever wish upon someone you loved, Riverpaw. Resurrecting the dead is an evil magic; it is no simple act of healing. Your father would be changed, Riverpaw, he would be incomplete. Do not wish for this."

Riverpaw dropped his head, too tired to fight any longer. The pain had won, and tears flowed freely from his eyes. "What would you have me do?"

"I would have you honor your father's memory."

Riverpaw looked back up. "Then I wish for the power of the wind. I, as well, wish to use it to create peace between bear and man. That is something that my father had worked toward. I wish to continue that work alongside Evercloud."

"Then you shall have it," said Tenturo.

And like Evercloud, Riverpaw too was enveloped by the wind and silver light. When the process was over, he stood to his full height, and without knowing that it was possible, launched himself into the air. He was flying. He soared through the air, above the mountain, diving and ascending again, making loops and rolls and finally, crashing into the rock wall of the alley. The mountain shook and Riverpaw stood from the ground where he had fallen, unscathed and smiling. A Riverpaw-sized chunk of rock had crumbled away from the wall where the bear had hit it.

"He's like a…like a…what do you call them?" asked Evercloud.

"A cannonball," said Ben.

"Yeah, he's a cannonball."

Riverpaw returned to the group and looked at Ben. "You plan to travel to Felaqua for clues to freeing Chera?"

"Yes," Ben answered.

"Do you mean to travel alone?" asked Riverpaw.

"I was hoping I wouldn't have to," said Ben with a grin.

Riverpaw turned to Evercloud and Evercloud nodded at him.

"I'm in as well," said Tomas.

"It's settled then," said Ben. "An alliance."

"What of you, Tenturo?" asked Evercloud. "What will you do when you reach your home in the Green Mountains?"

"That has yet to be determined," he said. "However, I believe that it is time for me to be going." Tenturo walked over to Whiteclaw's body and lifted it, in one massive paw.

"Please, tell my mother that I love her," said Riverpaw. "And tell her that I will return to her."

"And please, tell my parents the same," added Evercloud.

"Of course," said Tenturo. "Oh, and one other thing before I go. Which one of you was it that passed the Padre's test?"

Evercloud shyly raised a hand, still embarrassed for his being singled out. Then, suddenly, Tenturo touched his mind.

Anytime you should need me, Evercloud. No matter how far I am from you. You can always find me this way.

Evercloud nodded at the Ancient.

"Just wondering," said Tenturo. "Goodbye to you, and my thanks."

The griffin spread his giant wings and began to beat them against the air. The travelers had to brace themselves to prevent the draft from knocking them over. With one final push, the Ancient thrust himself into the air and began to fly away.

I will return to the mountain, Riverpaw said silently to his father as he watched Tenturo carry him toward the horizon. *I will see you again. I swear it.*

The travelers watched Tenturo fly in the distance, not quite knowing how to feel. Things were different now; *they* were different now. In the matter of a few hours, it had seemed as if the entire world had changed.

"There's something Tomas and I need to tell the two of you," said Ben to Evercloud and Riverpaw as he watched the Ancient disappear over the horizon.

"Excuse me," came a voice from behind. "But I was told that I might find the brothers Floyd up here."

The four travelers spun around to see a man holding a chain with a small, white stone hanging from it.

"Who are you?" asked Tomas.

"Me?" said the man. "I am a messenger."

31

Chapter 31: Confusion

The Messenger tossed the necklace at the feet of the newly formed alliance. "What have you done with Esteban?" asked Ben.

"*I* do nothing," said the Messenger. "I am what people do to themselves."

Ben was not in the mood for riddles. "If you don't tell me what you have done with Esteban, we will force it out of you, and trust me, you don't want that."

"That, Ben Floyd, would be a ridiculous waste of all of our time."

"And why do you say that?" asked Ben in confusion.

"Because, I've already killed Esteban."

All of their jaws dropped in disbelief. Tomas cried, "Why?"

"Come, come, Tomas. What is it mothers always say to their children? There's no use crying over spilled milk."

"I'll show you what crying is for," said Ben and pulled his blades from their sheaths.

"I wouldn't get so aggressive if I were you," said the Messenger. "Your sister wouldn't approve."

"No," yelled Ben.

"Well, first, let's be sure I have the right girl. Big, blue eyes, flowing, red hair, soft, pale skin, gets very upset when you kill her father."

"You monster!" screamed Ben.

•••

Iolana was laying on the top step of the passage that led to the top of the mountain. The Messenger had continued to paralyze her, repeatedly, since the desert. It had been a nightmare. Unable to even close her eyes as the Messenger killed Padre Esteban, the small man never standing a chance to defend himself against such a foe. She wished that she had just agreed to follow him while in the desert. Then, maybe, just maybe, she would have been able to stop him. *What is this man after,* she wondered? When they had entered the darkness of the passageway, she again had thought she would die. He had dragged her along the cold, rock floor, paralyzed. Her body being cut and bruised as they went along. After hours of moving, she had realized that he must need her for something, most likely to use against her brothers. A bartering chip. As she lay upon the freezing steps, she wondered if the man had found her brothers. *He could be fighting them now. If only I could move.* And then in her frustration and anger, her finger twitched. She tried with all her might to make it happen again. Two fingers twitched this time, and then her foot. The magic was wearing off. Minutes later, she slowly rose to her feet and hobbled out into the snow. And then she heard a man yell.

"Ben," she called. "Tomas."

With his blades raised, about to attack the Messenger, Ben heard something and turned his head to see Iolana, stumbling in the snow.

"Run," she called out. "He's going to kill you."

"Iolana?" said Ben.

The Messenger took the opportunity this small distraction had afforded him and shot his palm toward Ben, paralyzing the man in blue light. The Messenger moved in to strike him down, but Evercloud was quicker, knocking the Messenger to the ground. The Messenger looked back up at Evercloud in slight astonishment, but quickly jumped back to his feet, and then the fight began. The Messenger threw blow after blow at Evercloud, but he was quick enough and strong enough to block every one.

"I'm impressed," said the Messenger.

They moved through the snow, back and forth, no one able to land a strike. Suddenly, a roar came from the sky. The Messenger looked up to find Riverpaw, diving at him through the air. The Messenger dove away as Riverpaw crashed into the snowy mountain, shaking the ground.

Tomas ran over to Iolana, helping her to stand. "Are you all right?" he said.

"He killed Father," she cried. "He's here to kill you and Ben."

"Why?" asked Tomas.

"I don't know," she said. "But Tomas, he has powers, he's not normal. You must stop him."

"All right. Stay here," said Tomas and headed back toward the fray.

Evercloud was upon the Messenger before he had a chance to recover and slashed the man's ribs with his claw. The man grabbed at his torso to find that Evercloud had drawn blood. Unfortunately, it only angered the Messenger and he came at Evercloud with even more ferocity than before. As the Messenger attacked, a voice entered his mind.

Use caution. They have unleashed one of the Ancient Evils.

The Messenger never yielded in his assault, but his eyes widened in astonishment. *These are the first real foes that I have faced,* he thought.

Evercloud and the Messenger continued to battle each other, and Evercloud was beginning to lose ground. The Messenger was backing him against a wall of rock, pinning him with nowhere to go. The Messenger drew his fist back, ready to strike. But just before he could, Riverpaw hit him from behind, throwing the man through the air. His body came down in a heap, yards away.

"Thanks," said Evercloud.

"Don't mention it."

The Messenger got back to his feet, just in time to see Tomas releasing an arrow at his head. The Messenger watched as the arrow flew directly for him, it would not miss its mark. Just as the arrow was about to pierce the man, he reached into the air with incredible speed and ripped the arrow from the air. Without stopping his motion, he spun around and sent the arrow flying toward Evercloud.

It all happened so quickly, like a strike of lightning. Evercloud looked down and saw the arrow buried deep inside his chest. His face went blank and he fell to the ground.

"No!" roared Riverpaw and charged at the Messenger.

"Evercloud!" screamed Iolana and ran over to him, dropping to her knees beside his body. He looked up into her eyes and smiled, but the arrow had struck deep. He coughed and blood came from his lips. Iolana began to cry as she looked at him. She bent low, wrapping her arms around him, and then came the light. White light surrounded Evercloud; it was all he could see.

Everyone, including the Messenger, had stopped to stare at the white light that now enveloped both Evercloud and Iolana. Across the mountaintop, Ben fell to the ground, once again able to move.

"No," he said. "Iolana. No."

The voice once again returned to the Messenger.

It is time to leave. I am coming.

The light faded away from Iolana and Evercloud, and Evercloud looked down at his chest. The arrow and the wound were gone. There was no more blood. He was all right. Iolana stood up as if she were dizzy and stared down at him in confusion.

"Who? Who are you?" she said. "Where am I?"

Just then, in the sky, a blue light appeared and sped toward the mountaintop. Evercloud got to his feet and looked into the sky to see the figure of a man, seemingly made of lightning, inside an orb made of the same crackling energy.

"The Tyrant," whispered Riverpaw breathlessly. Then, collecting himself, called out in warning. "The Tyrant!"

Before anyone could think of how to react, the Great Tyrant had swept down and collected both Iolana and the Messenger and disappeared from the mountaintop.

"No!" screamed Ben as he knelt upon the snowy ground.

"No. No. No. No," said Tomas, walking in circles with his hands in his hair. "We've failed. Failed!"

Evercloud walked over to Tomas and shook him. "What are you talking about?"

"You don't get it," said Tomas. "You don't understand. That was the Tyrant. He has her! We've failed!"

Evercloud pulled Tomas close to his face so that he would understand him well. "We have not failed, do you understand me? We will find your sister. We will save Iolana. By the Everflame, I swear it."

Tomas hung in Evercloud's grasp, defeated.

"Iolana isn't my sister," said Tomas. "Iolana is Chera."

32

Chapter 32: The Cycle

Nikolas Floyd walked along the path that led home. The sun was far from setting for the day, but Nikolas had been fortunate in his hunting and figured he'd return to his wife early. Two brown rabbits hung over his back as he walked in the light of the mellow-gold sun. The light hit him at an angle that softened his wrinkles and yellowed his silver hair, making him look years younger than he was. It had been that kind of day so far.

Maggie will be happy, he thought. *She loves rabbit stew.* He thought about her beautiful smile, and in turn, thought of the sparsely toothed smiles of his two young boys, Ben and Tomas. Ben was eight and Tomas had just turned five. *Good thing I caught two rabbits. Growing boys. Such a handful. Good thing for Iolana.* Iolana was Nikolas' sister who lived with them in their forest cave, just outside the village of Hendrick. As he thought of Iolana, his happiness waned just slightly. Iolana had been noticing things lately, things that made for difficult conversations.

It had all started a few months ago when Nikolas' father had passed away. It had been hard for Iolana and she had shed many tears when he had been buried. It must have been all the thoughts of death and of aging that had brought about her new curiosities. One day, while the family had been down at the stream, she had made a comment about the ever-widening wrinkles on the faces of Nikolas and Maggie. Iolana had asked if they were becoming ill.

"No," Nikolas had replied, "just getting old." He had not even needed to wait for the follow-up question to be asked, in order to answer that too. "The years have been kind to you, Sister. Not so much, to us."

He wondered how long it would be before that excuse no longer worked. *I'll think of something,* he told himself. *I have to.*

He looked up ahead on the forest path and saw Iolana and his two boys coming toward him. Young Tomas ran to meet his father.

"Dad! Dad! Auntie Iolana said she'd take me and Ben to swim in the stream! Can we? Can we go?"

Nikolas smiled at the boy. "Sure," he said. "Just make sure the three of you are back before supper." Nikolas held up the rabbits for them to see.

"Yeah!" cheered Tomas, running circles around his father's legs with an uncontrollable energy that only small children possess.

"Don't worry," said Iolana to Nikolas. "We wouldn't miss out on Maggie's rabbit stew."

Iolana and the two boys continued walking to the stream and Nikolas headed home. When he arrived at the cave, he brought the rabbits inside and presented them to Maggie with a smile that betrayed his pride, and then he kissed her on the cheek.

"Rabbits," she said surprised. "Looks like those reflexes still have a little quickness left, old man." She giggled at her own teasing and smiled to show Nikolas that she was only playing.

"Very funny, Maggie. Very funny."

Unfortunately, Maggie's smile melted away too quick, as she had to deliver Nikolas some bad news. "She's asking questions again, Nikolas, and I don't know how to answer them. She's asking why we don't live in the village."

"She's asked that before, Maggie. Just stick to the story. We like our space, that's all."

"There was a new question today though."

"Oh?" Nikolas raised an eyebrow.

"She wanted to know if she wasn't supposed to find a husband."

"What did you say?" asked Nikolas.

"What could I have possibly said to that, Nikolas? What answer would have even made sense? I just changed the subject." Maggie put her hands on her hips. "She's noticing. She's figuring it out. It won't be long before, before…well I don't know what. I don't know how your family has kept it up all these years."

"I've wondered that same thing myself," said Nikolas. "We need to find the others, Maggie. They've got to be out there."

Suddenly, yells came from outside of the cave.

"DAD! DAD!"

Nikolas and Maggie rushed outside to find Ben, running down the path.

"What is it, Ben? What's wrong?" asked Nikolas.

"It's Tomas," said Ben, trying to catch his breath. "He fell on a rock, down by the stream. He's bleeding all over. Come quick."

Nikolas didn't slow his pace for his wife and son to keep up. He ran as fast as his aging legs could carry him, leaving them far behind. When he reached the stream, he saw Tomas, lying belly up on the ground, with Iolana kneeling next to him. Nikolas stared down at the boy in horror. Whatever rock he had fallen on had gashed his stomach open and he was losing a lot of blood.

"Dad, it hurts," cried Tomas in between gasps. "Make it stop."

Nikolas knelt down to the boy, knowing that there was nothing he could do. He pressed his cheek to Tomas' as tears welled in his eyes. "Shh," he said to the small boy as he ran his fingers through Tomas' hair. "It's gonna be all right. It's gonna be all right." Nikolas looked up at Iolana, who knelt on the other side of Tomas, and tears fell from his cheeks. Tomas was dying.

Then, without knowing why she was doing it, Iolana put her hands upon Tomas' wound. She closed her eyes and her skin began to glow white like the midday sun. Nikolas fell back as the light grew, until it enveloped both Iolana and Tomas. It was so bright that Nikolas had to shade his eyes. Then, she began to sing. Her words flowed soft and fast like the stream they knelt beside. Words and sounds reached Nikolas' ears that he had never heard before. Sounds so sweet they pulled at the strings of his heart, threatening to tear it from his chest. Then, as quickly as it came, it was gone. The light faded and Iolana collapsed, unconscious, next to Tomas' body. Nikolas scrambled over to the boy, his wound had disappeared, he was awake, blinking, alive.

"Dad," said Tomas quietly, "am I dead?"

Nikolas picked him up and held him tightly to his chest. "No, Tomas. You're alive."

Maggie ran over and ripped her son away from Nikolas, hugging him and kissing him and crying. Nikolas leaned over Iolana who was still unconscious.

"Iolana," he said. "Iolana?"

Without waking, she spoke:

> "In the world's most desperate hour of need,
> Earthly elements shall be set free.
> And evil tyrants should beware,
> The coming of an unlikely pair."

Then, Iolana slowly opened her eyes and stared, confused, at Nikolas. "Iolana?" he asked.

"Who are you?" she asked. "Where am I?" She sat up and looked around at everything, as if seeing it for the first time. Finally, Nikolas understood. This was part of the cycle.

"My name is Nikolas," he said, looking at her. "Your name is Iolana and you are my si… You are my daughter." She looked at him and blinked. "You had a bad fall, but you're all right now."

"Father?" she said.

"Yes, Iolana. Let's go home."